DEMON SLAVE
Published by Kiersten Fay
Edited by Rainy Kaye

Copyright 2010 by Kiersten Fay.
www.kierstenfay.com
All rights reserved.

This book is a work of fiction. All of the characters,
names, and events portrayed in this novel are
products of the author's imagination.

ISBN-10: 0983573336
ISBN-13: 99780983573333

DEMON SLAVE

(Shadow Quest - Book 2)

By

Kiersten Fay

This book is dedicated to Rainy—What an
amazing person you are.
And to my sister, Mariah—You are always
in my heart.

Chapter 1

Pain laced Marik Radkov's throat as he sucked in the freezing air. His legs burned with each long stride. The indigee followed close behind, hollering with each launch of their primitive arrows and spears. Marik thought about turning to attack—he abhorred running away from a fight—but he and his comrades had come to this icy planet with diplomacy in mind.

His captain, Sebastian, suddenly cried out as if in pain, though nothing had hit him. Marik followed his line of sight to the valley below, where Sebastian's mate, Anya, stood in what they thought would be a safe location. They'd left her there to rest, while they searched the area for her sister, Nadua. Now Anya was being threatened—by whom he couldn't see through the blanket of snowfall, but the outline of a craft rested behind her.

His blood turned to ice in his veins as Marik watched the strange man drag her toward the craft. He became enraged when her body went limp and she no longer fought her captor. Fire burned through him, warring with icy dread. He pumped his legs harder, as did Sebastian.

When an arrow embedded itself into Marik's calf, slicing past bone, he hardly felt it. His mind was focused on getting to Anya, and ripping apart whoever had her. The Edge was growing fast, making pain nothing more than a tickle. Horns glowing in rage, his fangs descend—ready to tear into flesh.

The snowfall, which only moments ago had dusted the ground, had grown into a furious blizzard before he realized. It must have hidden the approach of the small shuttle ship that Anya was being pulled toward.

A tug brought Marik's attention back to the arrow in his leg. There was a rope secured to the thick end. Another hard tug and the ground came rushing toward him as his calf slipped out from under him. He clawed at the frozen terrain to keep from sliding backward. Sebastian had stopped and turned to him, pain and indecision etched in his eyes. When a demon's mate was in trouble, nothing else mattered. The fact that Sebastian hesitated now was a testament to their friendship.

"Go!" Marik ordered. His claws sliced the layer of ice underneath him as another pull forced him back. "She needs you more than I. You know this." The rope went taut once more and when Sebastian hesitated again, Marik let go. He prayed that Sebastian made it to Anya in time.

The cold wetness of the freshly fallen snow, coupled with the hardened frozen ground, assaulted Marik's exposed skin as he was yanked backward. Sebastian's silhouette disappeared into a wall of gray and white. Marik geared himself up to meet his new friends. The pain in his leg became nothing as he invited the Edge, embracing the rage and the extra strength that came with it. He'd never been trained to use the Demon's Edge in battle, but he'd had more than enough experience losing himself to it over the years.

Once invoked, the Edge would trigger the release of chemicals, creating an intoxicating elixir that increased strength, lessened pain, and reduced one to little more than an animal running on instinct. Relief would come from either lashing out violently, or sexual release. Neither would be pleasant for whoever was on the other end of that rope.

Voices began to rise from behind the veil of white. They spoke a language he'd never heard before, meaning diplomacy would be impossible at the moment. It didn't matter anyway; Marik would soon be too far gone for rational conversation.

The pulling ceased when the group came into view. A small army of white haired, barely clothed warriors had weapons pointed directly at him. Some wielded arrows and others held swords that gleamed against the bright snow. They dressed as though it were a warm summer's day, rather than standing amid the freezing storm beating violently around them.

With his claws at the ready, Marik lashed out, making solid contact with the nearest body. A yelp, and a crimson trail of blood urged him on. Though his captor's skin was bluish, their blood still ran red. Marik needed to see more of it.

A group of the indigee leapt on him, yelling and attempting to restrain him with their hands, while others approached with ropes. With a roar, Marik slammed his body into them, successfully beating them away. A man with a sword sliced at him, the blade coming close to his neck, but Marik was quick.

Two more with swords rushed to the front. Twisting his body, Marik managed to avoid the sharp blades. At their backs, a group of archers notched their arrows, targeting him.

His vision blanched red as the Edge flooded through his veins, deadening his mind to anything but survival.

One of the assailants thrust his blade forward. Marik easily dodged, smashing his head into the other man's skull. With a small grunt, the man dropped to the ground.

Through the fog, Marik couldn't tell how many he was fighting, just that they kept coming—which was fine by him. He could do this all day.

Blood stained the unfallen snowflakes as Marik continued slicing through flesh. Soon he stood on a bank of red snow. He vaguely registered a few arrows embedded in his torso. When had that happened?

Footsteps charged from behind and Marik crashed his elbow into the attacker's nose, dropping him on the spot, but more quickly took his place.

A single voice rose above the rest, yelling in that language he couldn't understand, but the sound broke through his rageful mind. Marik faltered in his step, only slightly, but enough to lose his advantage. A barrage of hands and ropes surrounded him, and he was thrown up against a tree. He lashed out with his body and the ropes began to snap. Then that voice came at him, slowing his movements once more, only this time the voice spoke in a language he knew.

"Stop, demon!"

Marik blinked twice. More ropes came around him, fixing him to the cold bark of the tree, but he was stunned. Before him stood a small, fur-bundled creature holding a bow, arm stretched back, ready to release the arrow trained on Marik's forehead. The only identifying feature he could see through the thick layering of furs and skins was the eyes—ice blue, deep as a cavern, and sucking him in like a wild storm.

A heavy object knocked against Marik's skull and his vision went black.

* * *

Nadua gazed down at the unconscious demon.

While the creature had fought, she had marveled at his immense strength and fluid movements, even as her men were being cut down with ease. His injured leg hadn't hindered him at all.

Her gaze rolled over his powerful frame. His shoulders were packed with strength and his waist slim, the shirt under his long jacket was thick but tight against his chest. She had watched the cords of his muscles flex as he assaulted her elite guard. If he hadn't been hurting her soldiers, she could have admired him all day.

When she had finally noticed the blood being spilled, Nadua realized she needed to end the chaos. Loading her bow, Nadua aimed for the demon and yelled in the Cyrellian tongue for him to surrender. He hesitated slightly at the sound of her voice, but continued fighting as her men gained ground against him. She knew it would be only a matter of seconds before the demon broke free of their hold. On a whim, she'd switched to a language more commonly used by space travelers that she'd learned as a child, and ordered him once again to stop. Had he not stilled when she'd ordered, she would have put an arrow in his brain.

Now, as Nadua knelt beside the fallen beast, one of her soldiers called out, "Your Majesty, you should not get so close. It could wake any moment."

Nadua only waved away the concern and studied the demon further. His features were that of a warrior, strong, just like the rest of him. A small scar next to his ear that twisted down the back of his neck and disappeared under his collar was the only defect. His hair was reddish brown and cut unevenly short, as though he cut it himself and didn't care how it looked. A few arrows still jutted from his arms and legs. He hadn't even seemed to notice they were there.

Demon warriors were legendary, but this was the first one she'd ever seen. And she was impressed. She could use someone like him on her side, though she knew that recruiting him would be impossible. The last time demons came here, they had warred with the Cyrellians. The demons had attempted to claim Cyrellian land as their own, and had fought fiercely for it. In the end, the Cyrellians won, but the battle had been devastating.

"Take him back to camp and clean him up," Nadua ordered. "Make sure he's secure. I will be conducting the interrogation when he is conscious."

"I don't think that's necessary, Your Highness. We can call in a translator."

Nadua speared the guard with a look that ended his objection.

She may not be like the Cyrellians, who were able to ignore the freezing ice storms that constantly assaulted the land—whereas she couldn't go outside without layer upon layer of thick fur—but they would respect her rule.

"I will interrogate him," she said firmly, then changed the subject. "What of the rebel clan? Any sign of them?"

"No, Your Highness. The pack of demons must have frightened them off."

They'd been hunting the rebels for weeks now. She and half her elite guard—about thirty men—had been marching through the countryside hoping to find any sign of the rebel's stronghold.

The rebel clan had defected long ago. It was unclear exactly why, but there were whispers of political disagreements. They'd been terrorizing the kingdom ever since, invading the outer city and stealing whatever they wanted.

During their latest assault, a young woman had been kidnapped. The parents had implored *Her Royal Highness* to find their daughter Lidian and bring her home.

By the frequent caravan attacks and rumored sightings, they should be close to where the rebels made camp, but the only evidence they'd seen was a solo rebel male, spotted just across the plateau. The sudden arrival of the demons had caused her group to lose sight of him.

"And what of the other demons?" Nadua asked.

"It looks as though they too have escaped."

Tamir approached, the colors of his tunic a proud reminder of his high rank. She could see he had something on his mind.

"Your Majesty," Tamir began. "I believe the appearance of these demons could mean another invasion." The sneer in his voice indicated he still harbored a grudge, and she was reminded that he was old enough to have lived through it.

Nadua nodded, and scanned the depths of her mind for a vision. Unfortunately, they came whenever they came, no matter how many tantrums she threw.

"I agree, send word to Wren. He is to put additional guards on Ava immediately. Also inform him that we will be returning sooner than anticipated."

"Yes, Your Highness." Tamir turned and walked away, signaling to a lower-ranked soldier as he went.

Ava was the rightful ruler of the Cyrellians, and Nadua was sure she would one day prove to be a great queen. The only problem was Ava was only fifteen years old. Her father, Fineas, had, on his deathbed, charged Nadua with protecting the crown and keeping Ava safe from those who would see themselves on the throne. Ava had been only two years old at the time. When the decree was made that Nadua would be the proxy queen, not everyone had been happy about it.

Nadua, for one.

There had been an uproar from not only commoners, but those who were closest to the crown. Had it not been for Wren's loyalty to his king, and thankfully to her and Ava, she might not have had the power to take control of the situation.

Nadua hoped she was strong enough to safeguard Ava's crown until she came of age. She owed it to Fineas for taking her in when her own planet had come under attack, and for being so kind to her.

He had always treated her like a beloved daughter. It was a tragedy that he'd had four hundred years with her, yet only two with his actual daughter.

Though she owed him, and would do everything she could to keep her promise, Nadua was eager for the responsibility to be taken from her shoulders. She was never meant to rule. Kyra, her eldest sister, had been groomed from birth for the task, not her. If her home planet hadn't been attacked, and most of the royals ferried to safety among their many allies, then Nadua would have lived out a glamorous life as Princess Nadua and nothing more.

Oh, how I wish I were home.

But then she wouldn't be here to protect little Ava. Over the years, Nadua had watched her grow from innocent toddler, to the sweet and caring young adult she was today. After watching her, helping in her schooling, and joining in her childish pranks, Nadua loved Ava like a sister. But sometimes she felt more like a mother.

Nadua wanted Ava to be strong when she finally became queen. So whenever Nadua could pry Ava from her many tutors—not that they weren't doing a great job teaching her, in their soft she-might-break sort of way—she and Ava would "play swords": Nadua's way of testing Ava's fighting abilities, and making corrections if necessary.

Nadua's mind turned back to the unconscious demon, who was being carried away—not so gently—by a few soldiers. If his people were preparing for another invasion, she must prepare the Cyrellians for war.

* * *

The prisoner's tent was large and fairly empty, but for a raging fire pit, and a three foot thick, ten foot high stake jetting from the ground. The still unconscious demon's back was against it, and his hands were tied behind him, securing him in place.

Nadua stood close to the fire, gathering what heat she could, waiting for the demon to awaken. After sending a messenger back to the palace, Tamir joined her in the tent, followed by his favorite subordinate, Nakul. The two stood away from the flames; heat could be uncomfortable to them, just as the cold was uncomfortable to her.

She imagined, as she had many times in the past, what it would be like to have skin as cold as theirs. To find the snow pleasing as the flakes settled on their skin.

To be able to touch another without burning pain.

Because her skin was so warm and theirs so cold, if she touched the skin of a Cyrellian, both would burn at the contact. It often made her sad that she could never give Ava a simple hug without being careful there was no skin-to-skin contact. Nadua hadn't felt a true painless physical touch since she'd left her home planet more than four hundred years ago.

With her hands stretched out to the dancing flames, she gazed at the demon. His shirt had been removed, in order to clean and mend the many arrow wounds. Ancient scars of all sizes and shapes trailed along his torso, around his back, and down the length of his arms—blemishes on an otherwise perfectly sculpted physique.

Without his shirt, the demon looked even stronger than before. The light of the fire created shadows against the cords of his muscles, and the scars helped project a sense of danger. Though the marks were faded now, they must have caused great pain when they were made. Nadua watched his chest rise and fall with each slow breath.

Would his skin feel warm and soft?

The thought startled her, just as his green eyes flashed open and immediately found hers.

The drowsy demon was gone. A predator sat in his place.

Chapter 2

Marik quickly averted his gaze, and assessed his situation. Pain laced his body. He was slumped on the chilly floor, in a concoction of sludge and mud created from the melting snow, and tied to a thick piece of wood jutting from the ground. Lingering rage coupled with being tied down threatened to push him to the Edge once more. But the ropes they used to secure his wrists were brittle and could be easily broken.

It was obvious that these people didn't understand a demon's strength. The Edge receded. Marik decided to wait till he was fully in control before escaping.

Two men with straight white hair and a hint of blue in their skin stood to his right. The fur covered creature stood to his left, leaning over a blazing fire. The difference in their dress was extreme. The men wore hardly anything to protect themselves from the harsh cold. Perhaps they didn't need to.

The bundle of fur was openly studying his scars. For some reason, that caused a surge of embarrassment to run through him. Long ago, his scars brought him unmitigated shame—not born of battles won or lost, but of punishment. For most demons, wounds healed without a mark of their existence, but his *masters* had been harsh, wanting to leave their mark on him by making him bleed and not allowing him to heal properly. Marik thought he had left the humiliation of his scars in his past, until now.

He scowled at the mass of fur. Their eyes locked. Her iridescent blue eyes grew wide for a moment, before regaining their composure and turning away. An involuntary growl escaped him, successfully forcing those blue depths back to him. Why he wanted that he didn't know, perhaps a play for dominance. Pieces of the Edge still mingled in his blood, causing his mind to be muddled.

"Quiet down, demon," a lithe feminine voice commanded from behind the thick hides. Then, in another tongue she spoke more kindly to the two males, doubling his irritation.

Marik had learned a number of languages, due to his many diverse *masters* and their equally diverse speech, so deciphering this one should be a breeze. Unfortunately, Marik hadn't heard any dialect like it before. It would take some time to decode. Luckily, demons were quick learners.

The blue-eyed bundle turned back to him, speaking again in one of the common space languages, though her idiom was old-fashioned. "Demon, I have some questions, and you will answer them truthfully. Understand?"

Marik didn't move at first. He just challenged the creature with his gaze. She challenged him right back, rising to her full height. Of course, her bravado wasn't that impressive. She assumed he was securely tied down, and therefore harmless.

How would her bravery fare when he snapped the rope and took out her two guards, so he could have her at his mercy?

The thought jarred him as much as it pleased him. He wondered if that body matched the silky voice it belonged to.

Marik inwardly shook himself. The Edge, though dulled from

the earlier fight, still demanded release, and this female's scent was stroking his desire. He needed to take this situation more seriously.

Marik slowly nodded, curious what she would ask him.

"Are your people here to war with us?"

He wasn't expecting that. Shaking his head, Marik answered, "Not at all."

"Then why are you here?"

Marik wondered if it were wise to reveal that they came to Undewla in search of Anya's lost sister, Nadua, a Faieara princess who, according to a magical book, was supposed to be hiding somewhere on this planet.

Even in Marik's head it sounded daft.

According to the book, supposedly written by the king of the Faieara himself, who could see glimpses of the future, Nadua's presence was necessary in winning their war against the Kayadon—a race of warmongers in control of their home world.

Coincidentally, the Kayadon had destroyed Marik's home planet shortly after they'd captured him and his sister Misha, selling them both into slavery. Marik cringed at the memory of Misha's screams as they had dragged her away. He couldn't have more thoroughly failed her than if he'd sold her into slavery himself.

The bundle of fur cleared her throat, waiting for his answer. It was possible that these people knew of Nadua, but would they help him? By the nasty looks he was getting from the two in the corner, Marik didn't think so. If he revealed too much information, it could be used against him and his friends. But then, if he didn't reveal anything, these natives might turn to torture. Of course, Marik would destroy them first, but he'd like to avoid that route if possible.

Finally, Marik decided to keep it vague. "We are searching for someone. We have no intention of staying on this planet long. And we definitely do not seek war."

The woman eyed him warily before conversing once more with the two men. The men began to shout and sneer in his direction, until an abrupt command from her silenced them, making it obvious who was in charge here.

Incredulous, she asked, "Who is it you seek, demon?"

Shaking his head, Marik answered, "I'll not say more till I know I can trust you. And with me tied up and bleeding, I'd say you'll have a time of earning it."

The bundle of fur nearly choked on a laugh. "Oh, I must earn *your* trust? How am I to believe anything you say when you attacked my men?"

"As I remember it, they attacked first."

The woman waved away his comment and turned back to her fire. "You were trespassing on our territory. The last time demons came to this planet, they brought with them a reign of destruction not equaled since." She glared at him then. "I will not let that happen again. If your people are planning another attack, I will discover the truth."

Marik was stunned. "Demons have been here before?"

"Don't act stupid. Am I to believe you don't know the history of your own people?"

A low warning growl erupted from Marik, and both the white-haired males pulled their swords. The furry creature stilled them with a look, cutting off their clipped tones.

"Well?" She continued, unconcerned by the threat in Marik's eyes.

"Five hundred years ago my planet was destroyed and my people scattered through the universe. I have no idea how many survived or where they now reside. If a group of demons attacked your people,

I would have no way of knowing."

The woman's brows drew together in a surprising show of compassion, though he knew it to be contrived.

* * *

Surely the demon was lying, but his story was so close to her own. Nadua, too, was separated from her people and had no way of knowing what was happening back on Evlon.

Quickly, she turned away to hide any show of emotion. The demon would no doubt see it as a weakness. From what she knew of demons, they abhorred any emotion that wasn't anger or hatred, they were strong and stubborn, and they were incredibly lusty. Barbaric, one Cyrellian had said. She had to appear emotionless and prove herself equal, if she were to get any real information.

Nadua would need to use the worst of his traits against him. His stubbornness would be a problem and she couldn't fathom a way to manipulate him by his strengths. Her eyes followed the lines of his sculpted arms. No, that would need to be kept in check. Perhaps his lust could be her ally, but how? There were no other females in the camp besides her. Nadua shivered at the implication.

Could she lower herself in such a way?

She shook the thought away and nearly laughed—while other parts of her seized on the idea. She firmly ignored those parts.

He's quite possibly evil.

Her body didn't seem to care. But it had an excuse as to why it was being defiant. Seeing this male, fighting and winning against her greatest warriors, was one hell of a turn on. She supposed it didn't help that she hadn't been touched in centuries.

The last man she'd kissed had been a Cyrellian named Cyrus, Fineas' brother. It was the silly act of two drunken friends. And though it had been painful, it was her most tender memory. A few days later, Cyrus had died, at the hands of the rebels no less. Nadua had been devastated. A few of his paintings still hung on a wall in her room.

Nadua wasn't quite a virgin, but four hundred years out of practice, she might as well be.

Perhaps one of her maids from the castle could entice him, but by the looks of those burns on his skin, where the guards had handled him, he too couldn't touch Cyrellian skin without pain. The guard that had removed his torn clothing and tied him up had complained that the beast was boiling to the touch.

What would his skin feel like to her?

She scolded herself. Not going to happen.

"So, you claim you are seeking someone on my planet, but won't tell me who, and expect me to earn your trust in order to find out." Nadua couldn't help the twitch in her lip. The demon matched her smirk, and her amusement was lost. She couldn't imagine what business this demon had on Undewla that didn't involve deception.

Perhaps he seeks a fallen brother.

Unlikely, but plausible. Just after the war's end, demon sightings had been frequent, even though what was left of the demon invaders had reportedly been chased off this planet. Sightings were rare these days, but every now and again a farmer from the outskirts would run to the nearest pub, shouting about a giant beast with fire red horns that had pilfered one of his animals. Most people just laughed it off.

Was it possible that a demon or two had been left behind when his comrades took flight so long ago? And if so, had this demon and his small group been attempting a rescue? It would explain why he didn't want to reveal his target. And if that were the case, then he lied about not knowing demons had been here, and therefore he most definitely could not be trusted.

"Rest up, demon, we have a long journey in the morning."

"Oh?"

"I'm bringing you to my home, where you'll have free room and board, maybe a meal or two, and your choice of the many cells in our prison. There you can think about the whole trust issue and who needs to be the one earning it."

Chapter 3

"What a generous offer," Marik replied with a roll of his eyes.

Actually, it sounded like a pretty good deal. A free ride into town. He wouldn't need to wander around this wasteland trying to find life. Instead, she was going to lead him straight to it. Marik supposed he could stick around for a little while.

With an air of superiority, the bundle of fur left, speaking briefly with the two white-haired men in that strange language. In turn, they gave a small bow and then swung their angry faces toward him the moment she stepped out of sight.

Marik smiled and winked, causing their sneers to deepen.

That woman had mentioned demons coming here. Amazing that they would choose this place. Most likely, the group of demons who allegedly stumbled upon this frozen planet, and thought, "what a nice home that would make," were desperate for some reason. The conditions on this planet weren't suitable for anyone but perhaps these cold blue people. Any demon would have a hard time keeping oneself alive here, let alone thrive in a group.

He found himself wondering how Nadua was fairing on her own. She must have survived. Anya had sensed her just as they landed, right before the wave of blue attackers had interrupted their search. And from what Marik could tell, Anya was pretty accurate in her assumptions. It gave him much relief to know that once Anya was safely back with Sebastian, she would be able to help find him.

He had faith that Sebastian would succeed in rescuing her. *Sebastian must succeed.* If he didn't—

Marik frowned, dismissing the twinge of panic that laced through him.

His thoughts were interrupted by an argument that had started between the two guards. They spoke in hurried whispers while pointing at him every so often. When one of them bent to inspect his bindings, Marik grew curious. The other opened the tent flap wide, as if to exit, giving him a perfect view of the bundle of fur just as she entered her own tent across the way. Then they were gone, leaving the crackle of the fire as Marik's only companion.

Their strange behavior left him with brows drawn, staring into the flames. Their leader's position was revealed. Did they intend for him to see where she slept? Though the one had fiddled with Marik's ropes, the bindings didn't feel any tighter or more secure. He could still break them with a twist of his wrist.

If these people had known demons in battle, they must know how strong his kind could be. They couldn't be so ignorant as to think this meager rope could hold him.

Unless they wanted him to break free.

Now that he thought of it, those guards had been standing farther away from the woman than Marik had been. If he'd wanted her throat, he could have had it before they would have had a chance to react. Any guard worth his weight wouldn't have allowed a situation like that, even if the incredibly dangerous demon was properly secured.

Marik didn't really care if her guards wanted her dead or not. She was of no use to him anyway, if all she wanted to do was lock him up. But he wasn't going to be the one to end her life. Pockets of his past flashed in his mind, images of the arena. He fought the memories back.

No, he wouldn't kill her. Not unless she gave him a pretty damn good reason. And because she was unwittingly doing him a favor by bringing him to civilization, where he could begin the search for Nadua, he needed her alive for the time being.

He also suspected that he was still alive because of her. She only wanted answers, but he figured he owed her, at least a little.

* * *

A kick to his still-tender leg had Marik growling into consciousness. He bared his fangs at the offender, who scurried back. Behind the man, seven fully loaded guards stood ready. One of them came forward to cut Marik free from the stake.

Marik stretched his arms and their bodies went tense as they strained their weapons toward him.

"Look, I don't need any more holes in me. It'll just piss me off."

The men exchanged sideways glances, clearly not understanding.

Marik rested one arm on his knee and leaned back against the wooden stake. "Is something happening here? Or are we posing for a picture?" His shirt was tossed to him, and he caught it in mid-flight. "What? No seamstress?" He fingered one of the many tears. "I have a mind to lodge a complaint."

One of the men yelled something, urging him with a flick of his bow to put it on. When he did, the same man continued barking out orders. Though he didn't know what was being said, it didn't take a genius to figure out they wanted him up and out of the tent.

As he exited, five more guards were ready for him outside. "I'm flattered boys, but you're still a little understaffed." Marik glanced around. Everyone was packing up. Most of the tents were already disassembled.

Across camp, the walking rug caught his attention. She was kneeling next to an obscenely large brown animal with an angular leather face, filling a sack with supplies. The animal was twice her size in height, thick legs held up its massive body. On further study, he noted the beast sported fur like the woman's cloak.

For some reason, Marik grew alarmed when the giant's long neck twisted and its head came toward her, but it only pushed at her with its snout, as if being playful. She laughed as she went tumbling, and gently swatted its nose.

Marik wanted to watch her more, but a sharp point pressed into his back, while the guards in front of him parted. Ahead sat a small caged wagon, attached to another one of those large fuzzy beasts, this one with coarse gray fur.

"Great, I get the nearly dead oversized varmint."

A flare of unease rippled through Marik. Being caged was one of the many horrors from his past. He'd sworn never to let it happen again. But with more than a dozen armed warriors ready to pounce if he showed any resistance, Marik forced his feet forward.

He flicked the metal with his nail and noted the sound of low-quality workmanship. Gods, these people were making it too easy.

Lifting himself with the help of one of the top metal bars, he slipped inside the tiny entrance feet first and the door was closed behind him. "Don't I get a pillow or something? These accommodations are a little bare for my taste. And if you were wise, you'd get the hungry demon some breakfast."

Ignoring him, the guards went about their business, secure in the thought that Marik wasn't going anywhere. He slumped against the bars, and quietly observed his captors.

What was left of the camp was torn down and stored within

various wagons. Whenever an order was shouted, Marik paid attention to how it was carried out. Already he was beginning to learn certain words, associating them with the actions.

Marik craned his neck to see what that woman was up to, but she was gone, and so was her creature. A bit later, close to the edge of the gnarled woods, Marik caught sight of the two guards from the night before, speaking far away from the rest of the group. He didn't like that.

Before long, they were on the move. His ride was bumpy and he made the inconvenience known, but of course no one understood him. They wouldn't have paid any attention if they could.

Around midday, pellets of snow began to drift in the air.

At the same time, a familiar ragged beast trotted up beside him, with an equally ragged body riding atop it. "Morning, demon. How fare you?"

"I'm dandy, how polite of you to ask. Could use a fresh set of clothes, and hot meal though."

"Oh, absolutely, I'm here to serve. Would you like to look at a menu?"

"If you've got one."

"I'll get right on that, right after you give me the truth of your intentions here."

She rocked slightly as the beast kept pace, and Marik could almost make out the shape of her body under all that mess. His shaft took note as well. He'd obviously been far too long without a woman if that mere hint of a female form was turning him on.

"If you don't believe what I've said already, then I don't know what to tell you. Anything else I say would be a lie just to get what I want." He paused, waiting for a response. When he didn't receive one, he continued in a sarcastic tone. "Fine, here goes. My friends and I hail from a galactic-fun-ship, and we came to this planet in order to fill it with candy and cheese."

She narrowed her eyes. "Cute. I don't even know why I tried. The deception of your kind is legendary."

"Have you actually met one of my kind?"

"Aside from you? No. But you've already proven the stories to be true."

Marik couldn't help but roll his eyes at that.

They rode in stony silence for a moment. The only sound was from the crunch of snow, and heavy snort-breathing from the weird, furry monster. Its wrinkled gray face was the only part that wasn't covered in tangled brown fur.

"What's that thing you ride?"

"This is an edisdon.

"It smells."

"It's not that bad. Edisdons are a traveler's companion of choice. They're strong, and can endure long trips in the harshest weather. They don't eat much and their fur keeps them as warm as they need to be." The woman scratched the edisdon's neck. "And she's loyal. Aren't you, Sweetie?"

"She? It looks too ugly to be a girl."

She covered what must be its ears. "Shh, you'll hurt her feelings."

"Oh, forgive me. Let me amend. She's dazzling in her dreadlock do, her step, so light and dainty."

The edisdon let out a grunt as if protesting his sarcasm.

"And I'm sure the smell would grow on me eventually. How you match her radiance, lady, the two of you must be sisters."

Her posture straightened. "What a tongue you have."

"Oh, you have no idea what my tongue can do." Marik smiled as he sensed her unease. His teasing backfired and he inconspicuously shifted in his pants.

"Maybe we'll see what it can do once I've ripped it from your head, hmm."

"You'll need to put your finger in my mouth first." Marik flashed a fanged grin. Her blue eyes flared with disdain, which only worked to encourage him. "Tell me, do all the females dress like you and Eddie here? It must be hard for the men to decipher between the two. I can imagine the awkward morning when they've found they'd been fucking the wrong species."

After casting him a look of unmitigated hatred that seemed out of place in those blue depths, the woman rode away.

* * *

Nadua mentally scolded herself for letting him get to her so easily. The lying bastard was her prisoner, yet he was the one having fun. He must expect that his friends will come back for him. And perhaps they would, but her people would be ready. They were but two days from home.

"Your Highness," a voice called. Nadua slowed her speed to let Tamir catch up with her. "One of our sentries has spotted a rebel, just south of us."

Nadua pulled back on the lead and Sweetie obediently stopped. The rest of the party did as well. "I want to find the rebels too, but don't you think the threat of a demon invasion is more important right now?"

Tamir bowed his head. "Of course, Your Highness, whatever you think is best, but this could be our last chance to find the rebels. Surely they will move again with us being so close. And the demon is secure for the moment. I hardly think an extra day would hurt. Plus, I have already sent a messenger to the castle. They should already be prepared by the time we arrive."

Nadua supposed he was right. Wren would have everything taken care of before they even set foot into town. "How many were spotted?"

"Just one, but he could be a scout, not too far from the others."

Nadua's eyes followed the horizon. It was already midday. With a sigh, she pointed to a high bluff. "We'll make camp there. After everything is set up, I'll take half the men with me to search while the other half stays with our prisoner."

"I'll go with you, Your Highness."

"No, I'll need a leader to stay behind, in case the rebels attack."

"Of course. I'll relay your wishes to the others." Tamir bowed and rode ahead.

It took about an hour to reach the high ground. While Tamir supervised construction, Nadua gathered her group and headed out in search of the rebel outpost.

Silently, she prayed for Lidian's safety.

Chapter 4

Nadua sat in her warm tent waiting for a pot of ice chunks and packed snow to melt over the hot coals so she could wash away the grime from the day's journey.

The firelight illuminated her red locks, staining them gold. If she were home at the castle, Ava would be fawning over it while they sipped warm tea. As with Ava, Cyrellians only had hair as pale as the world around them.

Nadua could relate to Ava's envy. Back on Evlon, any gathering, no matter how minuscule, was always a spectacular feast for the eyes. Back then, she often thought her color dull and her curls wildly out of control compared to the elegant hairdos of the noblewomen.

Now, after four hundred years on Undewla, it was disconcerting every time she walked into a ballroom and her fiery curls stood out in a crowd of a thousand shades of white. By coincidence, Nadua's eyes were the only aspect she shared with the Cyrellians. Icy blue. But Ava would still comment on their uniqueness.

The expedition had turned up nothing. If there had been rebels nearby, they were certainly gone now.

Nadua sighed heavily. They were no closer to finding Lidian, and she was battling a strong sense of failure. Once they returned to the palace, she would send Wren to continue the search. The only redeeming factor about the trip so far was the discovery of the demon presence. But she hadn't been able to procure much information from their tight-lipped captive.

She knew he held important information about the coming invasion. And because of this, she was about to do something that would cause her great embarrassment—unless her plan worked.

The stubborn demon may not submit to questioning, but his earlier behavior suggested he could be tempted by other means. If she failed tonight, she would be forced to hand him over to her warden. And she didn't want to think of all the ways Renzo got his prisoners to talk.

Choosing her outfit carefully Nadua tried to dress as nicely as possible. With a slight tremble, she slipped on her finest fur cloak, which spanned the length of her body and cinched at the waist. A small train brushed the floor.

The robe fell open in the front, and she usually wore her riding clothes under it. Not tonight. Tonight it would serve as a dress of sorts. Holding the bottom of the fabric up she glanced down at her bare legs. It was surprisingly elegant. She blushed and let the material fall back into place.

Was she really going to go through with this?

Accessories were scarce, of course. While packing for this trip, she hadn't realized she'd be in need of finer adornments—who would pack for a fight and think, *where's that necklace I love?* So she was stuck with a clean pair of gloves, and boots with laces to match.

It didn't matter what her hair or face looked like, for it would remain covered, as usual, to protect her from the cold. Besides, it shouldn't be her face the demon would be looking at.

A mirror wasn't necessary for her to realize this was a lackluster attempt at dressing for seduction. Everything she wore was made, in some part, from edisdon fur—it was the only material that could keep her warm—and he'd already expressed his distaste for it. But it would have to do.

* * *

Marik leaned back against the familiar stake, hands behind him once more, with the same flimsy rope in place. A soldier entered, carrying a stool and set it down next to the dimming fire pit. With shaky hands, he added a few logs and then rushed away, sparing Marik an uneasy look as he went.

The day had been fairly productive—as productive as a day in captivity could be, anyway. He'd been able to learn quite a bit of the language by the simple act of observing those around him. Not enough to decipher complete sentences yet, but he could at least gather the gist of a conversation. It was sure to be useful, since no one spoke any other language that he could understand. Except that woman, of course.

She had proven distracting while she was near him, though. Even while they were silent he was too focused on her, rather than keeping to his task.

His curiosity had driven him mad. What was her name? Why does she speak a language of the stars when no one else could? What the hell was under that cloak?

Getting rid of her had been easy enough, but then keeping her in his sights had been a full time occupation. He didn't know why, but if she disappeared from view—which she managed often—Marik couldn't concentrate till he knew where she was in the group. To keep tabs on his enemy, he reminded himself. Not because he feared for her life. The two guards had also been out of sight most of the day.

After his crude remarks to her earlier, Marik was genuinely surprised when the woman entered his tent. Oddly, something in the pit of his stomach relaxed at the sight of her.

She was still covered from head to toe in that fluff, but something was different: her outfit was tighter, revealing her figure and giving him an even better idea of what her body might look like under that damn fur.

Tempting.

A thick scarf tucked into her hood and hid her features. Her lovely eyes glimmered in the glow of the flames as she sauntered to the fire.

A chair had been placed close to the flames and he expected her to take it immediately, but she remained standing. She looked a bit uneasy. By her swift glances to the exit, he had the feeling she was contemplating leaving without a word, and the thought bothered him.

"Are you here to continue our conversation about how talented my tongue can be? I assure you it . . ." Marik trailed off as she finally sat. The fabric of her outfit parted around long shapely legs, coming together again just below the apex of her thighs.

His cock jerked at the sight and he wished she'd move this way a bit, only an inch more. She crossed her legs with a deliberate motion, causing the fabric to fold elegantly closed, but one slender thigh was revealed instead. Marik's mouth went dry, while other parts of him sprang to life.

Her eyes gleamed with amusement and that alone gave her away.

Saucy chit.

Marik composed himself and tried to keep his eyes off her succulent pale skin.

Pale?

"Your skin isn't blue, like your male counterparts." He shrugged and gave her a leering smile. "Not that I'm complaining. I'm not really partial to blue."

* * *

"How convenient for you." Nadua had been nervous when she'd first walked in into the demon's tent. So much so that she hadn't been able to speak at first.

How could she have thought this was a good idea?

She felt like a fool coming here. It was unlikely the demon would be tempted by her. And this jaunt could end up being incredibly embarrassing if any of the guards discovered her plan. Doubts continued to swirl in her head and she had almost left without a word.

Then she'd seen lust in the demons eyes and knew she could pull this off.

"Is that why you females need to cover your bodies? You haven't adapted to your environment properly?"

Ass.

"Oh th . . . we've adapted just fine." She tried to make her voice sensual, but feared she was doing a poor job of it. "Why don't you tell me a little about yourself?" She rubbed her crossed legs together for effect.

With alarming intensity, his gaze went directly to where she intended it to.

"Well, let me think," he began. "You already know I'm a demon, and I'm sure you've heard of the dangers of teasing one such as I."

Nadua swallowed, but kept her back straight and suppressed her rising alarm. She could do this.

He continued. "I'm a great warrior . . . and a genius when it comes to preparing food. My favorite color is clear. And I love your legs. Why don't you come closer so I can sink my teeth into them."

Irritation flashed though her, but she tamped it down. "You are a very good fighter. My men can attests to that. You've been trained, obviously. I find that attractive." Nadua was surprised at how steady her voice was as well as the accuracy of the statement. She rubbed the back of her fingers over her thigh. "I find myself wanting to know more about you. Perhaps we can . . . chat a little?"

He gave a slight nod, eyes riveted to her caressing movement. She could see by the bulge in his pants that her actions were inspiring the exact response she was going for.

Easy.

"Can you tell me about the craft that brought you here?"

"A shuttle's a shuttle. What else do you need to know? It gets you where you're going, and in many cases back again."

"And why did it bring you here?"

"Look, I know what you're doing." His voice went guttural. "And you have no idea what you're tempting here."

"Don't I?" She was growing warm from the anxious rushing of her blood, induced by the knowledge of what she was about to do next. Somehow, she needed to calm herself down, but she was making progress with the demon. Stopping now was not an option.

She began removing her gloves, pulling at each finger and making sure he was watching as they slipped down her arm. Next came the shawl pelt that covered her shoulders and hid the deep V-neck of her outfit.

"That's better. You were saying?"

His teeth were grinding. Nadua couldn't tell if that was a good thing or not. Her pulse spiked at her own actions and her cheeks warmed. Good thing the demon couldn't see that.

"Well, if you're going to continue removing your clothing . . . perhaps we should have more logs brought in. Guard! More logs for the fire!"

"Shh!" Nadua shot forward, scrambling to gather her clothes, getting ready to redress if anyone entered. She would be mortified if she were caught trying to seduce a demon, even if she didn't intend to go through with it.

"Let me guess, no one knows you're here. Do you think it's wise to rile a demon's lust without backup, girly?"

"I think I can handle you."

"Why don't you untie these ropes and we'll find out." He stood as if she would do as he asked. "I would love to test your theory."

Her eyes widened when she saw his bulge had grown bigger, straining against his pants. She swallowed heavily.

Damn, she was losing control of the situation. In one last attempt, she took a step closer, playing with the lip of her collar.

Heavy lidded, his emerald gaze dipped to her cleavage.

"I want to help you, demon," she cooed. "I want to trust you. I just need you to tell me the truth."

"And I just want to taste you. I don't need my hands free to do that."

Why was she breathing so hard?

She eyed his lips, looking for a hint of his fangs. "I'm afraid you'd bite me, first chance you get. I need something from you first. I need to know I can trust you. Tell me who you're looking for?"

They were standing so close, if his hands weren't tied behind him he could reach out and grab her. Nadua couldn't help but imagine what that might feel like. Fathomless green eyes bore into hers with such intensity, she knew she had him.

"You, luv. I've been searching for you all my life." Sarcasm dripped from his words. He smirked.

"Bastard!"

"Come on, let us have a taste."

Nadua pulled out her cleverly placed dagger, hidden by a nearly invisible thigh holster, and set the point at his throat.

"Wow, what else do you keep down there?"

His lack of concern was maddening.

"This was your last chance, demon. Tell me what I want to know, or else."

"Or else what? You'll remove your top? I think I can hold out for that."

Nadua had never been so enraged by a single person in her entire life. With an irritated huff, she turned back toward the fire and slumped in the stool, silently admitting defeat. Slicing the demon's throat would have been gratifying, but irrational. She would learn all she needed to know. Eventually.

The few moments away from the fire had chilled her, though she hadn't realized it until now, and she rushed to replace her gloves and shawl.

"When we get back to the castle, you'll be turned over to Renzo. He lived through the first demon invasion, so I'm sure he'll know how to deal with you." Nadua glanced up when she heard a menacing snarl coming from the demon.

"Torture, you mean."

Nadua shrugged. "I suppose so." She had hoped to avoid it.

"And after all the torture, if I don't change my story, what will you do then?" In a flash, the previously lusty green irises morphed into an angry blood red.

Nadua stood with a gasp, not sure what was happening to him. The horns that peeked out of his sandy brown hair began to alter their color as well, taking on the cast of burning embers. Razor-sharp fangs peeked out from his lips, twisted in rage.

This was how he had looked when he was tearing through her men.

"What are you doing?" She stepped backwards, stumbling into the chair. She could swear there was heat coming off him. When the demon's lips curled back to bare his teeth, she screamed, "Guards!"

Chapter 5

Nadua stomped around the campground and shoved her supplies into her satchel with a little more force than necessary. Sweetie's body rocked as Nadua tightened the straps, preparing the edisdon for riding.

She strapped on her sword and quill, and placed her bow around one shoulder.

Last night had been a complete disaster. The guards may not have suspected her reason for being in the demon's tent alone, but it was still humiliating to have called on them for protection. And for what? A couple of red eyes and burning horns? On this morning's reflection, she decided he hadn't been *that* frightening.

"Your Highness, we're ready to move out," Tamir called.

Nadua looked around. All that was left of the camp were pockets of disturbed terrain. The demon was caged once more, leaning lazily against the bars as if he hadn't a care in the world. His eyes and horns were back to their normal state.

"Then let's go home," she said, mounting Sweetie.

The tightly packed landscape crunched under the beast's heavy feet, as she moved to assume the lead. Behind her, Tamir called the order and the men quickly fell in line. Taking up the rear was the prisoner's wagon, accompanied by four riding guards.

She'd felt the demon watching her all morning, but had refused to look at him. Now, with the heat of his gaze on her once more, Nadua leisurely glanced back. His eyes bore into her, revealing no discernible emotion. She gave him a lewd gesture before turning away. The bastard probably didn't even know what it meant, but she didn't care. All she wanted to do was return home, turn the demon over to Renzo, and forget about him.

The wind began to pick up. Nadua raised her eyes to the sky.

Great.

It looked like they were in for another storm. This time of year, the weather was usually mild. Well, mild for Undewla, which meant a little less ice falling from the sky than normal.

Storms were frequent and expected, but Nadua had been hoping to make it home before the next one hit. It seemed unlikely that was going to happen.

"Listen, all!" she shouted, pulling Sweetie to a stop. "We will be riding fast! I'd like to make it to the cliffs if we can."

Her men hollered in unison at her order, and increased their pace.

The steep ridges of the Cliffs of Ashtel would provide some protection against strong winds, as well as give them the advantage in case of attack.

Nadua stroked the edisdon's neck. "Come on girl, we've got a ways to go."

* * *

The chit hadn't looked at him all day, besides some strange gesture toward him that he didn't think was meant to be a, "Hi, how are ya?" No doubt she was licking her wounds from the night before.

A seductress she was not, although those long legs of hers were mouthwatering. Marik cursed. Remembering her silky thighs had his body aching again. She might need work when it came to seducing a man, but that didn't mean he wouldn't have her writhing under him in an instant, her screams of passion in his ear.

He hadn't meant to frighten her so badly, but her indifference toward torturing him had pushed him to the Edge almost immediately. His memories had closed in, nearly choking him with their revulsion.

To his surprise, he had calmed enough to keep himself in check. He'd never been on the cusp of the Edge and had it stamped out so quickly.

He wasn't sure, but he suspected the terror in her eyes had something to do with it. In his hazy mind, he remembered feeling like it was wrong for her to fear him—which was ridiculous. Of course she should fear him. She was his enemy, and all his enemies should fear him. It was every demon's motto.

He'd watched her through the cold bars all morning, trying to figure out why he should be so conflicted over her. Women never enticed him this much. It had been a while since he'd last taken one, but that wasn't unusual.

She remained at the front of the pack, riding on top of her creature and ignoring him thoroughly. Her clothing was the same as always, thick fur that looked similar to the thing carrying her. Didn't she realize it made her stand out among the group?

Yesterday, she'd rode out as if on a hunt, but came back empty handed. Marik could smell nearby wildlife, even now. If they had been hunting for food, they should have come back with something. Surely they could at least hunt.

Unless the creatures on this planet were more intelligent than he was currently giving them credit.

Next to him, one of the guard's overgrown rodents stopped to lower its head to the ground and began rummaging its snout in the snow. Cursing at the edisdon, the guard pulled hard at the reigns, but it didn't budge. Another man rode past in high spirits and smacked it on the ass with the flat of his sword. The beast grunted as it jumped forward, bits of snow covering its face.

Nope, not intelligent, at all.

As morning shifted into late afternoon, they entered an expanse. The path dipped between a thick forest of gnarled trees with thick black trunks and empty branches.

Something in the crisp air caught Marik's attention. He peered past the thicket, into the snowy depths. There was movement there, so subtle he almost missed it. Marik eased onto his knees to get a better look. It could have just been an animal.

Suddenly, the woman stopped, raising her left arm in the air. Like a wave, the solders halted and all eyes focused in the direction she was looking.

It was the same direction that claimed Marik's interest.

She eased her bow from her back and nocked it with an arrow. Following her example, the guards pulled their weapons.

For a moment, everything went still. Marik listened hard but heard nothing. Yet the woman seemed to have zeroed in on something past the trees.

Slowly, she pulled back her bow. A few guards with arrows mimicked her, while others looked back and forth, unsure what to do.

Then, from behind the trees came a unified cry. Bodies rushed out of the forest, brandishing swords and daggers. All were on foot. Their skin gleamed with the same blue tint as his captors.

Finally, the woman let her arrow fly, planting it firmly in the forehead of her target. He went down instantly. She reloaded and shot again, as did the other archers. Together they must have taken

down twenty men, but the swarm—Marik estimated fifty or so—
were still coming.

"Hold position!" she yelled, while continuing to fire arrows
into the horde. Another three down. Those who didn't carry a bow
had their swords at the ready. After a few more seconds, she hollered,
"Now!"

Her men surged forward, slamming into the oncoming barrage.
The familiar sounds of metal clanging against metal and flesh ripping filled Marik's ears while his heart picked up speed. An odd urge
to get to the woman, to protect her, nearly overcame him. But he
should remain where he was. It would be wise to wait out the melee,
and not let his captors know he could break from his cage.

He glanced over the crowd, toward the woman. It seemed that
she was properly guarded, a half-circle formed at her front, blocking
the attackers from coming near.

It was hard not to notice how well trained she was in the art of
battle. She'd taken the high ground and was dropping her opponents
with ease. For some reason, the sight made him smile, until he noticed the movement at her back.

More attackers were emerging from the forest behind her. No
one else noticed.

Then suddenly, with a sound like lightning, a thick sheet of ice
sprang out of the ground, separating the woman from her guards.
Marik blinked twice.

What the hell?

* * *

Nadua let her last arrow fly before she noticed the threat at her
back. The damn rebels had them surrounded. She should have seen
it coming: this was the perfect location for an ambush.

Suddenly, Sweetie's head shook and the edisdon's footing became erratic.

Nadua held on. "Shh, Sweetie. Steady." A thick chill tickled the back of her neck.

She gasped.

It couldn't be possible!

But when the ice began its swift ascent, she knew it to be true. Her heart sank. A Kaiylemi was with them, a master of ice.

As the small group of rebels closed in, another ice sheet burst from the ground behind them. A frightening sound boomed from the demon's direction, causing Sweetie to buck underneath her.

"Tamir!" she called, her voiced laced with panic.

Tamir, along with all her other guards, were on the opposite side of the ice. But before any of them could make their way around it, more gleaming towers exploded skyward, their path clear.

A glacial cage was forming around her, trapping her to face approaching rebels alone.

Quill empty, Nadua stowed the bow on her back and unsheathed her sword, urging Sweetie toward the six attackers.

Gathering speed, Nadua swung her sword, slashing the throat of the first she reached. Red spilled down his torso as he fell. The next one wasn't far away from the first, and she jabbed her sword into his jugular.

Sweetie slowed to a stop, corralled by the remaining four Cyrellians. Before Nadua could pull her blade from the rebel's spewing neck, hands were pulling at her from both sides. Cold metal sliced through her right leg, running all the way through to the edisdon's flesh. The beast made a horrific sound and reared back, knocking off both her and her attackers.

Nadua landed hard, losing her grip on the hilt of her sword.

After a quick sweep around the snow with her hands, she scrambled to her feet empty handed.

Her four remaining adversaries had recovered as well. She reached for her dagger, but found the holster was empty.

One of the rebels smiled then, holding her own dagger in his hand. "Looking for this, Highness?"

Nadua backed away, contemplating her next move. With no weapons at her disposal, she would resort to hand-to-hand combat. With four armed opponents, she knew she hadn't a chance, but she would do as much damage as possible while she could.

Ava's image flashed in her mind and Nadua wished she had told her how proud she was of her before she'd left. She mentally apologized to Fineas for failing him. Her father's face came next, flanked by her mother. She was struck with regret that she would never again see their smiles.

From the large opening above, a stray arrow landed at her feet, still intact. Before the rebels could react, she had her bow out, loaded, and aimed at the men. "I'm taking one of you with me, at least. So which one will it be?"

A massive roar shook the ice walls. From the corner of her eye, she noticed a blur of motion through the translucent barrier. A harsh bang reverberated around her. Where the shadow was, the ice cracked. Unsure what was happening, Nadua kept her arrow trained on the rebels, who were slipping each other confused looks.

Another loud crack thundered out. A section of the barricade splintered in all directions and began to crumble. An immense body stepped inside.

A quick glance told her it was the demon, red eyed and horns ablaze.

Stomach churning, she took in the sight of him. He looked as he had the night before and she remembered now why she had been so frightened of him.

Great! How do I get out of this one?

What was better: being killed swiftly by rebels, or ripped apart by an angry demon?

One of the men called out, "What the hell is that?"

"That's a fucking demon!" another answered. "Kill it!"

They all turned to him, momentarily forgetting Nadua. She glanced at the rebels and then turned her gaze to the demon. His sharp fangs were prominent, and his body seemed to have increased in mass. Bulging muscles strained through his torn shirt. He looked at her then, and her eyes met with molten fire. The unimaginable pain promised in their depths had her heart slamming to her throat.

She released her arrow.

"Damn it, woman!" the demon grated.

Her arrow had landed in his neck.

Lurching forward, he plowed through the four men. The one who had snatched her dagger used it to slash at the demon's side just before the demon tore out his throat. In the same instant, the demon's hand whipped out and snapped the neck of another rebel. The last two fled for the exit.

They didn't get far. The demon lunged after them and kicked out his leg, planting it directly in the middle of a rebel's back. The last Cyrellian made the mistake of looking back at the sound of his friend's spine cracking. The demon caught hold of his head with the palm of his hand, ripping it back, and twisted until a loud pop rang out.

Nadua hadn't taken a breath. The whole scene had left her frozen in awe and fear. Now the demon turned to her and she forced herself to gather her wits.

Kneeling in the snow, she frantically searched for her sword.

He was approaching her slowly, probably figuring she couldn't put up much of a fight. And with the exit at his back, there was no way she could make a run for it.

Sword, sword, where is that damn sword. Ah, there you are.

Her hand gripped cold metal.

Just as she lifted it, a voice called from behind him in the Cyrellian language. "Halt, demon!"

More of her soldiers poured into the enclosure. The demon, whose red eyes were beginning to dull, was still focused on her.

Speaking so he could understand, she said, "Don't move, demon, or my men will kill you where you stand."

He ripped the arrow from his neck. A stream of blood began to drip. "You shot me!"

"Of course I shot you! You may have gone for them first, but I have no doubt that I was next."

"I just saved your life, woman!"

"And I'm so sure that was your intent. How did you get out of the cage?"

The demon looked incredulous for a moment, then his gaze slid to the small, yet growing, stain of blood at her feet. "You're hurt."

Some of her soldiers noticed too and began looking her over.

"It's nothing," she assured them. She had always been a fast healer. Though the wound was deep, it should be healed in a couple of days. "Tell me how you got out?"

For a moment, she thought she caught amusement flash across the demon's face. "Faulty lock I guess."

"Your Highness!" Tamir approached, hauling one of the rebels along with him. "We've captured one."

"Only one? Is he the Kaiylemi?"

"I don't think so. We killed many, but most ran off like cowards when . . ." He motioned with his head at the demon.

Outside the ice, Nadua glanced around at the carnage. Fallen bodies—some her own men—were strewn everywhere. White stained with red. They would gather their fallen before moving on, and bring their bodies back to their families.

What a useless war this was. So much wasted life, for nothing.

And what a perfect time for the first signs of the storm to show itself. Small flakes began to settle around them.

Chapter 6

The tent walls snapped as they fought the strong wind. The storm had started mild but quickly turned fierce, forcing the group to stop and take shelter.

Marik sat in what was fast becoming his usual place, tied to the stake in the ground. The captured bandit sat across from him in a similar position. Surprisingly, he spoke Demonish. Said he'd learned it during the demon war.

Marik had been trying to gather information from him for hours, but the bandit, Jedar, seemed disinclined to converse with him—his prejudice was just as deep as the others. But then Marik had promised to free him when he was ready to escape, and the man started talking.

After learning that his people were called Cyrellians and that they were at war with each other, Marik convinced Jedar to teach him more of his native language. Still, he was in no way fluent, but he was able to gather a basic understanding.

Speaking with Jedar kept Marik's mind from drifting to that ungrateful fur ball. At the time, he'd been shocked that she had used her last arrow on him.

On him!

That infuriating fear back in her eyes. Later, when he calmed, he realized what he must have looked like.

Worse, she continued to treat him with the same disdain, as though he hadn't just taken out four of her heavily armed foes. The burns he'd received from their frozen skin were just beginning to heal. Marik thought she would have shown some appreciation. Instead, she went to inspect his broken cage and ordered him placed in another.

Why had those bandits singled her out, anyway? And where the hell had that ice sprouted from? He posed the question to Jedar but the bandit just narrowed his gaze and jutted his chin in the air.

"Then tell me, why are you fighting each other?"

"The false queen," Jedar replied. "The one you saved today." He spat in the snow.

"That sasquatch is your queen?"

"She is no queen of mine. You see how she binds herself in hides. She is not one of us, yet she rules absolutely. She must be removed from power, so the true queen can lead us."

Marik spoke his next words in Cyrellian, testing out his knowledge of the language. "Interesting. Where they take us?"

"You learn fast, demon." He sneered. "So did your brothers, as I recall."

Marik switched back to Demonish, "I'm sure they did. So, where are they taking us?"

"The palace, in the city of Sori."

"Is that where the queen lives?"

"The true queen lives there, as well as the false queen. It's a city of luxury and advantages, but not for us, demon. We will only see the dungeons unless you get us out of here. You'll have a place with my people if you vow to fight for our cause. I promise."

"Won't they want me dead for preventing the 'false queen's' death?"

"I can explain to them. You didn't know what you were doing.

You saw only violence and had to partake, as is your nature."

Marik kept his eyes from rolling. "As promised, I'll get you out of here, but I only want to find a lost girl and to leave this planet. Have you ever heard of someone who goes by the name Nadua?"

Jedar tilted his head quizzically. He opened his mouth to speak but shut it as the tent flap flew open and two guards entered.

* * *

Tamir stepped into the prisoner's tent, followed closely by Nakul. The two captives turned a glaring gaze at them, and the demon bared his fangs.

Tamir ignored him. If he had not escaped by now, then it wasn't going to happen. What a disappointment he'd turned out to be.

The demon should have been able to free himself from those ropes. If he had, his primitive mind would have sought out the closest female body. And since Nadua was the only female around, it should have been the perfect plan. Even if he didn't kill her afterward, Tamir would have done it, and made it look like the demon's doing. Now, with the arrival of the rebel, a new plan was forming.

Beside him, Nakul asked, "Shall we set the demon loose since he can't seem to do it himself? I thought you said they were strong?"

"Apparently this demon is not like the others. He's had his chance and failed. We have a rebel here who would not hesitate to kill her if he were free to do so."

The rebel turned eager, watching them with hopeful skepticism.

"When everyone wakes in the morning, she will be found with his dagger in her chest, and the rebel will be gone. The obvious will be assumed, and we will return home with the sad news of the queen's assassination."

"You wish me to kill the false queen?" asked the rebel.

Tamir scoffed. "Do you think I'd trust someone so easily captured with such an important task? The only thing you will be doing is running back to your clan with your heart still beating."

At Tamir's gesture, Nakul moved to cut the rebel's bindings. "Now leave, and tell your friends who to thank when the rightful queen is finally in power."

The rebel bowed. He made a comment to the demon in its crude language, before stepping through the exit. Peeking his head back in, the rebel asked, "What about a weapon?" Tamir gave him a dangerous look and the rebel backed away. "Right. Good luck, then."

Nakul spoke up. "What do we do with the demon? Should I kill him?" He palmed the hilt of his sword.

"Not yet. In the morning, the soldiers will look to me for leadership, and his death will be my first act. It will raise the spirits of the men after they find their beloved queen dead."

"I can't believe how many are loyal to her. It sickens me."

"Not to worry, Nakul. Once the true queen and I are wed, I will cleanse the palace of these traitors. Now take this." Tamir placed the rebel's dagger in Nakul's outstretched hand.

"You honor me, My Liege."

"Wait till she sleeps." Tamir put a warning in his tone. "If you're caught—"

"I will not be."

* * *

It was obvious to Marik what was happening. He didn't need Jedar's parting words, "Guess I won't need your help after all, demon. The false queen dies tonight," to know they were going to murder the woman who was their queen.

Marik didn't understand why the idea sat in his stomach like a heavy weight. This political animosity was none of his business. His first priority was to find Nadua, and he was only tagging along with these people for convenience.

He could leave now, go it on his own, but he still had no idea where he was, or where to find civilization, or where he should begin his search. Even if he did come across a town, the people there would probably only try to kill him.

A thought sparked in his mind. He could warn this *queen* of the plot against her. Save her life—again. Perhaps this time she'd be more inclined to help him. At the very least, he could demand some food for his service. They hadn't bothered to feed him. And if they didn't yet know it, they soon would: a hungry demon was a dangerous being.

The two Cyrellian betrayers quietly left. Marik waited a few moments before snapping the rope around his wrists. Easing toward the flap, he peeked through the small opening. The campsite was almost fully shaded in darkness, but for a few lit tents.

The storm had died down to a thick, but otherwise peaceful, snowfall. A few distant shadows drifted about. Possibly guards on patrol.

Feeling secure no one was close, Marik stepped from the tent and weaved his way through camp.

Of the few brightly lit tents, only one featured a guard posted outside. Marik spied another one patrolling on the other side of camp, coming his way. All others were likely on the outskirts, keeping watch for another ambush.

Sticking to the shadows, Marik moved closer. The fine coat of the newly fallen snow helped hide the sound of his footsteps. Just as the patrolling guard approached, Marik crouched behind a tent. To hide the white puffs from his breathing, Marik sucked in a breath, held it, and waited.

Clearly in no hurry, the man strolled by, his attention on the dark patch of trees just ahead of him. The man stilled for a moment, listening, and then turned back the way he came. Marik exhaled slowly.

Now was his chance. He shot toward his target. The guard only had time to widen his eyes before Marik knocked him unconscious. Holding the man's weight, he dragged him into the tent, and tossed him to the side.

The urgency to explain himself stuck in his throat the moment Marik caught sight of the *queen*.

His throat went dry and the only words he could manage were, "Oh shit."

Chapter 7

The welcomed heat of the fire warmed her body, freed from the confining furs. She had traded the skins for a lighter, more comfortable outfit: a sleeveless tan shirt and loose fitting trousers tied at the waist.

Nadua found these fabrics were easier to sleep in. Once under her edisdon fur blanket, she would be adequately warm through the night. She kept her boots and gloves on, however, not only for added warmth, but just in case she needed to quickly dress. The rebel menace was still looming.

The location of camp wasn't what she had hoped. The cliffs were still half a day's ride away and, in her opinion, they were too close to the mountains—where the Caves of Kayata held any number of threats. But the storm that was now but a tickle on the wind had beaten them to a stop. Even the Cyrellians had been shivering. The men had put up their tents in record time.

Staring into the burning embers, as she often did when she had much to think about, Nadua brushed a thick strand of hair behind one pointed ear.

Why had the demon hesitated to kill her? By the speed with which he took down those rebels, he'd had plenty of time to do it.

The fire popped and tiny sparks floated up before quickly burning out.

She'd inspected the cage lock after the fight. It had been cracked, almost clean through. She supposed it could have been faulty. Age combined with constant chill could cause almost any material to break down.

Or was it the demon's strength that had broken the lock? He was obviously much more powerful than she initially thought.

Nadua had questioned Tamir about this, but he assured her that the demon was secure. Besides, if he could have escaped so easily, why would he not have done so sooner?

His actions today had been ruthless, fortifying all the horrible stories she'd been told by those who had witnessed the brutality of his kind long ago. Never would she forget the savagery in his face as he dispatched those rebels without mercy. But when he turned toward her afterward, she recalled that his expression had changed. Became softer. As if he truly had been fighting for her.

Maybe he wasn't as horrible as the old stories suggested. But then she remembered his fierce anger from the night before and shivered.

It was too confusing. Nadua decided the demon needed further study before she let Renzo have him.

The tent rustled and someone pushed their way inside. Odd, usually they called for permission before entering.

Nadua rose to greet whoever it was and gasped at the sight of the demon dragging . . . a body? Spikes of fear shot through her.

When the demon caught sight of her, he froze, looking almost as shocked as she was.

* * *

Marik couldn't believe the sight before him. A description of Nadua hadn't been provided in the book, but he knew instantly that it was her. Her oddly shaped ears were prominent, the most obvious trait. Her eyes . . . how could he have not seen it before? They were nearly identical in color to Anya's.

Marik couldn't keep his gaze from followed the line of her body. Glossy red hair fell softly over sleek bare shoulders, leading his eyes to her breasts, rising and falling with every breath.

Her body—Marik had to stifle a hungry groan—was full of luscious curves that made his lower regions take immediate notice.

A creature from his deepest fantasies stood before him.

She recovered from the shock faster than he did and bent down, reaching for something. Whatever she was going for wouldn't be good for him—her eyes said as much. He was to her in a second, yanking her away from the dagger she'd pulled on him the other night.

Tricky female.

As soon as he had his arms around her, she began to thrash. Marik covered her mouth as she prepared for a scream that he was sure would have alerted the entire camp. Still, she hollered through his palm while continuing to struggle. The sweet scent of her filled his nose and a wave of desire swept through him, so strong he nearly doubled over. And the way she was moving her body against his wasn't helping.

Simultaneously kicking her legs and screeching like a wild woman, she smashed her elbow into his stomach, which helped to dampen his baser instincts. It also helped him to focus on the seriousness of the situation.

Nadua was the queen to be murdered! How the hell was that possible?

He no longer needed her help. She needed his. Only she didn't know it, and the way she was trying to scratch his eyes out told him she was in no mood to listen to anything he had to say at the moment. If he didn't get them both away from here, the Cyrellians were going to kill him. And then her.

Marik pulled her out of the tent and tore for woods. The mountain in the distance might provide a place to hide until he could get her calm enough to explain everything. If only she wasn't fighting so ferociously.

A voice shouted from behind. They must have found the guard knocked out and Nadua's tent empty.

Marik hurried his steps, slowing every so often to regain his grip on his captive, who was doing everything in her power to get away from him.

"Calm yourself, woman, you'll thank me later."

She made a doubtful noise and squirmed harder.

More voices rose from behind, but Marik was already deep into the trees. He got the sense that these Cyrellians didn't have the kind of night vision he did. Nadua's however, might be a little better, because she was continually trying to drive him into a tree, with surprising accuracy.

A sharp pain shot through his finger and he pulled it away from her mouth with a curse.

The wench bit me!

"I'm here! I'm here!" she screamed.

Silencing her once more with his hand over her mouth, Marik paid more attention to where her teeth were headed. Unfortunately, her outburst was successful in alerting her guards of their location and the voices began to grow louder.

At the same time, Nadua was doing too a good a job of slowing him down with the combination of her thrashing legs, whipping body, and trying to find the soft spot of his nose with the back of her head. If she had been captured by anyone other than him, she would have freed herself by now.

Finally, they reached the base of the mountain and he began

dragging Nadua up the rocky incline. She managed another bite, but he swallowed the pain.

There was a cave about twenty feet up. Hopefully it would be large enough to hide them.

When the wench bit him yet again, he contemplated knocking her unconscious.

"Damn it, woman!"

The voices from behind seemed to be moving off into another direction, growing distant. Nadua must have realized it too because she began to whimper as her struggles grew weaker, her breath labored.

At the entrance to the cave, Nadua gave one last desperate burst of energy, flailing and bucking her body. Marik held tight, waiting for her fatigue to kick in. When it did, he moved them deeper inside.

After a few minutes, the darkness almost became too much for him, but his eyes adjusted and he could still see well enough to push them forward. There was a maze like quality to the cavern, it broke into many chambers.

Marik used his sense of smell to decipher the best direction, one where the air flowed free and wouldn't turn stale or poisoned. Nadua had gone limp, and she was shaking uncontrollably.

Finally, they were far enough into the cave that he didn't think her voice would carry to the entrance. He removed his hand from her mouth.

Cyrellian insults flew from her like water down a slope. Marik understood a few words and had to laugh when she called him an edisdon dicksucker.

"Calm yourself. I'm not going to hurt you."

"No, you're g-going to k-kill me!" Her shivering was growing worse. "I'm f-freezing. I n-need f-f-fire!"

"I can't make a fire just yet. They may see the light and find us."

* * *

Gods, if only!

"We need to keep hidden or they'll kill us both," came his voice from somewhere in the sea of black. "I'm not going to let that happen. You're safe with me." He sounded like he was trying to reassure her.

The demon is psychotic!

Nadua tried to tell him so, but the piercing cold leached away her voice. Wrapping her arms around herself wasn't enough to keep the last of her warmth from slipping away. Her teeth began to chatter uncontrollably. She knew she wouldn't last much longer.

The demon cursed under his breath.

She heard a rustling and then something came around her—the demon's coat, which she had so graciously allowed him to keep. It was huge on her, falling past her knees. The thing might help a little, but it was in no way equal to her usual garment.

"Stay here," he said. "I'll be right back."

As if she had a fucking choice! She couldn't see two inches in front of her face. They were deep in the Caves of Kayata, where no light was allowed.

"D-Demon?"

Apparently he was already gone. The only sound left was her own shallow breath and the chatter of her teeth. Who knows if he would even return for her?

Suddenly, there was another noise. Footsteps? Was she imagining it?

"D-Dem-m-mon?" she called again. No response. Gods, it could be any manner of creature that the demon had left her with. There was a reason why the Cyrellians avoided these caves.

The spike of fear had her stumbling toward what she thought

was the exit. Blindly, she inched forward, placing her arms in front of her. Her legs ran into something and she used her hands to identify it. A large boulder.

Feeling her way around it, she attempted to walk again but came to what must be a cavern wall, or possibly an even larger bolder.

Weakness filled her bones along with the frigid air. Her fingers burned and prickled. She shoved them against her mouth, blowing as much warm air on them as she could. When her shivers overtook her, Nadua curled into a ball, hoping someone would find her in time.

So tired.

Somewhere in her dreary mind she realized her exhaustion was a bad sign.

The sound of falling pebbles roused her. Too cold to be afraid, she waited for some cave dwelling creature to attack.

"Are you alright?"

She let out a relieved sigh, though she didn't know why. It was the demon. Probably had come back to kill her. The sound of sticks hitting the floor echoed around her. It seemed as if the demon was methodically breaking them up and moving them around in a pile.

"This will keep us off the cold floor."

Us?

"It's the best I can do for now."

She heard him stand and move toward her. Obviously, the demon didn't have a problem seeing in this darkness, because there was no running into boulders for him.

In one easy swoop, he pulled her off the ground. Nadua didn't even have the strength to protest. As it was, her traitorous body instinctively curled into him for the heat he was giving off.

After he laid them on what turned out to be some sort of pallet, he slipped his arms around her. She weakly tried to push away, but at the moment she couldn't have pushed a snowflake off of her.

"Put your arm around me," he said.

"Fuck you!" she managed, though she did move closer. The heat of his body was already starting to sooth the chill in her.

And he smells good.

She was losing it.

"Use my body for the warmth you need. I tried to get back to your tent to find those skins you wear, but there are too many guards. I'll try again in the morning. This is what I can offer till then."

With her mind reluctant, but her body screaming for warmth, she placed her arms on his chest, burrowing into him as close as possible. Thick biceps cradled her.

Eventually, the worst of her shaking abated, while her mind began its exhausted descent. Her last thought—which later she blamed on her delusional state—was how wonderful it felt to be within his arms.

Chapter 8

Rising from a heavy sleep, Nadua adjusted her position on the bed, which, for some reason, was less comfortable this morning, and snuggled deeper against the warm . . . *muscular chest?* Stiffening, she opened her eyes to a wall of black.

Her heart jerked as the events from last night played back in her mind. The side of her face was pressed intimately against the demon's bare chest, his musky scent and heat enveloping her.

Afraid she'd wake him, Nadua tried to remain still.

Unexpectedly, his grip tightened around her. Panic nearly engulfed her, making her pulse burn through her veins. She had to get away, get back to camp, signal her soldiers. But how was she going to do any of that? She wasn't sure exactly how long she'd slept, but she assumed there should be some light outside by now—or perhaps it was already midday—yet the cave was still pitch black. He must have taken her farther inside than she thought.

Somehow, Nadua would need to get the demon to lead her out. Without him, she might never find her way. The Caves of Kayata were said to be a complex labyrinth of passages, mostly unexplored due to the many dangers. Pitfalls, cave-ins, and toxic air. And those were the non-superstitious obstacles.

"How are you feeling?" His deep voice rumbled in his chest.

Nadua tensed in surprise. She hadn't realized the demon was awake. His voice was soft and drowsy, which probably made it easier for him to fake the concern she heard in it.

"Take me back, demon, and I promise not to have you killed."

He touched his chin to the top of her head, pulled her closer, and breathed deep. "You're not going back there, ever."

"Is that a threat?" Preparing to push away from him, Nadua placed one palm against his skin, but as she felt the ridges of his muscles—the first warm flesh she felt in a long time—a completely inappropriate surge of desire came over her.

Am I so deprived of another's touch? And where is his shirt!

Then she realized there was some kind of fabric wrapped around her legs. He must have given her his shirt at some point during the night.

"Completely the opposite. I plan on keeping you safe and alive until *Marada* comes for us."

"*Marada*? Is that one of your gods?"

His body shook with amusement, which brought back the awareness that she was still pressed tightly against him. His hand was on her back, lightly rubbing.

It felt odd arguing with someone, fearing him, while holding on to him for dear life. The air around them was still as cold as it was the night before.

"*Marada* is my home. It's a ship." He sounded so reasonable, but what he was saying was that he planned to abduct her and take her away.

"So you want to take me there, and what? Have tea? Introduce me to the family?"

"Aye. Mine *and* yours."

That got her attention. "What?"

"Your sister Anya is . . . well, was aboard the *Marada*." His tone went serious with heavy sorrow. "Hopefully, Sebastian got to her in time. We found her—or rather, she found us a few months ago."

Nadua nearly balked, but managed to keep it to herself. She didn't have a sister named Anya. The liar must have gotten his facts wrong and confused the name with Ava, Fineas' daughter and future queen of the Cyrellians.

However, keeping him talking might be in her best interest. Perhaps she could discover his true agenda, as well as keep herself alive.

"What do you mean you hope he got to her in time?"

"Just as your soldiers were playing pin cushion with my leg, Anya was being taken by someone very bad, someone who would want to hurt her. Sebastian went after her, and if all went well, Anya is safe, and they're on their way to find us right now."

Nadua didn't think it was wise to mention that it was she who played pin cushion with his leg. Her soldiers had just reeled him in. Better to let that drop.

"What if they're not on their way to find you?"

He was silent for a moment. "Then a very dear friend is dead, and possibly so is your sister."

Not my sister, psycho!

"Your friend, I assume he's a demon?"

"Aye."

"And Anya is like me?"

He raised a brow. "Uh . . . yes."

"Tell me, then, why would a demon risk his life for someone like me?"

"Because she is his mate," he said simply. As if that explained anything. "Look, I can tell you're skeptical. Let me start a fire and we can talk face-to-face."

Nadua let go of him with a combination of eagerness and regret. The latter was only for the warmth he provided. As soon as they parted, the cold air assaulted her.

"How is it you're so warm?" she found herself asking.

"It's evolutionary," he replied, while gathering part of their bed into a pile. "Our home planet had very extreme winters, not unlike here, from what I've seen so far. We also experienced very hot summers. For survival, our bodies adapted to adjust to both temperatures."

A spark flashed in the dark as he struck two rocks together, and then again. After a short time there was a decent fire going, warming the space around them.

Finally seeing the demon felt awkward. He didn't know it, but he was the first male to touch her, without causing pain, in nearly four hundred years. She could still smell him on her, and she hated herself for savoring it. He was still shirtless, and it didn't help that his chest was sculpted to perfection, even under all those scars. He was unnervingly attractive.

"There, that's better," the demon said, when he was satisfied with the fire's size. The chamber was larger than she initially assumed. The ceiling curved into an uneven dome, and sporadic columns of rock formations cast ominous shadows every which way.

No ice or snow was present. It had been a long time since she'd seen sand and dirt, or bare stone. Outside, the temperature never grew warm enough for the snow to melt down. It just grew in layers, the landscape ever changing.

The demon took a seat on a boulder, watching her as she studied her surroundings. She should be looking for a weapon, not marveling at the walls, but they were strangely fascinating as the firelight bounced off them, creating shimmering pockets of light and dark.

"The reason we came here," the demon began, "was to find you, Nadua."

She stilled at the use of her name. She hadn't told it to him, but it was possible he heard it from one of her guards. "Is that so? What a coincidence that *I* be the one you're searching for. And that I was there just when you landed."

"Where your father is concerned, I don't think I can believe in coincidences. And it was Anya who sensed where you might be."

Nadua claimed a seat across from him, keeping the fire between them. "Ah, you know my father, as well as my sister . . . *Anya*."

"No, I've never met your father, and why do you say her name like that?"

She hadn't meant to sound so dubious, but his story was so poorly strewn together. "Why did you not tell me any of this when I asked?"

"I had no idea who you were. I figured you were one of them." His eyes unabashedly skimmed her body. "I should have known when you gave me that peek show."

Nadua's teeth gnashed together. "That wasn't . . . That was just . . ."

"You left me aching bad that night. Left me wondering how the rest of you would look." He gave a sexy grin. "I must say, I'm not disappointed."

Cheeks flaming, she scrambled for the closest fist-sized rock. "I will fight you if you try anything."

His features hardened. "I'm not going to hurt you. Just like what I see, is all."

She relaxed a bit, but held onto her primitive weapon. "Please, just continue."

The demon proceeded to tell her how this Anya person had found her way onto *Marada* after being enslaved on a ship called *Extarga*. Which was absurd. Not only would her father never allow that to happen, but Nadua—master of eavesdropping on her father—had learned the intended locations of all her sisters, and a ship named

Extarga had not been one of them.

He continued with details of their lengthy journey through space—expedited by *Anya's* ability to provide energy to the ship, nearly dying in the process—to find a book, written by their father, King Alestar. The book provided them with her location on Undewla.

Then he went into a tale even less believable. "I overheard your men conspiring against you. The two that were with you, the first night we spoke, were plotting to kill you last night and blame the rebel, who they had also set free. That's why I took . . . extreme . . . measures to get you out of there. I don't believe all your men are in on it, but I can't be sure."

Nadua took it all in, and tried not to laugh. "But according to you, you didn't even know who I was before you rushed to my *rescue*. Why bother risking your life to save a stranger who threatened to torture you?"

"Before I knew you were Nadua, I was hoping you would be appreciative enough to help me find her . . . well, you. Now that I have found you, I just need to keep you alive. And that means keeping you away from any blue tinted would-be murderers."

Nadua couldn't help the skeptical sound that escaped her. "And are we just going to sit in this cave, hoping your friends will find us here?"

"No, when things settle down out there, we'll go back to the place where you captured me. That's where Sebastian would start looking."

"I can't travel without my furs! I wouldn't last an hour."

"Don't worry. I plan to sneak back into camp and get them for you."

"How gracious of you, and while you're there can you pick me up a couple of edisdons and something to snack on, because walking all the way back there is going to take some time."

The demon looked thoughtful. "I can try, but I can't guarantee it."

Nadua felt her mouth drop open. "Demon, I was kidding. This is crazy. We can't just go wonder off by ourselves. That's a death wish on this planet. What would we eat, where would we sleep? You may be full of warm fuzzies, but the edisdon fur only goes so far at keeping my temperature up." She took in a frustrated breath. "I'm sure whatever you heard, regarding the plot against my life, was a misunderstanding. If we go back to camp now, I'll set everything straight."

"Did you not hear anything I just said? I've come to take you off this planet. Whether or not someone wants you dead doesn't change that. Besides, it was not a misunderstanding! I was there when they released the rebel. They spoke of how his dagger would be found in your chest and the one—what was his name?—Tamir, seemed to be in charge."

Impossible.

"How could you possibly understand anything Tamir might have said? He doesn't even speak your language!"

"They weren't speaking Demonish."

"Okay, so you've learned to speak Cyrellian in a few days."

The demon just shrugged, and Nadua scoffed.

"Last night, you were cursing me in Cyrellian right?"

"Yes." She repeated a few of those curses for him now.

With a bit of amusement, the demon said. "You called me an edisdon dicksucker."

Nadua gaped at him. He couldn't have learned the language in just a few days, her mind rationalized. The deceitful demon must have known the language all along and pretended not to.

Realizing what her trail of thought must be, the demon added, "My kind can learn almost anything in a short amount of time. An advantage of our race that helped many of us survive after the destruction of our planet."

Nadua stared at him, not sure what to say.

Her disbelief must have been evident, because he made an irritated sound.

Throwing what was left of their pallet on the dying fire, he said, "I don't know why you're having such a hard time believing me. I know facts. Stuff that I shouldn't know. Stuff about your family, your race." He scrubbed his hand down his face. Shaking his head, he stood silent for a moment. Then he changed the subject. "How is your leg?"

Nadua had been ignoring the dull pain from where she'd been stabbed. When she didn't answer, he crossed to her.

"Let me see."

"What? It's fine."

Her heart rate spiked when he knelt in front of her. Peeling the rock from her grasp, he tossed it over his shoulder. She was contemplating running, but he gave her a look that said she wouldn't get far.

He placed her calf on his bent knee, gently lifting the hem of her pant leg to reveal her upper thigh. The cloth that had been wrapped around her wound was soaked in blood, but it looked worse than it actually was.

As he began undoing the knot, Nadua marveled at the lightness of his touch, as if he were trying his hardest not to hurt her. He set the ruined cloth aside and began inspecting the gash.

Her breath hitched at the feeling of his palm on her thigh, holding her still for his examination. Luckily, the demon didn't seem to notice how fast her heart was beating, although to her it seemed like the sound of it should be echoing off the cavern walls.

"You heal well. I can see it's almost fully closed."

"See. It's fine." She tried to remove her leg but he held her firm, still not hurting, but keeping her in place.

As his thumb rubbed her inner thigh, their eyes met. "You really do have lovely legs."

Jaw dropped, she shuddered at his touch. But as quickly as it appeared, his heated expression morphed into something unreadable and he let her go.

He moved toward a darkened passageway and ordered, "Stay put while I get your furs."

"Wait! Take me with you, demon! Don't leave me in this cave!"

Halting by the chamber's exit, he glanced over his shoulder. "The fire should last until I return."

Then he was gone. No sound for her to follow into the dark, not that she didn't try. With a few new scrapes to show for her effort, she returned to the flames, once again chilled to the bone.

After her teeth stopped chattering, she slumped on the same rock he'd been sitting on and was instantly slammed by a vision.

As with most her visions, it was like being jolted into another realm, then a fuzzy image appeared, coating her sight, and morphing into something more tangible.

Years ago, she was used to her sight suddenly not belonging to her, but since she hadn't had a vision in quite a while, it startled her at first. She forced herself to calm and allowed the vision to take over.

Menacing red eyes, fangs seeking blood, a face twisted in a snarl. An army of her men held the demon back as he tried with all his might to get to her. The depth of his gaze was hollow, both unseeing and focused through their unwavering panic and rage. Nadua's heart lurched as his body sliced through the line.

A blinding white light broke the vision, leaving her stunned and gasping. Her nails were digging into the rock beneath her.

Slowly, the disorientation that came with every vision dissipated. It had been decades since she'd had a vision so intense. She could almost feel the need for bloodshed rolling off the demon.

Though the vision had been short, the message was clear. Sometime in the future, the demon was going to try to kill her.

Chapter 9

The tail end of twilight kissed the sky. Darkening shadows were encouraged by heavy cloud cover.

On the way to the Cyrellian camp, Marik had mused about the stubbornness of women. Well, one woman in particular.

Nadua had her mind set on not believing him. Why? He'd been a bit rough when spiriting her away, but that was only because she had been fighting him so fiercely.

He'd feared all her thrashing had reopened her wound but it looked to be healing as it should.

Unfortunately, being that close to her, touching her, had caused his desire to make its vicious return. He would have loved to take things further, but was sure she wouldn't appreciate his reaction to her. Not when she resisted the truth of his words so persistently.

He supposed being informed by a stranger that someone she trusted was scheming against her could be hard to accept. Marik wondered how close Nadua was with Tamir. A spike of irritation sprang to life inside him. He hoped she had better taste than that, but she'd already proven her judge of character to be a bit skewed.

With far too much ease, Marik slipped into camp. Nadua's tent was as he had left it, minus the crackling fire. The furs he came for were draped over a line that ran the length of the enclosure. It looked as if she had attempted to wash them. Their scent was not as bad as before, but was still strong enough to mask her natural fragrance, a fragrance that had kept him up all night fighting the need to roll her to her back and warm her body in other ways.

A frustrated sigh escaped him. It would be a shame to cover up that physique, but necessary. Not only because she needed protection from the cold, but because his desire for her was already at a dangerous point. He'd been hiding it well, and for good reason. She didn't trust him.

Though demons were mostly civilized, and could usually control their more primitive impulses, they were still slaves to their baser instincts, as Marik was well aware. And his baser instincts were telling him to go back to that cave and explore every inch of the woman he'd left inside, before taking her up against the wall.

Once he got back to *Marada*, he'd need to find a willing female fast, to relieve the building pressure.

Marik snatched the furs and gathered a few more items before making his way to his next target. The scent of cooked meat guided him to a fire pit, manned by a solitary soldier who was twirling a carcass on a spit. Procuring an edisdon would be far too conspicuous, but this meal would be easy to pilfer, and might be their last for a while.

Using a nearby tent as cover, Marik stalked closer. But voices from inside had him halting in his tracks.

"—and I both witnessed her final moments. Continuing the search is pointless. I have no doubt that the queen has left this world. We will resume our journey home at first light."

"But to return without a body? We will be unable to perform an honorable burial."

"The demon is long gone. Who knows if we will ever find a body? No, we must return home quickly and look to our new queen for guidance."

So, they're claiming Marik killed Nadua, anyway. That would enforce the heavily ingrained prejudice against his kind. Of course, it didn't really matter. Both he and Nadua would be off this planet soon. He hoped.

A small prick of fear tingled his nerves. What if the *Marada* never came?

* * *

Crouching behind a large boulder, Nadua waited. The rock in her hand was growing heavy, but soon it would be the instrument of her survival. The sound of his footsteps echoed through the passageways, warning of his approach. She would need to be fast.

He stepped through the threshold, arms filled with a heaping pile of logs and twigs. By the looks of it, her fur blanket was being used as an oversized satchel, heaped full of stuff. Adrenalin coursed through her as her arm swung out.

"Ow!" The demon dropped his bundle, and reached for his head.

Damn!

She was counting on him going down with the first hit, but she'd planned for this, just in case. Reaching down to her pile of rocks, Nadua readied to strike again.

Before she could release her second throw, he was ripping it from her grip and positioning his body firmly behind hers. Her arms, easily restrained with one of his hands, were drawn above her head as he effortlessly twirled her body, pushing her back against the cavern wall.

In a low but threatening voice, he said, "I'm losing my patience with you, luv."

She struggled as best she could but it was no use. He used his body like a steel cage.

His lips came to her ear and his voice went even lower. "You are not going to get away from me. Our journey will be long, and I will drag you kicking and screaming the entire way if I have to." He seemed to take a moment to gather her scent. The act made her shudder. "I was hoping to give you your furs, but now I know you'll try to escape while I sleep. But if you promise to be good, I'll give you your other present."

"Fuck you, demon!"

"That's another thing. I have a name, and you will use it. It's Marik, since you've never bothered to ask."

"I'll call you whatever I want. *Demon.*"

He let out a frustrated sigh. "Stubborn wench." Releasing her, he went to the scattered pile. He'd gathered more twigs and sticks to replenish the makeshift pallet, and more logs for the fire. On top of the pallet, he spread out her blanket.

Nadua eyed her fur clothing, buried in the mess. When the demon noticed her line of sight, he grabbed them and placed them high on a ledge where she could not reach. Then he turned his attention back to the jumble of items, ignoring her nasty glare.

He retrieved a carefully wrapped package. Her stomach grumbled when she caught the sweet scent of roasted meat. The demon took on a mischievous grin.

"*Acta,*" she grumbled. If he really did understand the Cyrellian language, then he should know she'd just called him an asshole.

By the disapproving look he gave her, he did, but his only response was to tear off a piece of meat and pop it into his mouth, making a show of enjoying himself.

"Your men have stopped looking for you." He took another bite.

Nadua rolled her eyes. "You expect me to believe that? They

wouldn't stop searching after so short a time."

"They would if they've been told you're dead."

"And who would tell them that? I suppose they let you stroll into camp to give them the news."

"I overheard your friend Tamir claim to have seen me kill you with his own eyes."

"Whatever you say, demon." Tamir wouldn't betray her like that.

They sat in silence for a long while. The demon enjoyed his meal as the fire grew dimmer and dimmer. She assumed he wasn't going to give her any food until she called him by name.

Ha!

There was no way she was going to give him the satisfaction. She wasn't that hungry, anyway. Her stomach made a sound in dis-agreement.

"Hungry?" He smirked.

"Not at all."

When the fire grew dangerously low, a chill ran through her. He didn't look as though he had any intention of adding logs to the flame and she wondered if he was about to demand she call him by name or freeze to death.

Pulling herself off the ground, she reached for a log, but he stopped her. "Come on, demon, are you really going to let me freeze?"

Eyes sparkling with amusement, he teetered the meat between two fingers. The smell made her stomach grumble. "Are you sure you don't want something to eat before bed?"

"So you're going to make me starve, as well as freeze?"

"Food is here for the taking, if you really wanted it. I'd willingly give it to you—"

She reached for it, knowing he would just snatch it away. She was right.

"Do you have something you'd like to say?"

"No."

"Ah, well." He took another bite and added, while chewing, "I promise you won't freeze, but there will be no fire tonight."

"If there's no fire then how . . . oh, no. There's no need for that. We have plenty of wood for a fire to last all night. I . . . I only allowed that last night out of necessity. You can't expect me to cuddle up to you for warmth again!"

"You brought this on yourself, luv. Fire is just another weapon for your scheming mind to use against me. And I plan on getting a good night's sleep." He held up the meat in one last attempt, but all he received was an indignant glare. With a shrug, he wrapped the meat and placed it with her furs on the high ledge.

Her stomach rebelled, as if angered by her refusal to submit. She knew the demon could hear every ireful grumble. When he turned back to her there was something new in his grip, but it wasn't an offering of food.

Nadua backed away from him. "What do you think you're doing?"

"I told you." He caught one of her wrists and snugly wrapped the rope around it. "I plan on getting a good night's sleep tonight." As he reached for her other wrist, she jerked it away, along with the rest of her body. He easily used her captured arm to pull her back and subdue her, wrapping both wrists tightly together.

"You son of a bitch! Release me!"

"I won't have you slipping away in the night and bashing me with more rocks."

Nadua thrashed her body, trying to land a kick; she was usually skillful at kicking. In an embarrassingly easy maneuver, he lifted her entire body off the ground and deposited it on the pallet. Her back met the soft fur of the blanket and heavy muscles came on top of her, holding her in place.

His body, as usual, was warm, and something inside her eased against her will. Then she felt something she hadn't felt in a long time. The demon was . . . turned on!

"Hold still and just let me finish."

Heart slamming against her chest, she squeaked. "Finish what?"

His smile was wicked in the dim light, and he began moving down her body. The ability to breath suddenly became difficult. Her whole body seemed to blush as his hands trailed down her sides, over her hips, leaving a line of fire in their wake. She should be fighting but she couldn't seem to make her body respond properly.

Wide eyed, she watched him, trapped in his gaze. He continued his course, his hands stopping briefly at her upper thighs. As if he couldn't help it, a soft masculine groan escaped him, making her body clench in places she'd long forgotten about.

When he made it to her calves, he revealed more rope from seemingly out of nowhere and began binding her legs. Head dropping back, Nadua let out a harsh sigh that she was sure sounded like relief rather than disappointment, but after the demon's soft chuckle, she wasn't so sure.

Then reality slammed back into her and she realized what he was doing.

"Stop this! I won't run away, I promise." Unless she could get to her skins. "This is not necessary."

"Sure it is. This is the only way to make sure you stay put." He sat back to examine his work. "Look, I don't like having to tie you up." At her raised eyebrow, he teased, "Well, I do a little. But I know what it's like to be helpless and at the whim of someone you don't trust. Believe me when I say I don't want to hurt you. I promise to do everything in my power not to, but if you don't stop making me have to be so close to you . . .when you smell as you do . . ."

Nadua tilted her head in confusion.

"Your scent, it calls to me . . . to my most primal need."

"Yeah, I felt your primal need, and don't you dare. I would never permit that."

His grin grew teasing again. "Then why did your luscious scent grow stronger a moment ago?"

Nadua's jaw dropped. "It . . . no, it didn't!"

"I think maybe your primal instincts are reacting to me too."

The demon crawled up beside her, wrapping one thick arm around her waist, and pulling her against his body so that she was practically in his lap, primal instincts and all.

His warmth engulfed her, though his next words made her shiver as he spoke next to her ear. "I can only hope that one day you will perform your leggy seduction act for me again, because I can't get it out of my head."

Chapter 10

Despite the lumpy pallet, her hands and legs being tied, and the constantly aroused demon at her back, Nadua had slept better than should be expected.

The demon was up and about, and had already lit a fire, though he hadn't bothered to untie her yet. She had the feeling he was leaving her bound for his own sick pleasure, evident by the vexing smirk on his lips. When she'd asked him to loosen the rope, she'd called him demon again, and his eyes flashed with annoyance.

"You can't keep me tied up the whole time. What are you going to do? Cart me over your shoulder like some barbarian?" When he evenly met her gaze, she cringed. "You can't be serious!"

"You just need to say one little word." He produced the leftover meat from last night and began warming it over the fire. "Then I'll untie you and let you eat."

Nadua caught a whiff of the roasted meat and her stomach twisted. Damn it, she *was* hungry. And there would be no escaping him if he continued to keep her restrained like this. She would have to ignore her pride on this one.

"Fine." She clenched her teeth and pushed the words out. "Please untie me . . . Mar-im . . ." She trailed off.

"Wow! That was almost close."

Nadua grumbled under her breath. It was nearly inaudible to her own ears. "Marik."

"What?"

"Marik! Marik! Marik! Damn it, untie me!"

"As you wish, Princess."

"Queen," she corrected.

"Not anymore."

Nadua shoved her arms out at him as the demon moved to undo the bindings.

"Tamir was talking about looking to the new queen for leadership, so they already have a replacement lined up."

Once the ropes were lose, she hurried to untie her legs, pushing away the demons helping hands. Then she practically ripped the meat from his grip. It was half eaten in seconds. Through her angry chewing, she had hardly tasted it.

"Ava is not yet old enough to take over," Nadua blurted, and then regretted the statement.

"Who's Ava?"

The person you've confused with my sister.

"She's the real queen."

"Ah, so you two are in battle over the crown? She wants you out of the way?"

"Of course not! She'll be crowned in a few years and I'll gladly step down."

"You don't covet the title?"

"Gods, no! I don't enjoy ruling at all. I wish she could take over now."

The demon looked considerate for a moment. "It doesn't make sense. If the true queen is going to take over in a few years anyway, then why bother trying to kill you?"

Nadua rolled her eyes.

He's really sticking with that story.

"Do you mind if we get out of this cave already? You may be

right at home in these dingy surroundings, but I need sun. Or at least what little sun I can get."

"Oh, aye," he said bitingly. "Give me dark and drafty and I'm content. Obviously we demons are too dimwitted to understand the concept of comfortable living." He snatched her furs from the ledge and tossed them at her.

Nadua began slipping them on at once. "I'm sorry, *demon*. Did I hurt your feelings?"

Without warning, his hand was wrapped around the back of her neck and the hard muscles of his body pressed against hers.

She gasped in surprise.

"That's the last time you use that word like a curse." Glowing red horns emphasized his sudden and dangerous anger.

Nadua hardened her features in defiance. In a dark part of her mind, she realized she should be frightened, but for some reason she wasn't. She couldn't say why. She also couldn't say why she had to struggle so hard not to focus on his lips, which were much closer to hers than they ought to be.

Unfortunately, by trying not to notice them, her mind began to take in other aspects of the demon, all of which were the last things she should be concentrating on at the moment.

With his warm hand against her nape, his thumb ever-so-slightly caressed below her ear. She didn't think he realized he was doing it. His deep green eyes, though trained on her in anger, were warm and green, like an Evlon summer. She hated him for that. His other arm had slipped around the small of her back. Unintentionally, she inhaled his masculine scent and shuddered, embarrassed to admit to herself why.

Just as she was trying to hide her reactions to him, his gaze turned hungry. "Your eyes," he murmured, almost in a daze.

Nadua swallowed hard, afraid her eyes had betrayed her and

turned violet with desire. That often happened with her kind; eye colors, shifting. It was difficult to hide at times. "Let me go."

He looked as confused as she felt, but he released her and turned away. No one on this planet knew what the shifting of her eyes meant. Not even Cyrus had guessed. She hoped this demon didn't know either, because in that brief moment . . . she wanted him.

Keep your senses.

After a short silence, Nadua remembered she had been in the middle of donning her warm skins and finished the process. Finally, she was ready for the rough conditions of Undewla.

They didn't say a word to each other as they traveled through the passageways, a torch lighting the way. Nadua mused at the difference between the way she'd entered the cave and how she was now leaving it. The demon was almost gentlemanly, offering her his hand over rocky terrain. And, though she refused his help each time, he didn't stop offering it.

At last, daylight grew near and a moment later they were outside. For the first time in ages, the sky was blue. The beauty of it drew her eyes for a long while. The demon's too, apparently. He was studying both the sky and the rest of the mountain landscape. He didn't seem to be paying any attention to her.

Without thinking, her fist closed around a heavy rock, and she used her whole body to swing it hard into the back of his skull.

He gave half a grunt and fell to the ground, limp and unmoving. Nadua waited a few moments to be sure he was out, surprised at how easily he went down. Then she was racing toward camp.

She decided that once she got there, she would have her men come back for him—to attempt a recapture, or to kill on sight, she wasn't sure.

Camp was a bit farther than expected but she made it without stopping. But the moment the trees began to thin she was unable to comprehend what she was seeing. Or rather, not seeing.

An empty space stood in front of her, no soldiers or tents waiting for her return. A dusting of loose snow skated across the barren land.

Perhaps she had headed in the wrong direction and camp was a little farther to the north. But as soon as she thought it, she knew it was a lie. There was evidence all around. Fire pits and muddied walkways. This is where they had been, and they had left without her, just as the demon said. And if he was right about this . . .

"It cannot be," she murmured.

A noise at her back made her whip around. The demon stood silent at the edge of the forest, leaning against a tree. He didn't look as though he'd just been knocked unconscious. She expected him to look smug, but he didn't. He actually looked a little concerned. The sight of it made her want to hit him over the head with another rock.

Nadua forced a strong tone. "This doesn't mean anything, dem . . . I'm sure there's another explanation."

Tamir couldn't have plotted against her. He had always been loyal. Always did as she asked without complaint. Why would he turn on her?

The demon shook his head. "How much more proof do you need?"

"You let me come here, didn't you? You wanted me to see this so I would believe you!"

He shrugged.

"Well, you should have done a little more research when you were digging into my background, because you don't have all your facts right."

He approached her then. "Oh? And what exactly have I gotten wrong?"

Exasperated, Nadua began stomping in the direction of the palace, determined to make her way home. "You've been very thorough, but for one small detail. Whatever made my men leave without me must seem like a lucky break for you. You must think I'll just follow you to your ship, eager to see my sister *Anya*."

He followed close behind. "Why are you being so difficult? You're being irrational, and stupid!"

"*Acta*! You want to know how I know I can't believe you? Because I don't have a sister named Anya!"

The sound of his footsteps ceased, and Nadua was ready to laugh at whatever lie he was about to come up with to cover his mistake.

"Oh, that's right. You would know her as Analia."

Nadua halted. A sickening heaviness rolled in her stomach.

Analia.

She hadn't heard the name spoken aloud in so long, but it instantly made her think of home. Her mind was bombarded with the striking contrast of this world compared to her own. All around her stood perpetually dead trees, blinding white ground, choking cold air.

Her throat worked hard to hold in the emotion that threatened to overwhelm her as the image of little Analia, playing under the giant trees behind their family's home filled her mind. Her elder sister, Kyra, standing beside her. It was the last memory of her sisters together.

The demon at her back hadn't said a word, but she could feel him watching her, waiting for something. A light breeze alerted her to the wetness on her cheeks and she worked fervently to dry them.

It hit her then, that her dream of finally going home, of seeing her family once more could become a reality.

When she was once more composed, Nadua turned around. "Okay dem . . . um, Marik. Tell me more."

Chapter 11

It took Nadua a while to fully accept the sudden change in her situation. It was a lot to take in. The possibility of going home, leaving this planet, leaving Ava. It was all giving her mixed emotions. Not to mention the alleged betrayal of one or more of her men, which she still wasn't fully convinced of, but the demon was sounding more credible by the minute.

She sat on a raised patch of snow and listened to what Marik had to say. It was disturbing to hear what had happened to her sister. From what Nadua remembered, Analia and their mother should have been en route to stay with one of the Faieara's strongest allies, among the dragon clans. But, according to Marik, they were betrayed and sold to a loathsome man, who had abused Analia until the day she escaped onto the ship, *Marada*.

When Nadua asked about her mother, the demon lowered his head and gave a slight shake. Nadua couldn't speak for a time after that.

Her father's book sounded fascinating, said to be large and lined in gold. Apparently, once closed, it could only be opened by Nadua or her two sisters—some sort of magical lock, possibly bespelled by the Serakians.

Inside it had been a letter to Analia, describing their father's vision of the future. He believed if they all returned home, there may be hope of rescuing their people from the Kayadon, who coveted the many gifts of her people.

Every Faieara used some form of magic, though some were more powerful than others. Her father's visions, for example, were much stronger than hers, and he could call on them whenever he liked, through quiet meditation. Hers came at the whim of the gods, and were about as helpful as them too.

Marik was eager to get moving. He wanted to get back to where he though his friends would begin their search, but Nadua thought it would be best to go to her palace—not only because it was nice and warm there, but she wanted to face Tamir, and learn the truth from him.

"I'm not letting you anywhere near that place without proper backup. We don't know how many are involved."

"I can't just leave without addressing this issue. If it is as you said, and Tamir has plotted against me, then he should be tried for treason. And Ava will be furious! Even if he claims to have done it for her benefit."

"Still, I'd have to insist on waiting for my friends. I'm strong alone, but your army still took me down. If we wait for *Marada*, you'd have four demons and Ethanule to safeguard you, among others."

"Ethanule?" Nadua's heart leaped. She and Ethanule used to flirt when he was tasked as her guard. She thought him very handsome. "Ethan is with you?" There was no stopping the little smile that slid over her lips.

The demon sat back, a strange look covering his features. "He's the one who translated the book and found your location."

"If Ethan is with your friends, then I feel much better about waiting till we rendezvous with them. He is a considerable warrior among my people."

"My kind isn't enough?"

Nadua looked up, wondering at the dark tone in his voice. "It's not that. It's just, I don't know your friends. Or you, for that matter." She recalled her vision of his enraged visage and wondered if she was doing the right thing by going along with him. "I don't even know my sister," Nadua continued. "She was very young when we were separated. But Ethan and I . . ." She could feel heat enter her cheeks. "We used to—"

"I don't need to hear it." Marik interrupted in a tone meant to end the conversation. He stood and brushed his pants clean. "We should get moving before we lose the light."

The sudden surliness was odd to her, but maybe it was a demon thing. From the stories, they could change moods with the fall of each snowflake.

* * *

It was obvious to Marik what Nadua and Ethan used to do. The chit grew red with embarrassment just remembering. He didn't know why learning she had been with Ethanule made him suddenly want to murder the man. It was none of his business.

They did need to get moving, though. Nadua figured it would take quite a few days to walk back to the location where Marik had been captured. But as they began their journey she continued to make the argument for going back to the palace, which would take roughly the same amount of time.

"Once we get there," she offered, "I can send soldiers out to find your friends."

"Like I said, we can't trust your soldiers."

Clearly Nadua wasn't used to not getting her way because her bottom lip stuck out every time he refused to give in. Marik found it sickeningly cute. At least she wasn't trying to assault him with rocks anymore.

Traveling near the mountains provided a good amount of cover. The area was thick with trees.

Although Marik felt they were adequately hidden from wandering eyes, he couldn't be sure. There was nothing on the wind, no sound that alerted him to danger, but something was making him uneasy. He kept glancing behind them to be sure no one was following.

According to Nadua, the mountains housed countless caves where they could find shelter, though she was admittedly anxious about going into them. When he asked why, she just said that many souls were lost to them.

As they traveled, neither made the effort to hold a conversation, which was fine by Marik. Staying focused was more important than idle chit chat, though he found the sound of her voice pleasing.

There was an apprehensive truce between them. He worried that she was only pretending to go along with him to force his guard to drop. And, in order to discover any such pretense, he watched her closely—which turned out to be a bad idea. Seeing the way she moved over the uneven terrain made him constantly visualize the body hidden by all that fur, and had him fighting to ignore his swollen shaft. When she bent to adjust the lacing of her boots, he barely kept himself from palming her backside.

Forcing his eyes in another direction, Marik realized what was happening to him, and he needed to get a hold of himself. There must be some residual chemicals flowing through him from when he'd been driven to the Edge twice this last week. It wasn't enough to make him crave violence . . . but physical release . . .

He couldn't allow it. Not only because it would lead to further awkwardness between them, but blacking out now would leave them both vulnerable to attack.

Cale would tell him that it was because he forced himself to abstain too long that he could never remember a night with a female.

"Demons are made for sex," Cale would say.

But that wasn't the reason Marik's mind retreated during his sexual encounters. It was the disturbing flashbacks of the arena, from his days as a slave. Too many times he'd been forced to the Edge by his *masters*, only to supply them with an evening's entertainment by becoming some poor female's nightmare.

Luckily, the gods had taken pity, and the worst of those memories were deeply suppressed. But bedding a female always ended the same. Marik would wake up next to some random sleeping woman, make sure he hadn't hurt her—as he always feared—and then sneak back to the *Marada* without waking her. His body would recognize that its lust had been slaked, but he could never recall what they'd done together, or if either of them had even enjoyed it.

"Are you alright?" Nadua asked.

Marik schooled his expression. "Yeah, I'm fine. Just thinking of the past."

"What is in the past that has you looking like that?"

"Nothing of importance." He looked to the dimming sky. "It's getting dark. Keep an eye out for shelter."

Nadua actually giggled at him then. "Whatever it is, it has you pretty distracted." She pointed to her right.

A large-mouthed cave stared bluntly back at him. At his dumfounded expression, Nadua laughed again, a beautiful sound that soothed something inside him, and he couldn't help but smile too.

As they entered, Marik noted how quickly Nadua's mood changed. A sense of unease floated from her.

"You fear the caves that much?"

"The Cyrellians have many stories regarding these caves."

Marik snorted. "Those people sure love their legends."

"What does that mean?"

"Well, from what I can tell, they've painted a horrible picture of demons in the minds of everyone."

"That's because demons are . . ." Nadua trailed off, as if suddenly remembering that he was one.

"I'm not so bad, am I?"

Nadua shrugged, a slight curve to her lips. "I'm holding off on my judgment for now."

"I'll bet the stories have gotten progressively worse over the years, probably to scare children into going to bed. Right?"

"It's possible."

"Then it is possible that the stories about these caves are overblown, as well. Don't you agree?"

"You're just trying to make me feel better about having to sleep here."

"Maybe. Is it working?"

"A little."

Suddenly, Nadua jerked her head toward the trees, as if she caught sight of something. A light breeze carried the scent to Marik a second later. On instinct, he pulled Nadua against him and twisted his body to shield her. Pain speared him when two sharp objects embedded themselves into his back. Cold objects.

Nadua gasped. "Kaiylemi."

Was that a person? He didn't have a chance to ask. Just as another sharp item found his calf, the Edge took over. He managed to pull Nadua farther into the cave and set her behind a large boulder along with their sack of supplies. When she looked at him, her eyes widened in fear. He nearly growled in frustration at that, but the urge to protect her swallowed him.

Following the scent, Marik raced into the forest. He sniffed and realized there was more than one that he hunted. Three at least.

Something flew toward him and his shoulder was pushed back as it made contact. Removing the weapon from his flesh, he tossed it angrily at a thick trunk. It shattered on impact. A shaft of ice?

There was movement behind the trees. Marik shot forward, ready to use his claws on those who threatened Nadua. Whoever it was, they were fast. Dodging through thick trunks, Marik attempted to gain ground. A couple more ice daggers shot at him, but this time he knocked them away.

Just ahead he heard a roar followed by a yelp, and then silence. Marik came to a drastic stop as he nearly tripped over a lifeless Cyrellian male body. Four deep gashes marred his chest, and his head was twisted unnaturally. Still gripped in the man's hand was a sharp piece of ice. Scouring the surroundings, Marik tried to scent if someone else was near, but there was nothing.

In the distance, Nadua screamed. Like a blanket, the Edge wrapped is mind so that only a single thought pushed his legs into action.

Protect Nadua.

* * *

Nadua put her hands in the air as the glossy tip of the sword poked at her. Soon after Marik had disappeared into the woods, two men had appeared. Nomads. She'd heard Marik roaring and feared the Kaiylemi had killed him with the ice arrows.

While one Cyrellian held her at the end of his blade, another rummaged through the makeshift fur sack.

"Just grab the whole thing and let's get out of here! I don't want that creature coming back."

The one pilfering the pack replied, "Dedrick should be able to take care of him."

Neither Cyrellian noticed the shadowy figure growing behind them.

Nadua gulped at the sight of Marik's slow approach. When the men finally saw him, their attention shifted. Nadua used the distraction and kicked the man with the sword, right in the jaw. He stumbled back into Marik, who was like a monster from a thousand nightmares.

Unmitigated rage rolled off him in palpable waves. Nadua managed to turn away just as Marik snapped the man's neck. The sword he'd been holding crashed to the rocky ground. The second man only made a soft gurgling noise. Next came the sound of the bodies being dragged away. Braving a look, she realized she was alone.

Nadua didn't know why she couldn't watch. She'd killed men herself, plenty. Would again, if she needed to. But seeing Marik in that wild state had seemed wrong.

Her heavy breathing echoed off the thick walls, her body frozen in shock, but when Marik reappeared in the mouth of the cave she reached for the sword. He was still in a state of bloodlust and was, what she could only describe as, stalking her.

"Marik?"

His head tilted to the side, as if he didn't recognize his own name.

What would he do to her?

Unfortunately, she knew the answer to that question by the way his desperate gaze was traveling her body.

Ominously, he inched forward and she rose to her full height, lifting the sword toward him. Determined red eyes scanned the metal before sweeping back to her face. His expression said, "I am getting past that sword." And he probably would, but Nadua wasn't the type to become prey to a crazed demon without a fight.

He took another step. Nadua swung the blade, forcing him back. His eyes narrowed.

"That's right, demon. I'm not so easy, am I?" As soon as she said it, she knew she made a dangerous mistake. At the word "demon", a fearsome sound rumbled up from within him. When he moved again, Nadua tried to strike, but he was much faster than she. He had her down on her back in seconds.

She expected pain next, but when none came she peeked open an eye. Marik was gazing down at her, his features unreadable. As if trying not to alarm her—as it was, her heart was ready to burst from her chest—one callus hand unhurriedly reached for her face. Afraid it would provoke him, Nadua stifled a flinch. His thumb caressed her cheek while the rest of his fingers threaded through her hair.

Nadua was stunned by the gentleness, when he looked as though ready to tear the flesh from her throat with his lengthening fangs.

Even after she agreed to journey with him, she'd been in constant fear of encountering this side of him, with no way to defend herself. The Cyrellians called it the Demon's Madness, where a demon loses all sanity and is no more than a primitive beast.

Well, they were right. Marik looked beastly. But she didn't think he was going to hurt her. Then he shifted his hips, giving her a better idea of what he had in mind. Her throat went dry.

Earlier, while they were traveling the forest, she had to work to keep her eyes from drifting his way. It was hard not to marvel at his strong, fluid movements. He oozed power. And every time he looked at her too, it had felt as though he were consuming her with his eyes.

And she had liked it.

So long has it been, since a man looked at her in that way. It made her stomach flip and her mind drift to all the things she could do with him. Things she often feared she'd never experience again. For the last few centuries, Nadua had tried to force herself to forget what it was like to be with a man. How good it could be.

Could she trust Marik not to hurt her?

Just as his eyes dipped to her lips, his hand moved to cup the back of her neck. Nadua's heart rate spiked uncontrollably, while the rest of her body relaxed for him.

She knew it was going to happen, was ready for it, but when he pulled her to his lips, nothing could have prepared her for the heavy rush of desire that slammed through her. Her breasts grew sensitive against the material of her shirt. Liquid gathered between her legs. Her head turned to deepen the contact.

Then his kiss, slow and testing at first, became something more. Bodies pressing deeper, his tongue delved to meet hers. Nadua answered back in kind, lost to the moment. She'd never been shy about things like this; her only apprehension was that Marik wasn't himself. He was animalistic and unpredictable.

And oh, how she loved it.

Her body arched when his tongue trailed the line of her jaw to play with that sensitive area of flesh at her neckline. When he pushed his hips closer to hers, she felt his budding erection. Her body clenched in anticipation.

But then his hands grew impatient, roaming the thick fur of her outfit, he clutched a handful of the material as though he were ready to rip it from her.

She gasped, "Marik, no!" If he tore her furs, she'd have no way of repairing them.

Body shaking with need, he stilled and his molten eyes found hers. Their normal color slowly started to bleed back into the red. After a moment longer, they were once more fully green.

He eased back. A shadow of regret lingered behind his eyes.

Letting go of her completely, he crouched a few feet away. When he looked her over, as though seeing her for the first time, there was no more heat in his gaze. "Did they hurt you? Did . . . I . . . ." He trailed off, his unspoken words lingering between them.

"No. I'm fine, really." She reached out for him but he shot to his feet. To avoid her touch? "Are *you* okay?" She noticed a small trail of blood at his shoulder. The Kaiylemi must have gotten him.

Instead of answering her question, he said, "I'm sorry I frightened you. It won't happen again." It didn't sound like he believed his own words. He looked at his hands then, as if suddenly remembering something. "Tell me, what kind of animal can claw a man to death?"

Besides you?

"I . . . don't think there are any on Undewla. Why?"

At length he said, "Something had gotten to one of them before me."

His concerned expression was alarming. Whatever a demon feared would not bode well for her.

"I'm going to search for something for us to eat while it's still light. I don't sense anyone else near. Will you be alright here?"

"Of course." She reclaimed the hilt of the sword.

He nodded and then hesitated, looking as though he was contemplating making her tag along with him. "You won't run?"

Nadua tilted her head. "I have nowhere to run to."

"And if you did?"

Her brows drew together as she considered his question. There was something deeper in it. "I don't know," she finally offered. "This is unlike any situation I've ever been in." The last few days played back in her mind. "You may think abducting me was the right thing to do, but can you honestly protect the both of us out here? What if there had been more than one Kaiylemi just now? And what if you lose yourself to that madness again? Could you keep yourself from hurting me next time?"

His features grew dark, and she feared her questioning had upset him.

"I won't hurt you," he grated. A sliver of uncertainty crossed his face, but was quickly replaced with determination. "I won't."

"Are you trying to convince me? Or yourself?"

She waited for an answer, but, fists clenched, he only turned and left without another word. That was probably the most revealing conversation they'd had thus far. He was unsure of his level of control, and so was she.

Chapter 12

From a window in the palace, Ava watched with unbridled excitement as the troops marched closer to Sori. She'd spotted them as they appeared from behind the low hills, just outside the city. Her loud screech alerted Wren, who entered her room, weapon drawn, as though to face an army.

"We must go meet them!" she cried, rushing toward the door.

"My queen!" Wren caught her arm.

Ava bounced with impatience. "What?"

"You should not be seen in this manner."

She looked down at herself. "Oops." She was dressed in her sleeping gown and slippers. After calling for her maid, Terina, Ava ransacked her closet, choosing a deep blue gown that Nadua always said went nicely with her white hair and drove the boys nuts. Ava held it up against her body for Wren's inspection.

"That would be lovely," he said, and then, as always when women things were about to happen, he retreated from sight. But she knew he'd stay close by in the hall.

With Terina's help, she dressed and had her hair up in an elegant style in no time. Then she was out the door, startling Wren once again with her speed. Keeping up with her eager pace, he followed close behind.

"My queen, slow down. Watch your step on the stairs," he warned.

Wren was always trying to get her to be more responsible, but she would be queen soon—the ultimate responsibility. And Nadua had told her this was her time to be reckless, and irresponsible. So she would be.

A stuffy voice halted her step as Ava entered the great hall. Wren had to stop abruptly to keep from running into her.

"Avaline, why are you running, child?"

Ava huffed in a breath. "Aunt Idesse, the troops are back."

"That is no reason for you to act like a commoner. The House of Dion is an ancient and respected family line. Take care to do us honor. You are lucky my sister, Odette, is not here to see." Idesse was dressed, elegant as always, in purple flowing gown. The royal tailors probably spent months preparing every little detail to her specifications. Her long white hair shone like silver spun with ice. "Come." She wrapped her arm with Ava's. "Let us greet them together."

Inwardly, Ava groaned, knowing she would have to walk at Idesse's regal pace. She could practically hear Wren grinning behind her.

"How is your education progressing, darling?"

"Very well, Aunt Idesse."

"And your gown for Sir Baret's ball?"

"Uh . . . I don't know. You would have to ask Terina."

"You must keep on top of these things. How dreadful would it be if the wrong thread were used, or a button out of place. How embarrassing. I pity Nalphia, for one, poor girl has no taste at all. She is forever walking around in the most hideous garments. I asked her once who her tailor was, just so I would know who never to commission."

As if doing her a great service, Idesse divulged the name of the offending tailor, and warned her to keep clear. Ava nodded, as she always did with Idesse, and tried to tamp down her eagerness to see Nadua.

Finally, they reached the palace entrance. The troops were coming up the long walkway. Ava smiled and waved at the men in greeting, but dropped her arm once they came closer, and their solemn faces came into view.

Her smile faded completely when Tamir came forward and dismounted his edisdon to kneel before her. "Princess, I regret to inform you . . ."

Ava couldn't recall his next words. Her world had split in two and the sound of it was deafening. She backed away, not wanting to hear any more. A warm hand clasped her shoulder—Wren—but her eyes were too blurred to see him clearly.

A moment later, she found herself racing through the halls of the castle, not quite sure where she planned to go. Anywhere to get away. Anywhere where she could see Nadua again.

* * *

Marik trudged through the darkening forest with growing frustration.

He'd been so close to taking her. Her soft lips had been so welcoming, and surprisingly eager, making him imagine what else her lips might be eager for.

Marik groaned, his shaft hardening once again, even though he had just brought himself to come, twice—the whole while watching her from a distance, as she explored the shallow cave.

And still he couldn't keep his thoughts from Nadua. Even now, his instincts were clamoring for him to race back to her and bury himself inside her. A hint of her arousal still swirled in his head.

And she *had* been aroused, almost desperately. At least at first.

Her eyes had gone stark when Marik was ready to strip her of that damn cloak, and she'd nearly begged him to stop. Snapped from the Edge, he'd gone from thinking he would die without feeling her flesh against his, to releasing her and drawing away.

The astonishing thing about it was that Marik hadn't blacked out. He'd been almost coherent, which, for being as deeply on the Edge as he was, was unusual. Perhaps she had some sort of power over him. Maybe that was her gift . . . Some kind of inherent control over those around her. It would explain her rise to power over those archaic people.

Or maybe it was that he was finally learning self-control.

He could only hope for the latter, because the next time the Edge claimed him, he feared nothing would stop him from satiating his lust on Nadua's firm little body. Not even her lingering fear of him.

Clearing his head, Marik continued his hunt. He was searching for not only tonight's meal, but that mysterious clawed creature who had robbed him of his prey. If it had been a wild beast defending its territory, it should have stuck around to attack Marik too.

What was even more unsettling, all three bodies were gone when Marik went to check the markings again. No traces of footprints gave any evidence of who, or what, had taken them.

Marik hurried so he could get back to Nadua.

* * *

The demon came back to the cave just before darkness fell, panting like he just run the length of the valley and back. He had with him a small catch of yellowbacks—small furry creatures, about the size of Nadua's hand. They were mostly white, but for the line of yellow that ran along their backs. Hence the name.

When she was still learning this planet, Nadua had thought

them cute, until one of the nasty things had speared her with its teeth. They were razor sharp and excreted a mild venom. Her hand had been swollen for the rest of the day.

With twilight dwindling, Nadua and Marik built a small fire for cooking. Nadua cozied up to it as best she could. The cave wasn't very deep, and gusts of wind periodically swept the heat away. Marik sat across from her. Eye contact between them was minimal.

The meat was cooked to perfection, tender and juicy, with a hint of something Nadua couldn't describe. While Marik was cooking, Nadua had watched with curiosity as he crushed up a mix of hard roots and sprinkled them across the sizzling meat. He said he'd pulled them from the ground. It added a delightful sweetness.

"You have quite a talent," she said, recalling him mentioning something about being a skilled cook. At the time she assumed he'd been feeding her nonsense.

Marik shrugged in response.

His mood had been somewhat sour since his return. Every so often, he would glance through the cave hole, into the dark forest. She wondered if their earlier discussion still affected him. Or what had gone unfinished. She considered broaching the subject but decided against it.

They enjoyed the rest of their meal in silence. Nadua figured he would go the rest of the night without saying more than a few words to her, so when he spoke next, it surprised her.

"The one that threw the ice." He paused. "You called him a kay-something. What does that mean?"

"Kaiylemi. It's a master of ice. Not all Cyrellians, but a few, I'm not sure how many, can somehow manipulate ice. Make it do what they want."

"Then, it was a Kaiylemi who tried to imprison you in ice? Was it the same one as today?"

"A very powerful Kaiylemi had made that cage. I don't believe it was the same person. The one from today could only manipulate small pieces of ice, probably had been very young. No doubt those nomads felt very lucky to have had him in their group. Kaiylemi's are not as common as they used to be."

After another short silence, Nadua asked, "What is it like on *Marada*?" If she were going to be taking up residence there, she might as well know about it.

Her question must have pulled him from a deep thought because he looked up at her with an almost vacant gaze. "It's great. The ship provides everything we need, and then some. It's more like a high class cruising ship. You'll be right at home there, I bet."

Nadua forced a smile. For the longest time, she accepted that her home was with Ava, even though she'd always known her time here was temporary.

Marik continued. "There's entertainment, a large room for exercise, an entire deck called the Sanctuary, where plants grow to the ceiling—"

"Plants?" She leaned forward. "You have live plants on board?"

He nodded, adding, "And a heated pool."

A heated pool!

There was nothing like that on Undewla. The Cyrellian's had no need for such a thing.

"Well, we must find this *Marada* at once!" That pulled a large grin from him and she felt gratified by the small achievement. That is, until her next inquiry. "Do you have family there?"

The happiness seeped out of him. Pain flashed in his eyes before he schooled his features. Nadua got the sense that she'd asked the worst possible question.

"No family." is all he said, and then he began arranging the pallet. One pallet, she noticed, even though she had her furs and the fire had finally risen the temperature around them to a comfortable degree.

But when he motioned for her to join him, the protest on the back of her throat died away when she grudgingly admitted to herself that was where she wanted to be. The realization had her questioning her own sanity—amending that it was only because she hadn't been with a man in over four hundred years that she yearned for the possessive way he held her during the night.

Once she was in place, Marik lazily fingered the material of her pelt.

"I hate this," he declared. "I don't like the way it covers your scent. Once we're on *Marada*, I'm burning it." Then his arm came around her, pulling her close.

Nadua was of a similar opinion. At times her cloak felt like a cage she couldn't escape, though she hadn't known about the scent thing. However, she was grateful for the protection it provided.

"If I feel I won't ever need it again, I might just let you." It was unlikely that she would ever come back to visit Ava. "Marik?"

"Hmm." He sounded half asleep already.

"Promise me I will be able to say goodbye to Ava before we leave."

There was a heavy silence. "I don't know if I can make that promise."

Her body tensed. "I won't leave without seeing her."

At length he replied, "Perhaps we can come back, sometime in the future."

We?

"Not good enough. Promise me." When he made no sound Nadua added, "She's like a sister to me. Please."

He sighed. "Alright, Nadua. I'll do what I can."

* * *

Nadua looked up at a raging crowd. She was standing in some sort of pit while the onlookers screamed and shouted from their seats. It reminded her of the plays and tournaments that were performed back at the palace, but there was something much more sinister going on here. The people's faces were twisted in anger, their eyes shining with malevolence.

Movement to her right pulled her attention to a bleeding, broken mass. The man's slashed back was facing her, his body struggling to pull itself off the ground. She realized who it was before he turned.

Bile rose in her throat.

Two men with whips were striking him again and again from behind the safety of thick shafts of metal.

With a snarl, Marik launched at them, only to be thwarted by the bars. The whipping increased with enthusiasm, pushing Marik back in the middle of the pit. The sounds of agony he made tore at her heart. She tried to look away, but couldn't.

The crowd cheered with Marik's vicious roars, making her hate every one of them. Nadua could see in his vacant red eyes that he was lost to madness, filled with such hollowness that she couldn't picture this demon as the same Marik she knew. He wasn't the man who held her with surprising gentleness.

He was a beast, nothing more.

I don't want to see anymore.

Unfortunately, Nadua had never been able to control her visions. She couldn't make them start, and she couldn't make them stop. She had to keep watching.

To her horror, at the height of Marik's torture, a woman dressed in poor clothing was dropped into the pit. She scrambled away, screaming and clutching the walls. Her foreign pleas echoed in the arena. The crowd went mad with excitement. A sick feeling nearly forced Nadua to double over.

Marik's gaze settled on the woman. The girl cried out to those who were standing above her, looking over the edge and laughing.

Nadua begged her mind to make it stop.

When the booing began, Nadua looked at Marik, who had moved as far from the woman as he could get. His face was twisted in rage, his fists were opening and closing with the anticipation of violence, but he remained frozen.

Then he charged. It wasn't the woman he went after, it was the walls around him, the ground under him. The cement splintered as he cracked his fist into it over and over, bloodying his knuckles. He went on like that until he collapsed from exhaustion. The crowd was riotous, denied the brutality they craved.

Four massive bodies entered the pit. Nadua kept an intense focused on the two that held Marik still, while keeping her back to the other two, who were working on placating the deranged mob.

After it was all over, the people threw rocks into the pit as they left. Marik took each hit huddled with his back to the broken body left behind.

Her vision blurred and Nadua hovered in that mysterious space between sleep and awake, every detail of the dream burned into her mind. Was it only a nightmare?

She opened her eyes to ask Marik about it, but an unfamiliar face was gazing down at her.

Nadua screamed.

Chapter 13

"I'll kill you, pirate!" Sonya lunged at the man pilfering her liquor.

He dodged quite well for someone who'd just been guzzling straight from a bottle. They were standing in the storage room of her pub, and she was blocking the only exit.

"Calm yourself, female. I was just sampling the product to see what would be best to recommend to our clients."

"*My* clients!" She growled as her horns began to glow against her straight black hair.

"I'll pay for the liquor, it was only a drop."

"Damn right you'll pay for it! And that bottle was nearly full till you got your hands on it."

The bastard had the gall to roll his eyes at her. "Very well, I'll buy you another bottle. What's the big deal?"

What's the big deal?

The big deal was she had to see this damn pirate every day! Had to train him to work in her pub, and even pay him a salary! A kindness forced upon her by her big brother, Sebastian.

Ethanule brushed his blond hair back, revealing his slightly pointed ears. The pirate was from the same race as her best friend, Anya, but they couldn't be more different from each other. Anya was sweet and loveable. Ethanule was arrogant—almost more so than Sonya's other brother, Cale, if that were even possible—and thought himself superior to demons.

With a slur in his voice, Ethanule tipped the scale of her anger from enraged to murderous by saying, "You know, you're rather attractive when you're pissed off. You should remain that way all the time."

She swung at him, but again she missed. How could he be so fast, especially drunk? Sonya blamed the confined space. She wasn't used to fighting in such small quarters. Besides, she didn't want to disturb the many bottles lining the walls.

"What's going on?" A soft voice that Sonya instantly recognized came from the doorway.

"Princess!" Ethanule greeted Anya with a smile.

Sonya took advantage of his temporary distraction. She latched her tail around the almost empty bottle still grasped in his hand, and then flung it hard into the side of his head. The glass shattered, and a smile spread across her lips as he went down.

Anya shrieked. "What are you doing?" She rushed past and knelt beside the pirate's limp body. "Ethan?"

"His head is far too thick for me to do any real damage." When Anya gave her a chiding look, Sonya whined, "He was stealing my liquor."

"You two have got to stop fighting. Sebastian and I are leaving for Undewla soon and you'll be acting as captain. If you want your pub to stay open, then you need him. Everyone else is occupied with their own jobs. Sebastian had to pull one of the mechanics to work the galley."

"Yeah, and the food just isn't the same."

With worry etched in her features, Anya's head dropped. She continued to blame herself for Marik's situation.

"It's not your fault. And you'll find him, don't fret. Marik can take care of himself. I'm sure he's fine."

Ethan grumbled from the floor, "That was a cheap shot, demon witch." Gripping his head, he sat up.

Sonya couldn't help but smirk. "But I thought I was oh-so pretty when I was angry? Change your mind, did you?

"Indeed."

Both she and Anya watched as he summoned his gift. Ethanule could heal himself and others. At the spot where blood was matting in his blond hair, he placed his hand. A bright light erupted underneath. Sonya shielded her eyes from it. When it was over he stood, a bit wobbly. Whether it was from the hit or the stolen alcohol, Sonya didn't know.

"That tail of yours is wicked. I'll be sure to keep an eye on it from now on."

"You do that!"

Wait, had she just given him permission to check out her tail?

"Just keep your eyes on my pub, and if I catch you sneaking drinks again, you might not be able to heal after what I'll do to you."

* * *

Marik woke fully on the Edge and found that his hands gripping the neck of someone threatening his woman. Cords of confusion tangle in his brain.

Not my woman. Nadua.

He roared at the man pinned up against the cavern wall. A pair of horns, similar to his own, poked through the man's sandy blond hair, causing Marik's murky mind to swirl.

A lithe voice urged him to cease, but he had to protect what was his. Marik's grip tightened.

"Marik! Stop! He just startled me." When Marik didn't back off, she added, "He's not fighting."

Nadua was right. His eyes had not gone red. His horns remained cool. He wasn't showing fangs, and his arms were limp at his side.

Marik pulled away from the Edge as best he could, easing his hold slightly, but not enough for the stranger to move. "Who are you?"

Nadua gasped. "What? You don't know him?"

Sucking in a breath, the man responded, "My name is Rex." After another breath he added, "Did Orson send you?"

Marik let go and backed away, placing himself in front of Nadua. "I don't know any Orson." Aggression still coursed through him, but curiosity started to overrule.

Rex snapped his eyes between Marik and Nadua, brows drawn in confusion. Apprehension shadowed his feature. With his shoulders slumping, he took on a hopeless expression. "But I thought . . ." Rex raised his head to study Marik's horns. Incredulous, he continued, "You haven't come for me?"

With Rex maintaining his nonthreatening stance against the wall, and the last of the Edge seeping away, Marik was beginning to comprehend. By the looks of him, this demon has been on his own for some time. His clothes were poorly mended and badly stained. His sandy hair, falling unevenly below his shoulders, looked as though it hadn't been tended to in ages. It wasn't difficult to guess his story.

"Was it you who killed that Kaiylemi?"

Rex nodded.

Nadua spoke. "Oh, no. You don't expect me to believe that you don't know who this is." She was backing away from them. She'd put up her hood and wrapped her face with the attached scarf so that Marik could only see her eyes. They looked annoyingly suspicious.

"Nadua." Marik took a step toward her, still keeping the other demon in his sight. "I promise, I don't know him."

She continued her retreat, looking as though she was ready to run. "It's just a massive coincidence that we suddenly find another demon? This is just too convenient. What is your game?"

"This isn't some silly trick."

At the mouth of the cave, Nadua stood against the darkness of early morning. Thick clumps of drifting snow sparkled in the space around her.

Marik growled, "You can run, but you won't get far. I'll just bring you back and keep you tied up for the rest of the duration."

"You expect me to trust you when you talk to me like that?"

Marik didn't answer. The manner in which he'd woke made him more than irritable, and the renewed fear in Nadua's eyes had him wanting to lash out.

When she edged out farther, he yelled in a tone that he'd meant to be pleading, but it came out as more of a demand: "Don't!"

Turning on her heels, Nadua took off down the hill. If he had forced her to remove her skins last night, as he wanted to, she never would have made the attempt.

Note to self.

Marik turned to Rex who was now slumped on the floor, ignoring them completely. His demeanor screamed despair. "Stay here," he ordered.

Rex gave the tiniest of nods without looking up from the ground.

Marik wasn't sure if the demon would obey, but he couldn't worry about that now. He needed to go after Nadua.

Outside, he spotted her tracks. She'd already disappeared into the dense gnarled trees. Marik plunged through the surprisingly deep snow after her. It must have stormed heavily throughout the night.

It didn't take long for Marik to catch up to Nadua, who was

plowing ahead of him, buried up to her chest. By her increased speed, she knew he was nearing. Still, he easily closed the space between them.

He leapt toward her. She let out a squeak when he caught her around the waist. He took her to the ground, turning at the last moment to keep from landing on top of her. Fluffy white flakes covered them both. She squirmed to get away, but Marik rolled her so that she was under him.

Nadua lifted her head to holler in his face. "Let me go!"

Through the melee, most of the snow under them had been pushed to the sides, creating a kind of private cocoon.

"Why are you running?"

"You're not being truthful with me!"

Marik stifled a growl. "Yes, I am!"

"No, you're not. I'm still just your prisoner, aren't I? Let me go! I just want to go home to Ava!"

"Well, that's not going to happen! Not now! In fact, you may never see Ava again!"

Nadua stilled. The look she gave him gouged his heart and ripped him out of his rage. Though it was said out of anger, he knew there was nothing he could do at the moment to take it back.

Her shock flashed to anger and then morphed into hatred directed at him. It didn't matter. He only needed to get Nadua to the *Marada* and then Sebastian and Anya could take her from there. If Nadua didn't want to go with them after speaking with her sister, fine. She could stay on this floating ice cube for the remainder of her days.

Surely they could defeat the Kayadon without her. Whatever her gift was, it couldn't be that influential. Thus far, the chit hadn't given the slightest hint that she even had any power, besides attracting people who wanted to kill her.

Inwardly, he cringed, realizing he'd never bothered to ask if she had a gift. And by the stubborn look creeping over her now, she wasn't about to answer any questions at the moment. He must remember to inquire, after she cooled down a bit.

He should have been pleased that she didn't fight when he hiked her over his shoulder and carried her back to the cave, but the relenting dead weight of her body irked him. Inside the cave, he set her down, and tried to avoid her hurt gaze.

Rex hadn't moved from his spot on the floor, and didn't even look up when they entered.

It crossed Marik's mind to restrain Nadua, but he couldn't stand to do that to her. Even though he needed her to stay put, he wouldn't tie her up and leave her defenseless. Not when there were so many unknown threats around them.

He turned to Rex. "You've been here a long time, haven't you?"

Studying the ground, Rex nodded.

"Were you involved in what they call the Demon War?"

Rex looked up, displaying a hollow chasm of loss in his dark gray eyes. "Is that what they call it? I remember fighting. I couldn't say how it escalated so quickly." He dropped his head. "I was left behind."

"Have you been living here, in these caves?"

Another silent nod.

Then Nadua chimed in. "You look quite tidy for a cave dweller."

Although Marik didn't appreciate her tone, she did have a point. His clothes and hair were a mess, but the rest of him looked as though he'd washed and shaved this morning. Marik felt his own stubbled chin.

"I've learned how to take care of myself over the years. Whatever I can hunt, I hunt. Whatever I can't hunt, I steal."

That sparked something in Nadua, her eyes going wide. "Steal from whom?"

"Whomever I can," he said simply.

Nadua's eyes worked back and forth, processing his answer.

"What is it?" Marik asked.

Her resulting glare was piercing and he wasn't sure she would respond to him.

"There is a legend," she finally said.

Marik threw up his hands in exasperation. "Of course there is."

Nadua stepped toward Rex, but Marik stayed her with a hand to her elbow and a look of warning. When she ripped away from him, he quickly convinced himself that it didn't make his heart sink a little. He wanted to pull her against him and demand she forgive him for his harshness, but that would most likely just aggravate her further.

"You steal from the outer cities, don't you?" she continued.

"Sometimes. It's easier there. Less people."

Marik grew hopeful. "So you believe me now that I've never met him before?"

With a coldness that equaled the entire span of Undewla, Nadua said, "Yes." Her answer wasn't reassuring.

Eyes blazing, she turned back to Rex. Her tone was hard. "Have you ever kidnapped anyone?"

* * *

Ethan poured drink after drink, chatting with the patrons and accepting a few shots from those who wanted to share their exuberance. Sonya would knock him in his fun-zone if she knew, but he figured it was rude to refuse. At least that's what he told himself. Besides, it was only a couple of drinks, and he was adding them to the client's bill.

The three hundred and fifty years he'd spent drinking as a pirate he had built quite a tolerance for the stuff. Usually his kind could only handle small amounts. But most of the individuals he'd dealt with in his guise as a pirate had insisted on discussing business over drinks that would tear the skin from his throat if he wasn't used to them. Ethan had nearly gotten himself killed the first time he choked after taking a sip. The pirates had not been impressed.

"Hey, Ethan!" Aidan sat down at the bar.

He was one of the ship pilots, and a dragon shifter. Ethan had nothing against dragons, but they could be tricky, and were known to have an extremely determined and motivated culture, which is probably why Aidan is one of the best pilots Ethan had ever seen.

"Hey Aidan, what can I get you?"

"Whatever. Surprise me."

Ethan began filling a large glass with one of his own favorite mixtures. "Did *she* send you to check on me?"

Sebastian and Anya had departed for Undewla this morning, and now Sonya was captain.

Aidan's silence spoke for him.

"Go back and tell her I've burned the place down, will you?"

"She definitely doesn't think much of you, does she?"

Ethan's teeth clenched at the statement. "What does it matter? She's only a demon."

Aidan's eyes widened. "Don't let her hear you say that. You'll be eating your own entrails for a week."

Aidan finished his drink and asked for another one. He wasn't much of a talker, which allowed Ethan to simmer in his irritation. If that female thought so little of him, then he thought even less of her.

Ethan was destined to be a prince, soon to wed one of the king's daughters. At first he thought it would be princess Analia. She was sweet and kind. But she had chosen a demon, which was only a little insulting since he happened to admire Sebastian as a leader.

There were two others, however, and the king had promised one of them would be his. So whatever Sonya thought of him was not important, though her attitude toward him was more than aggravating.

Ethan supposed it didn't help that he derived enjoyment from egging her on. The twistedness of it wasn't lost on him. To arouse her anger for fun and then despise her contempt for him was something only a seasoned psychologist could puzzle out.

Chapter 14

Nadua ignored the way Marik's eyebrows rose at her question to Rex. She had never been so angry at someone in her life. Marik's careless threat about her never seeing Ava again—even though he'd promised—had nearly brought her to tears.

But if Rex knew where Lidian was, then this horrible trip could be . . . well, a little less horrible.

"Well? Have you ever taken anyone? A Cyrellian female, named Lidian?" Nadua prompted, ignoring the hurt that still tore at her.

It wasn't from being kept from Ava. No matter what that demon thought, Nadua was going to see her again. What caused the painful ache inside was that she had actually begun to trust Marik, and enjoy his company. She was even starting to get used to her attraction to him.

Then he'd turned into a lying warden, threatening to take away what she wanted most. The bastard had even flashed his fangs at her!

Sure, she had run. But for all the gods, where was she going to go?

"Why would I kidnap one of them?" Rex brought her back to the conversation. He was looking at her as though she were a crossed eyed edisdon with no legs. "Their retched skin burns. What use would I have for a female I can't touch?" Then he raked his vision down her body. Luckily she was covered up, or she would be displaying a full body blush. "You're different though, aren't you?"

A low, menacing sound rumbled from deep within Marik. He clenched his fists and peeled back his lips to reveal his fangs. His black horns warmed to a glow as he glowered at Rex.

Nadua took a tentative step back, registering the difference between this Marik and the one who had tackled her in the snow. This Marik frightened her.

Rex raised his palms and uttered something to Marik in a language she didn't understand. Whatever he said made Marik go tense. His sharp gaze suddenly focused on her and a mixture of emotions raced across his features, so fast she could hardly read them. Astonishment. Confusion. Maybe even a little fear. And, finally, anger as he seemed to shake himself out of a trance.

Demeanor returning to normal, Marik gave Rex a short reply in the same language. Rex looked confused as he responded back.

Irritated at being left out of the conversation, Nadua asked, "What are you saying?"

"Never mind," Marik snarled. "We should get moving."

Nadua shook her head. "Sorry, but that's not going to happen."

Marik countered, "I remember saying something about kicking and screaming."

She jutted her chin. "I may have mistaken your intent, but I thought the goal was to deliver me to my sister *alive*." She shrugged. "But if all you need is a body, sans soul, then let's go."

"What are you talking about?"

She pointed to the churning sky. "This storm is just beginning. My furs only go so far to keep me from freezing to death, and if you take me out there, with no guarantee of shelter, you'll be carrying my empty shell back to your ship."

Rex sat up. "Ship?"

Ignoring Rex, Marik narrowed his gaze at Nadua, as though weighing the validity of her claim.

"She's right," Rex said. "The storms here rival those of our planet, and that one looks bad. You intend to continue south?"

Marik offered a tight nod.

"The next cave system is more than half a day from here, and that's in good weather. But once you get there, you can travel within the caves, rather than out in the open as you have been."

"Within?"

"Aye. It's safer than following the mountain's edge."

"How so?"

"We're on the cusp of two tribal territories. The one you want to avoid is more hostile and lives"—he pointed into the distance, past the caves entrance—"just that way." The direction was congruent with where Nadua suspected the rebels compound to be, but the news of a possible second faction of rebels was alarming.

"And the other?" she asked.

"The other lives within the caves, far south as well. But they are easily avoided. For many years these caves have been my home. I know them well. I could show you the way, if you like."

Marik leaned against the rocky side of the cave, arms crossed. "I'll consider it."

Rex nodded.

A gust of wind blew into their little crevice. Nadua moved to see a wall of darkness inching toward them from the north. She wrapped her arms around her torso. Unfortunately, the fire that had raged for them last night was no more than a mess of ash. But what was worse, the cave opening was large, and the chamber was not all that deep.

It was going to get cold.

Marik came to the realization too. "Rex, what supplies can you provide?"

Eyes darting side to side, he said, "I-I can provide pelts, such as she wears. I will need to travel back north to get them."

"Go, then."

"Wait," Nadua interjected. "Rex, can you make it back here in time?"

The wind whipped again. The coming storm could quickly grow dangerous, even for a demon. Rex must know that.

With a slight hesitation, he nodded, which only worked to worry her.

She felt guilty for jumping to the wrong conclusion so swiftly, and then for snapping at Rex. Everything about him screamed frightened and lonely, from the simple nuance of his movements, to the sadness in his eyes. It spoke to something inside her. Raising Ava must have brought out some sort of protective instinct in her, because she was actually concerned for a demon's safety.

* * *

Nadua stared after Rex long after he'd gone. For whatever reason, that bothered Marik more than the way she continued to scowl at him.

Turning to him, she snapped, "You do realize he just wants to please you so you'll take him with you."

"I know." Marik was counting on it. Another demon meant more defense for Nadua. And a possible ally on this strange world.

"He's one of your kind and you don't care what happens to him?"

Marik moved toward her. "Do you? You're very interested in his well-being, though you've just met him. I don't recall you being so concerned for me. In fact, you were ready to have me tortured at the first opportunity."

"That was when I thought you were here to hurt my people, and before I knew you."

She thought of those barbarians as her people? Marik glared down at her, but she refused to back away from him. "And now that you know me?"

She took a stubborn moment to answer. Marik realized he was holding his breath. Why should her answer matter to him? He briefly recalled what Rex had said to him, but instantly put it from his mind. It was impossible.

"Now I know you're as heartless as the stories suggest."

He gnashed his teeth and barked, "Heartless!" His loud tone bounced off the cavern walls. Nadua jumped, but continued to challenge his gaze. "If I were heartless, would I have risked my life to save you? Would I have come looking for you at all? Would I have kept you warm each night—"

"Oh, you enjoyed that. Believe me, I could tell. Just like you enjoyed nearly forcing me to—"

"Oh, aye, I enjoyed it."

Immensely.

"And I'll enjoy it when you come to me tonight as well. As for forcing? Perhaps next time you should respond as someone who is being forced, rather than kissing me as needy as you had."

When no sound came out of her gaping jaw, Marik turned and headed for the opening.

"Where are you going?"

"If I'm not mistaken, we will need fresh wood for the fire. And when I get back, maybe I'll have the heart to let you near it."

* * *

Anya trudged through the snow in the ridiculous outfit Bastian had forced her to wear. He refused to let her out of the shuttle until she put it on, though she had a decent cloak with her. She felt like some kind of snow monster in the thick rubbery ensemble, with a tiny built in heating mechanism.

After taking a few exhausting steps, she complained, "Bastian, this is completely unnecessary."

"I disagree. You're warm and safe." Blasé, he added, "And, if anyone touches you I can engage an electric charge that would run along the outer lining."

"But I can hardly move." Through the bluish window of her helmet, she tried to convey her irritation. She hadn't gone four steps before she was completely winded. Cale should adopt this absurd thing into his training regimen, but she wasn't going to be the one to suggest it.

"It won't be for much longer. Marik isn't here. And we will get nowhere in this storm."

While keeping Anya in his constant line of sight, Sebastian had been all over the plateau looking for clues. Unfortunately, the surface had been pounded with snow, so there was little evidence left for them to go on.

A few feet away, the shuttle awaited them. Anya had hoped her gift for reading energies would help them to quickly find Marik, but she wasn't sensing him or Nadua at the moment. She had thought she caught a glimpse of his energy to the north, but it vanished, as though from existence.

Please be alright.

Sebastian guided her back to the shuttle and it wasn't long before they were hovering over the planet's surface. "We'll need to wait out the storm. Did you get any feelings about which way Marik might have gone?"

Freeing herself of the chunky suit, Anya said, "North, maybe, but I'm not sure."

He glanced back at her. "Don't get too comfortable outside that suit. It's going back on as soon as we land."

"Uh uh. No, it's not."

* * *

The palace was dark in mood, its people mourning the loss of the false queen. Tamir tried to match their temperament, but in private he couldn't help but let his pleasure beam.

Emblems of the House of Dion mocked him as he walked the halls. Soon it would be his house's name that decorated the palace.

The true queen would rejoice with him. The prospect sped his step, as he was on his way to see her now and receive due praise for his success. How would she thank him?

As the day progressed, the light through the windows grew dim, and servants began tending lanterns. They bowed as he passed. He easily ignored them.

Straightening his tunic, Tamir tapped on his queen's door. He was greeted by a short-haired servant in a simple gown.

"I seek the lady's audience," he announced.

The small woman disappeared, returning moments later to usher him in.

"Leave us," a female voice commanded.

Offering an obedient bow, the servant girl rushed away, softly closing the door behind her and leaving Tamir alone with his lovely mistress.

Stepping farther into the room, he found his soon-to-be bride resting leisurely at her dressing table fixing her hair with the help of a large mirror. As always, she looked prim and elegant. Soft features surrounded piercing eyes. She was the most beautiful woman he'd ever had the honor to behold.

"Your Majesty," he cooed.

"Not yet," she snapped. "Avaline has yet to choose a successor. Daft child probably hopes Nadua has survived somehow."

Tamir remained silent, which only worked to alarm his mistress. He knew he was being studied when she glanced at him through the mirror.

She turned to face him, her pitch high. "Tell me she is dead, Tamir."

"There is no doubt that the demon would have disposed of her."

"Would have? You said you witnessed it."

"I said that so the men would stop searching. Their devotion is gravely misplaced."

"Yes, it is, isn't it? So, what did you seen then?"

"I believe the demon carried her into the caves."

His mistress looked thoughtful. "So, it is possible," she trailed off.

"But she was taken by a demon—"

"Don't underestimate her. She is . . . wily."

"Apologies, my love, I had planned to do the job myself that very night, and blame it on a rebel we had captured."

Or rather, I planned to have Nakul do it.

Her back went straight. "You idiot," she hissed.

"My lady?"

"I cannot have the rebels implicated. How would I justify bringing our people together once I am queen? It would be impossible, and all my planning would be for naught. It is a lucky thing indeed that the demon thwarted you."

"I was not thinking—"

"Obviously." She turned her back. "I want our spies notified of the threat. If she lives, I want it taken care of quietly. Now get out of my sight."

The dishonor of his dismissal was grating, but he bowed respectfully and made his way to the door.

"And Tamir?" she called.

"Yes, my love?"

"Do not fail me again."

Tamir pushed past the servant waiting outside. The female let out a grunt of pain as she fell into the wall. The sound of fabric rustling and the door closing indicated she had swiftly recovered.

His thumping footsteps projected his anger as the severe words chanted in his mind. She would not speak to him so when he was king.

* * *

Rex and Nadua had been correct: the storm quickly turned hazardous. The snow was so thick in the air that Marik had difficulty seeing through it, and inhaled a little with each breath, dulling his sense of smell. The volatile wind made the trees thrash around him, and though it was close to midday, the black clouds shrouded the harsh landscape in an odd darkness.

He'd spent much of the morning hunting, but it seemed the weather had driven any useful prey into hiding. Eventually he'd given up on the prospect of finding food and focused on gathering kindling for a fire, instead.

Marik returned to the cave with a cache of wood and was surprised that Rex had not yet returned. Nadua hunched in a corner, shivering with her knees to her chest. If she was shaking like this now, how would she fare when night fell? He had to admit, even he was starting to feel the chill in the air.

He sparked a fire near to where she sat; she'd wisely chosen a corner that blocked much of the wind.

He would need to make several more trips to ensure that they didn't run out of wood. About to demand gratitude for all he was doing for her, he looked up, but paused after seeing the misery in her eyes. Had she been crying? His harsh words came back to him. Was it he who had caused her this grief?

Before his arrival, she had been a queen, which usually included luxurious living and fawning servants. She must be feeling the loss now that she was stuck with him, surviving in a dank cave.

"Do you need anything?" he asked, not sure what he could do to cheer her.

Studying the flames, she gave a small shake of her head.

"Then I must go back out for more wood."

She looked at him then. "You won't go too far?"

Was she worried for him, as she had been for Rex? More likely, she feared what would happen to her if he didn't return.

"There's plenty of wood just down the slope. I'll be quick." It wasn't really a lie, but the good logs, the kind that would burn slowly, were a little farther out. No need to worry her further, though.

She nodded, but then shivered again although the flames were now high.

"Why have you not made use of your blanket?"

She glanced over at the pile of supplies, still a mess from when the men had rifled through it. Marik shook out the blanket, crossed to Nadua, and wrapped it around her.

"Thanks," she said, gripping it tight to her chin.

Feeling there was nothing more he could do, Marik stepped back into the blizzard. When he came back the second time to drop off his load, her stark expression was coupled with exhaustion.

"Sleep. I will know if anyone approaches." Then he noticed a shiny object peaking from under the blanket. "What do you fear that has you clinging to a sword like that?"

"It's dark, and there are noises coming from the cracks."

Marik listened. There were small gaps in the wall, no bigger than a fist, that could be connected to a thread of passageways. Each one seemed to moan eerily.

"Just the wind."

She nodded but kept hold of the hilt. "Could be."

He recalled her initial fear of the caves. She had said the Cyrellians told stories about them. Probably legends of monsters and such. Marik opened his senses but found nothing ominous close by.

"Look, I just need to make a few more trips."

"Then please hurry. The storm is getting worse and I don't need you dying out there."

"Ah, my little Faieara can't wait till she can be in her demon's arms," he teased, knowing it would rile her.

"That is not what I'm waiting for!"

Her sweet blue eyes flashed with indignation, and Marik held back a grin. He preferred her angered over distraught. He could deal with her anger.

After another trip of wood gathering and a renewed, but failed, attempt to catch dinner, Marik returned to the cave again. He warmed by the fire and studied Nadua. The sword had made it to her lap as she held her hands out to the flames.

Marik scented Rex just before he entered, covered in a thick layer of white, his arms full of pelts. With an accomplished grin, he dropped the furs near the fire.

Nadua expelled a relieved sigh. When Marik noticed the smile in her eyes—aimed at Rex—he had to restrain himself from attacking the other male.

I have kept her safe, kept her warm. And she smiles for him!

"We need more wood. Join me," Marik barked.

"But, Rex has been out there this whole time. Give him a moment to rest and get warm?"

Rex went tense. Marik gave a smug smile. Nadua just saved him the trouble of having to order Rex out of the cave. She didn't realize she'd just insulted him, by supposing he wasn't capable of gathering a little wood.

"I'll be fine." Rex smiled at Nadua.

After just a few trips, their stock of wood was a full days' worth, at least. Utilizing the new pelts, Marik arranged a pallet for Nadua and himself, leaving enough for Rex to make his own. Rex was proving to be helpful for the moment, but Marik would be watching the demon closely.

Releasing her death grip on the sword, Nadua allowed Marik to place it with their other belongings.

But when he stretched out on the pallet, she didn't move to join him. He thought it wise not to push her, though she looked near passing out.

Cocooned in her blanket, Nadua stared into the fire as if she could meld with it. She did that a lot. Marik wondered what was so fascinating about the flames. Then her eyebrows twitched and he realized she was deep in thought. Oh, how he wished he could know what was going on behind those pale eyes.

"Stare any harder and I do believe you'll become one with the flames, luv."

A hint of amusement lit her irises. "It helps me to focus on my thoughts."

"And what's on your mind?"

"I've been thinking about Tamir."

Marik remained quiet. The last thing he wanted was to start arguing with her again.

"Can you tell me exactly what he said? I wasn't really in a . . . trusting mood when you first told me."

He raised a sardonic brow. "And you trust me now? Even after running from me earlier?"

"I only ran because . . ." Her gaze shifted to Rex, then back to Marik. "Come on . . . meeting not one, but two, demons after four hundred years alone on this planet? It's a one in a million coincidence. You can't blame me for being skeptical."

"Alone?"

Nadua looked confused for a moment, retracing her words. "I didn't mean alone, I just . . . I don't know, maybe I did. Do you know what it's like to be without physical contact for so long that sometimes you thought you'd go mad?"

If she needed physical contact so badly, why had she still not come to him? He feared the reason was because he'd been too harsh with her.

"Yes, I do." Rex sighed, answering her.

Nadua turned her compassionate gaze on him.

Marik knew it, as well, but he wasn't about to bring up his past— which rankled him, because his instincts were telling him to outdo this male in every way, as if they were in competition for Nadua.

And in a way, they were.

Nadua was a beautiful, sexy, available woman. But Marik had a taste of her, and he would be the one to have more. Shaking his head, he worried his thoughts were turning dangerously possessive.

"So what were Tamir's words, exactly?"

"I may not recall exactly, but he mentioned something about the *true queen*. He and that Naky—"

"Nakul."

"Well, he and Nakul planned to kill you while you slept, and place blame on the rebel." Marik couldn't help a small growl. "Who, by the way, was happy to participate. Apparently, he and his clan prefer this true queen as well."

Nadua's brows knit together. "The rebel said that?"

Marik nodded. "That's what he told me."

Nadua looked troubled. Marik had an idea what she was thinking. If Tamir had the same goal as the rebels, then Ava was probably not their intended queen.

Which meant Ava was in danger.

Chapter 15

The next few days were grueling. The storm rampaged outside the shallow cave. Usually Nadua would be within the safety of the palace during a storm like this, watching through a reinforced window with a warm cup of tea and plenty of soft blankets to keep her content.

Rex had come up with an ingenious way of using the rope and many of the pelts as a sort of barricade against the wind. It did help quite a bit.

Marik never failed to sense her discomfort—even though at first she'd tried to hide it, not wanting to be a burden.

She was still a bit angry with him, but she needed his heat—this storm was unusually cold for this time of year—and Marik's attentiveness was starting to soften her. Whenever the fire went low or the chill became too much, she would lean into him, and he would obligingly wrap his arms around her, enveloping her in his warmth.

She hated she could not do more for herself. It made her feel weak and helpless. She, who had led a nation of people and fought alongside her soldiers in battle.

But she was grateful to Marik and Rex. They were both destroying her idea of what a demon was supposed to be. Especially Rex. A bit withdrawn, and somewhat shy, he often looked to Marik for approval, as if he were the younger of the two, but it was revealed that they were nearly the same age. And though Marik treated him gruffly at times, Rex continued to regard him as his leader.

Around the fire, they would regale her with stories of their home planet, before the Kayadon had even been a thought in their minds. They talked about their summer heat waves and how they would strive to keep cool.

"After this," Marik declared. "I will never again wish for a freak snow storm."

In turn, Nadua told them about her planet. Near where she had lived, the double suns allowed for mild weather almost all year. And the most it ever did was rain, which created breathtaking forests blooming with every color imaginable.

Rex gazed at her in awe. "I would like to see that."

She smiled at him. Their situations were similar in some ways, but where she had only felt isolated on Undewla, Rex actually had been. She still had people to talk to, friends to confide in and share her time with. Rex had none of that.

But his eyes lit up when he spoke of his family next. Five wily older brothers and three older sisters. He was the youngest. Out of all of them, only one had been mated, and out of all of them, Rex knew the location of only two—one sister and one brother.

"At least I *had* known where they were, before I got stuck here. Now I can't be sure."

Nadua sat with Marik on a small boulder that the demons had maneuvered by the flames. Her back was pressed against his front.

"If you get off this planet, will you search for them?" Nadua asked Rex.

"If they have moved on, I will continue to seek them out. But I'm afraid only luck will be my guide."

"You think it would difficult to find them?"

Marik's deep voice rumbled from behind. "He would do well to forget them. Concentrate on rebuilding his own life."

"Marik!" She turned to him and scowled.

Marik shrugged. "I've spent much of my life in space, luv. And short of coming across an enchanted book with their locations detailed, it's nearly impossible to find any specific person." His tone held a hint of remorse.

"I agree with him," Rex replied. "I would love to reconnect with my family, but I would also like to start one of my own. I crave a mate and young ones."

"Not me," Marik replied. "I prefer my freedom."

Nadua assumed "mate" to a demon must be akin to the joining of two people.

Her brows furrowed. "You don't want to fall in love?"

* * *

Love?

Marik scoffed in answer.

Matehood had nothing to do with love. Cale and Sebastian thought otherwise, but Marik believed when a demon recognized his mate, he became trapped into an obsessive need to claim her, whether love was involved or not. It meant leaving oneself open to the possibility of being tied to a horrid creature. Calic was a prime example. He still fancied himself in love with a woman who had torn his heart out and smashed it under her heel.

Then there was Sebastian's constant worry and endless desire to protect Anya. Marik didn't want to be so responsible for another person's well-being. Not after he had already failed in protecting his sister, and so many others.

Suddenly, Nadua shivered in his arms and he tightened his grip.

"Rex, throw another log on, would you?"

"Thanks," she said, as Rex moved to obey. She burrowed her back into Marik's chest, and he found himself reveling in the feel of her. "I think the storm is finally starting to wane." Defiantly, a gust of wind whipped against their wall of pelts. "Or maybe not."

Nadua's stomach continued to grumble, but she said nothing. Her refusal to complain was both admiring and irksome. If she would just tell him what she needed, he would find a way to get it for her.

Hearing it too, Rex stared at him, waiting for orders. Finally, Marik nodded. Rex pulled to his feet and slipped behind the pelts.

"Rex?" Nadua called after him.

"Just getting some more wood while I can," he answered.

She always protested when they left, especially if it was to hunt. Rex had made the mistake of boasting to her that demons could go months without sustenance. Before now, Nadua probably hadn't gone a day, but she was more than willing to deny herself if it meant Rex or Marik didn't have to leave the cave.

Her compassion was heartening. But they had set some traps for the elusive creatures outside, and it was time to check them.

Marik had no doubt that if she could get all her warmth from him alone, she wouldn't even let them out to gather wood. That would be fine with him. He was finding that he liked being so close to her, even though the side effect was a painfully hard shaft, and her scent burning a spot into his mind, possibly for the rest of his life.

He had never spent so long with a female and enjoyed it half as much as he was with Nadua. It made no difference that the conditions around them were miserable.

And now he had her alone.

"So, you didn't answer my question," she pointed out.

"Hmm?"

"You don't want to fall in love?"

* * *

Marik's tone went low. "Do you?"

She tried to call up an image of Cyrus, but time had eroded the accuracy of her memory. "I thought I was once." Nadua became aware of the sudden change in Marik. He was cocooning her in his arms, and his head dipped so his lips barely brushed the tip of her ear, making her shudder.

"And who was this lucky man who almost had you?"

She thrilled at the word lucky, but suspected he was only trying to distract her and evade the question. But she answered, anyway. "He was a soldier. A truly great fighter. He taught me to use a blade and shoot a bow. If circumstances had been different, we would have wed I think."

Marik's arms shifted with his palms flat on her stomach, caressing her soft skin. He spoke into her ear. "And if you see him when you return to Evlon?"

Why were his hands so distracting? His lips found their way to her neck and he slid them back and forth in such a way that she had to concentrate on breathing correctly.

Her clothing suddenly felt very tight. "He was from Undewla, and he died in battle a long time ago." She paused, trying not to notice how incredibly warm Marik had become "Your turn. Wait, what are you doing?"

He was unfastening her cloak.

"I'd rather not talk when I finally have you to myself." He slipped his hand into her hair and turned her head to him. Hooded lids covered his lusty gaze. "I'd rather be doing what we've both been thinking about."

"I haven't been thinking about having sex with you."

"What a saucy mind you have. I was talking about a kiss, but if you have other things in mind . . ." His lips descended, pressing against hers, and preventing her outraged reply.

Rational thoughts abandoned her as his tongue came out to taste her lips. A heady rush of adrenalin sparked in her brain, making her dizzy with a desire for more.

He demanded entry and, with her heart slamming, she relented. Pressing her lips firmly against his, their tongues met. She had been daydreaming of kissing him like this since their last encounter, but had feared he'd only wanted her then because of his demon madness.

Now he was himself and his need was flowing off him like water. Her body was responding in kind.

Feeling her submit completely, Marik's hands found the entrance of her outfit.

Nadua gasped at the first touch on her skin, first on her stomach, and then slowly inching higher as his kiss consumed her. Struggling to keep her wits, Nadua stammered through breaths, "Marik . . . this isn't . . . we can't."

His responding growl reverberated from his chest and traveled down through her spine. The sound of it made her breath hitch, and her body quiver, putting an end to her protests.

One callused palm covered her breasts and she couldn't prevent herself from arcing into his touch. Another desperate sound rumbled out of him, causing her to grow damp. Heat rushed through her, creating a warm thrumming sensation that rivaled the fast beat of her heart. She leaned back against him and offered herself to his roaming hands.

His other hand slipped inside her fur cloak and all she could do was concentrate on its slow descent.

"Marik?" Her voice shook.

"What, luv? Tell me what you need."

The sensation of his lips on her neck shot hot liquid to her core.

Between breaths, she said, "Rex."

Marik stilled then pulled away, "What?"

"He'll be back soon, we need to hurry." She was suddenly aroused at the idea of being caught.

Lips curling back into a smile, his voice rumbled with promises. "My Faieara wants to come badly, I can tell."

"Gods, yes." Nadua melted against him, needing this more than she realized. The way he gazed into her eyes, she suspected they must be deeply violet, and this time she didn't care if he knew why.

Thick fingers found her center, making her jerk in surprise.

He groaned when he discovered her wet. "Later I will taste you here. When I have more time."

Her eyes rolled back in her head, her breathing erratic as she imagined him doing just that. "Please."

It's been so long, she added to herself.

While his fingers played, his other hand fondled her breasts, teasing the sensitive flesh of her nipples. He took her lips again, stealing her breath with his masterful kiss.

His slow, maddening strokes began to build a steady pressure. Panting, she gripped the fabric of his pants. A finger breached her entrance and the first hint of an orgasm rippled through her. She moaned softly into his mouth.

Her hips undulate in rhythm to his movements and her head fell back against his shoulder as she gave herself to the moment. Marik found the spot that ripped sounds from her and he captured her in a cage of pleasure. Her body went tense and she screamed as it tore through her, taking her over until every cell exploded in ecstasy.

Marik held her tight, kissing her neck and circling her sex, until she went boneless.

"Been dying to see that," he said when it was over.

Fiery heat spread through her cheeks, as embarrassment replaced desire. No one had seen her like that in ages. But the only thing running through her mind was what he would feel like against her palm.

Finally, her breath returned to normal and she turned to ask, "What about you?"

He chuckled. "I nearly came from watching you. One touch and it'll be over for me."

* * *

Her wicked smile sent even more blood rushing to his sex. Though she was as red as could be, she wasn't shy about breaching the waist of his pants to find him hard as steel. They both shuddered when she gripped him hard. The way her eyes widened, she was probably thinking he was too large for her. And he couldn't wait to prove her wrong.

She freed him from his trousers. Her sapphire eyes traveled his length as her hand began moving on him in a rhythmic motion. Sharp pleasure jolted through him like a current of lightning. A faint smile tugged at her lips, making him want kiss her again, but the molten color behind her heavy lids had him mesmerized.

She looked as though she were enjoying pleasuring him as much as he had her. The sight was more erotic than her soft hand stroking him from root to tip.

He wasn't lying about nearly exploding when she had fallen apart in his arms. When her tongue darted out to lick her lips, Marik couldn't hold out another second.

As his seed spilled, the orgasm that raked through him was nearly blinding. He pulled her up to kiss her hard and demanding, delving his tongue between her lips—a warning that next time he would be inside her when he came.

If Marik hadn't heard Rex approaching he would have pressed her to the floor and used his tongue on her further. He didn't care if Rex had to wait out there all night, but Nadua wouldn't like it. Nor would she like it if Rex walked in while her hand was still absently stroking him.

After righting their clothes, Marik sat up and pulled her back against his chest, as they had been. Only he couldn't keep from burying his face in the soft red tendrils of her hair, inhaling her sweet scent. To his dismay, he went instantly hard again.

Pausing thoughtfully for only a second after he entered, Rex laid the wood in the pile and then crossed to his pallet. Evidently, their traps had yet to catch anything.

Chapter 16

Nadua awoke resting against Marik. It was becoming so natural to wake in his arms. Going back to a solitary bed would be difficult.

The nearly constant howling that had poured from various cracks over the last few days had stopped. Silence.

The storm was over.

"Good morning," Marik's deep voice rumbled.

Nadua rubbed the sleep from her eyes, allowing them to get used to the glorious sunlight seeping past the pelt wall. She wanted to run out and soak it up, but just because the sun was out didn't mean it would be warm.

Looking around, Nadua realized Rex was gone.

As if reading her thoughts, Marik said, "I sent him out to hunt." His green eyes were glinting with dark thoughts, but then suddenly his lips thinned in disappointment.

Footsteps sounded just before Rex entered, harboring a big smile. In his arms were a couple of neatly skinned carcasses and a bundle of long sticks.

"I told you the traps would work." He beamed.

"Oh, thank goodness, I'm starving." Nadua sat up.

It must have been Rex who had kept the fire going all night because she didn't recall Marik leaving her side for an instant. Although, she'd been blissfully exhausted and probably wouldn't have noticed if he had, anyway.

Working together, they crafted a spit from the sticks. Soon after, the smell of cooked meat teased Nadua's rumbling tummy.

When the meal was over, Nadua barely remembered tasting it. Marik had even offered her some of his portion, but she refused, reassuring him several times that she was quite full.

They were all eager to finally leave their little cavern and get moving to the cave system Rex spoke of, where they would continue traveling south till they reached place she'd captured Marik.

Spurring Nadua's excitement, Rex claimed there was a naturally warm spring where they were headed. Once they began their trek, the other two had to practically force Nadua to pause and take a break.

They'd been making good ground, when Marik stopped for the third time.

"I don't need a break," she lied. She'd been pushing through snow that often came above her waist. Not to mention she kept tripping over random obstacles like stumps and rocks, hidden under the snow.

I miss my edisdon.

"Well, then, *I* need a break," Marik said, seeing through her.

Rolling her eyes, she slumped down on what she assumed was a rock covered in snow. A squeak burst from her as a sudden wave of white enveloped her.

Nope, not a rock.

She pulled herself out of the snow and ignored the demons' snorts of laughter as she dusted herself off.

Through his amusement, Rex said, "The entrance to the cave isn't much farther. We'll need to start climbing from here, but then we still have a ways to travel once inside."

Nadua surveyed the mountainside. It looked steep. She supposed a little rest would be alright, although Marik's continued snickers wouldn't do.

She spied a branch above him, full of icy flakes. She sauntered past him, and then, without warning, kicked its base. The pack of snow tumbled down, making contact with Marik's head and sprinkling over his shoulders.

She laughed out loud at his astonished expression, but quickly reigned it in when his features morphed into something menacing.

"Wait a second." She put her hands up as he inched toward her.

Darting behind a thick trunk, she managed to keep him at bay for a moment. Then his speed caught her by surprise and once again she was covered by snow. Marik heartily laughed alongside her.

Pulling herself up, Nadua noticed Rex was a little too dry. Stealthily, she began packing snow into a ball. Marik registered her intent and followed her lead. Far too late, Rex realized what was happening and he was already being pelted by both of them. Soon sides became blurred and they were all out for themselves, throwing snowballs at whatever moved.

The fun ended when both demons snapped to attention. Their gazes turned toward the forest.

"What is it?" Nadua huffed.

"I heard something," Marik answered.

Rex waved them toward the mountain. "It could be nothing, but we should move on."

Moments later, Rex was leading the climb. It was as steep as it had looked and Nadua had to utilize both her arms and legs to help her along.

Marik was at her back and at times it was as if she could feel his eyes on her. She told herself she was just imagining it. When she braved a look, she saw he was transfixed by her backside, as she was bent in an almost inviting position. She jerked her body straight, nearly slipping on an icy rock. Marik latched an arm around her waist, easily righting her, a guilty grin in place.

He held her for a moment longer than was needed and they started their ascent again, only now her body was throbbing with awareness. Her heart rate spiked and a flood of heat washed over her, even as the chill in the air grew worse. Another storm was on the heel of the last.

As if the gods flipped a switch, puffs of white drifted down around them, adding to the fresh layers of already fallen snow. Luckily, they reached the cave before it grew any worse.

Inside was similar to the last cave, except there were a couple of shafts that faded into darkness.

Right away, Rex produced a lantern he kept stored behind a rock—most likely stolen. He said he left them, whenever possible, in the caves he used most.

They all took a moment to dust away any clinging flakes before Rex directed her and Marik to the passage on the left.

Like any cave, the walls were jagged and the ground was hard with stones. As they continued on, a musty smell became increasingly stronger.

Again, Marik stayed behind her, aiding her through the tight spots. Shockingly, the farther they traveled into the cave, the more humid it became. Narrow walls became juicy with muck, and the ground was no longer frozen solid. It actually squished under her boots.

The air was heavy in her lungs, and so thick it felt as if she were pushing her way through it.

A small amount of sweat dripped down her back. The cave held a natural heat that felt completely foreign after so many years in her frigid surroundings. And for the first time in four hundred years, her furs were causing her to become overheated. She paused for a moment to remove them, leaving her in her thin sleeveless shirt and long pants.

Marik motioned to the bundle in her arms. "Would you like me to carry those for you?"

"I've got it, thanks." She folded the pieces under her arm and proceeded to follow Rex through a small opening. Briefly, she had to crawl on her hands and knees—hobbling forward as she held her furs in one arm—then the shaft morphed into a generously wide and equally tall tunnel.

Rex waited for them a few feet ahead. The dim light of his lantern offered a measure of visibility, then tapered into darkness.

The tunnel opening had been spacious for her, but Marik had to wiggle and push his big shoulders through. Nadua glanced at Rex, noticing how much smaller his frame was compared to Marik's, though he was nearly as tall. The result of living off this desolate land, she supposed.

A smoky haze suddenly fell over her and she went tense. The gray puffs parted in her mind as if moved by a delicate wind. Sighing, she relaxed and let the vision come.

A rift in the floor. A thunderous echo. The walls shook.

Still in mid-vision, Nadua whirled around. "Marik!"

He looked up at her just as his feet hit the floor. Then she heard it. The sound was terrible. Louder than in her vision, like a viscous lightning storm from below.

The ground began to fall away. She tried to scramble back but her feet slipped on the unsteady terrain. A plume of fine dust obstructed her sight and she blindly reached out as she felt herself sinking.

Catching hold of what must be a newly created ledge, Nadua clung to a wall of stone and dirt. Her feet thrashed for solid ground.

There was none. She was on an overhang that could break off any second. Her fingers dug painfully into the rock to keep herself up.

"Marik!" she called again, fearing he had fallen to his death. With the dust in the air, she couldn't see anything but floating specs lit by the amber light of the lantern above.

"Shh," came Rex's soft voice. "Any extra vibration could make it worse."

As if to prove his point, the cavern rumbled ominously. Bits of gravel cascaded all around her, and the sound of clattering rocks finding the end of their journey rose up from the pit.

"Nadua, hold on," Marik whispered.

Oh, thank the gods!

"Where are you?" She kept her voice as low and as steady as her raging heart would allow.

"I'm on the other side. I could jump, but you need to climb up first or I'll risk causing you to fall."

Another tumbling of rocks echoed from below. Her cheek was pressed against the ledge, and her heavy breath disturbed the powdery soil. Some of the fine dust coated her lungs, but she suppressed the need to cough.

"I can't." Her arms were already beginning to shake from holding her weight, and it felt like the rocks were about to slip.

"Rex?" The hint of panic in Marik's voice made Nadua's heart thump painfully faster.

"I think I can reach her," Rex whispered back. "Nadua, I'm going to climb down."

His movements caused a river of lose soil to descend on her. She finally coughed as she was forced to breath in more dust.

A moment later, a strong hand wrapped around her wrist. She mimicked the hold. Quicker than she expected, her body was yanked up to a flat surface. They both scrambled to a more stable location.

Nadua turned to see Marik in mid leap, his body slicing through the cloud of particles.

Landing with a heavy thud, he rushed forward to collect her in his arms, right as the ledge collapsed behind him. Relief swept over her and she held on to him just as tightly as she had the rock face.

"Thank you," he said to Rex, who must have only nodded in return.

"I've walked this path over a thousand times," Rex murmured. "I thought it would be the safest route." He seemed to be talking to himself more than to either of them.

Marik put Nadua at arm's length, looking her over. He studied her palms, which were scratched and bleeding from the sharp rocks. "You've lost your furs."

"Damn it." Nadua looked back to the sink hole. If the cave grew cold again, she would be screwed.

Marik guided her away. "We'll think of something."

"The rest of our supplies are gone too," Rex reluctantly added. "I had set them down over there." He pointed to the gaping hole.

When the shock subsided and they finally began moving again, Nadua couldn't seem to let go of Marik. She didn't realize till later that, in her vision, she had watched him fall.

* * *

Being captain of the *Marada* at a time like this was like being a glorified babysitter. There were no merchant deals to be made, no negotiations for contracts. All they were doing was floating in space, waiting to hear from Sebastian. Other than that, to stave off boredom, Sonya wandered the ship and made sure all was well with the crew.

With the ship idle, she often caught the engineers sitting around, offering tales of past conquests, in anatomical detail. Most everyone had nothing else to do, besides visit the salon or entertainment rooms.

Sonya had just finished the rounds and was hoping to sit back and have a drink at The Demon's Punchbowl. After a long warm shower to relax her muscles, she dressed in her regular clothes: short black skirt, black corset with glossy red string woven down the front, and stockings that crawled up to her thighs. Her heels were tall, which she loved because she was shorter than most other female demons. Not that there were any on the ship to compare herself to.

Sonya made her way to the pub. She shouldn't have been surprised when she got there. Should have expected as much. But the blasting music, and the sight of two busty crew members, who were allowing her good ale to be poured down the front of their white blouses, was a shock nonetheless.

The crowd was cheering at the show as she stomped her way to where Ethanule was mixing a drink for one of the inebriated patrons waiting at the bar.

When Ethanule spotted Sonya, his smile dropped a bit. But then his gaze traveled her body and another expression came over him, nearly freezing her in mid-step. Surely he didn't find her attractive. His eyes settled on her bodice where, she had to admit, her cleavage was looking damn good.

"What do you think you're doing?" Her outrage was buried under the blaring music. Ethanule stopped pouring when the glass began to overfill and he set it down as though he'd meant to fill it that full.

"It looks like I'm serving this fine gentleman," he said. The man paid for the drink and blindly grabbed for the glass, unable to take his gaze away from the now soaked women who had begun kissing each other. Between the masculine groans and hollers from the crowd, Sonya was contemplating how best to murder Ethanule and make it look like an accident.

"I am not running a brothel here!"

"That's good, because if you were, you'd be dangerously low on employees."

Sonya pointed to the sexual display. "Was this your idea?"

He lifted his thumb and forefinger together. "I may have made a tiny suggestion."

Sonya grabbed him by the collar, bringing his face closer to hers so that they were both leaning over the bar. "This is not one of you pirate dens. This pub is my life and I will not have you defiling it."

As if unsure where his attention should be, he alternated between looking at her face and ogling her chest, pissing her off further.

"You're fired! Get out!"

"Wait, wait, hold on." He reached up and gently removed her hands, which had been itching to move around his neck. "Look around for a second."

She did so grudgingly, and saw exactly what she did before. Sonya shrugged, waiting for further explanation.

Ethanule pointed past the melee of overly excited men, surrounding the two females. "Those two are in a committed relationship. They're just having some fun with the boys, and putting a little spice into their relationship."

"You're kidding."

"Not even a little. They came in during a lovers' quarrel. I got them to kiss and make up, and they just didn't want to stop. Who am I to stand in the way of true love?"

"And how did you get them to kiss and make up?"

"The same way you get any two females to kiss. You get them drunk."

Sonya almost laughed at that, but she swallowed the urge. Then her gaze slid around the rest of the room. Besides the drunken horde of testosterone, every table was full with not only men, but women too. And many of them were reveling at the show as well.

A little surprised, Sonya plopped down on a stool, still watching the crowd. The Demon's Punchbowl hadn't had a turn out like this in a while.

The mood on the ship for the last few weeks has been low at best. With the loss of Marik, and nearly losing Anya, the tension was as thick as it had ever been. Anya's return had given everyone something to cheer for, but now she and Sebastian were out risking their lives to find Marik.

Aside from all that, there had been little down time until now. They'd gone from double shifts, to almost no shifts at all. The ship was in a constant state of waiting, and the crew was growing antsy.

Normally, Sebastian would allow *Marada* to dock at a space city every so often, where the entertainment was a little more extravagant. But no one had been off the ship in months, and Sonya supposed this was the crew's way of letting off a little steam.

Flipping around to face Ethanule, Sonya grumbled, "Fine. You're not fired."

Ethanule gave a theatrical bow.

"Just get me a drink," she ordered.

"Of course, my liege."

Sonya couldn't tell if his blatant disrespect of her authority was supposed to be insulting or comical. Then she found herself pondering the fact that Ethanule had been given the opportunity to remove himself from her employment, and hadn't taken it.

While his attention was averted, Sonya openly studied him. Ethanule may claim to have put his pirate life behind him, but he still dressed like one. Over his loose white shirt, he wore a tan coat adorned with gold buttons and multiple buckles. A small, thick gold hoop hung from one of his pointed ears. A couple of beaded braids peaked out from under his light blond hair.

Sonya sneered.

She sipped her drink, tasting a heavy hand. "Ethanule, you had better not put this much alcohol in everyone's drinks."

"Special for you, my captain."

Rolling her eyes, Sonya took a large gulp. The mixture was a bit off regarding flavor, but it wasn't much different than the way she mixed her own drinks. Demons had a higher tolerance for alcohol than most other races, and they needed more of it to feel its effects. Did Ethanule know that? Or was he just trying to get her drunk?

She'd often been surprised at Ethanule's knowledge about demon culture. When Anya had mated Sebastian, he'd acted as though he knew what that meant. Most races outside her culture had no idea how sacred the mate bond was.

She gulped the last of her glass and signaled for another. The kissing twits had moved to the makeshift dance floor and were thoroughly ignoring the ring of testosterone that had followed them. Maybe they really were lovers. Who knew?

Sonya mumbled to herself, "I might as well have a little fun while my bar is being used as a nightclub."

Dancing had always reminded her of fighting, only slower and with less blood. After downing her second drink, she sashayed onto the dance floor, searching the crowd for a willing partner. She spotted one of the least drunk looking males, and pulled him onto the floor with her. She searched her memory for his name. Rick, or Rok maybe.

Rick/Rok wasn't bad looking, a little taller than her, not a load of muscle, but not really scrawny, either. He was a technician, and didn't often hang out at her pub, which supported her theory about the crew needing a little excitement. She wasn't about to admit that to Ethanule, but her desire to punish him was waning.

It became clear that Rick/Rok was just this side of wasted, because as they danced he was blatantly staring at her body every chance he got. Usually—due to her family ties—men tended to shy away from her. Especially when it came to anything sexual. It dawned on her, that with her brothers off the ship, she might actually get to have a little fun. For once.

His appraisal was flattering, but she was rather shocked when his arm came around her waist. So much so, she almost stopped dancing. Then he actually dipped her, and the move was surprisingly smooth.

She laughed when he brought her back up, and teased, "You'd better watch out, you might be mistaken as suave."

Rick/Rok just gave her a crooked grin and pulled her against him. Then he began moving one hand down the curve of her back as they danced.

Just when he was about to reach his destination, Ethanule appeared behind him. The next thing Sonya knew, Ethan had decked him so hard that he slumped to the floor.

"What the fuck!" She pushed Ethanule away to examine the unconscious man's swelling face. There was no reaction from him when she touched the fresh cut on his cheek. "Why did you do that?"

"He was groping you!"

"No kidding! If I had wanted him to stop I would have hit him myself! Heal him!" she demanded.

"Sorry, sweetheart, my power isn't working at the moment."

A small crowd had gathered around them. Sonya pointed to two almost sober looking males. "Take him to sickbay. Now." She dragged Ethanule behind the bar and into the storage room. "What the fuck, Ethan! Why did you hit him?"

The expression on Ethanule's face was a mixture of astonishment and bewilderment. "I don't know why I did that. I just didn't think you wanted him touching you."

"You deduced that from the smile on my face?"

Head shaking, Ethanule threw his arms out to the side. His voice was confounded. "I just didn't like it."

A suspicion arose. "Did Sebastian order you to keep an eye on me? Keep guys away from me?"

He just looked at her.

"It is none of Sebastian's business if I decide to—"

Ethanule pushed her back into the door, and before she could protest, his lips were on hers.

The abruptness of it had her frozen in place. The feeling of his body pressed against hers caused a tingling sensation that traveled through her stomach and took control of her mind. His kiss was nearly punishing with its forcefulness, and when his tongue demanded entry, she surrendered, taking him in her mouth.

She'd kissed guys before, but she'd never experienced anything like this. This was like a claiming of her lips. They belonged to Ethanule as long as he wanted them. His hand found its way to her backside. She gasped when he pulled her lower half into his and she felt his stiff groin. He rolled his hips, pressing her harder against the door as his grip tightened from behind.

Images of the wicked things they could do in this position assaulted her mind. She flipped him around to take control, but he wouldn't have that. With speed and skill that rivaled her own, he twirled her body and had her front heading for the wall. She put her hands up to stop herself from slamming into it. With him at her back, he quickly pulled down her bodice and covered her breast with his hands.

His aggressiveness was furthering her arousal. She pressed her ass against his crotch. A satisfying sound ripped from deep within him.

"Ah, fuck," he groaned. Once again he flipped her, taking her lips again and rubbing a thumb over her hardened nipple.

A cold button of his coat pressed into her flesh and she made the mistake of reminding herself who was kissing her so deeply. She was bombarded by the memory her younger self, peeking through a crack as those men slashed her father to death.

It was like fire and ice collided in her body.

Pushing him away, she straightened her outfit, and wiped her mouth in disgust. Ethanule grew cold at the sight.

"Don't ever do that again," she warned, in a tone filled with the depth of her loathing.

She was out of there before he could respond, racing through the halls in a confused fury. Back in her room, she leaned against the wall, vehemently telling herself that she didn't want to go back.

Chapter 17

After what must have been hours, they came upon a sight that made Nadua want to fall to her knees and rejoice.

The passage opened to a tall cavern, a pool of clear steaming water at its base. She estimated it was waist deep, maybe more. Around it was a naturally made path, wide enough for a single person.

Kneeling on the edge, Nadua reached out for the water, but paused to give Rex a questioning look. He nodded and she tentatively put her hand in to test the temperature, and groaned. It was warm!

Exuberant excitement made her giddy. She nearly stripped right then and there, but decided tearing off her clothes in front of two sexually starved demons wasn't the greatest idea.

Trying to suppress her excitement, she asked, "Will we be stopping for the night?"

Rex pointed to a small opening on the opposite wall. "There is a steep climb to a space large enough for us to sleep and make a fire. It also leads to an exit."

"Show us," Marik ordered.

Nadua got the sense that Marik didn't fully trust Rex. She wondered if he ever trusted anyone.

She may have had her suspicions about Rex before, but after

seeing how easily that ledge had crumbled, she knew he had risked his life to save her.

The fissure was narrow, even for her, but easy to climb. As she slowly ascended, the air transformed into the familiar crisp chill of Undewla. The change was so drastic she could almost believe she'd walked through a portal.

At the end of the tunnel, a massive room came into view. Rex motioned toward a long corridor to his left. "That's the exit."

It must have been a straight shot because Nadua could see a dim light in the distance.

"I'll go start gathering wood for our fire." He handed the lantern to Marik, then crossed to pull something from behind a pile of stones. "Here are some supplies. Cloth, soap, razor. Feel free to use them."

Marik nodded in thanks.

Back in the blissfully warm cavern, Nadua eagerly turned to take the lantern and supplies from Marik. "I'll go first and come up for you when I'm done."

He lifted it out of reach. "I'm not leaving you alone down here."

She gaped at him as his words sank in. "You don't expect me to bathe in front of you?"

"If you want to wash, then yes. I do expect that."

"You can't be in here while I bathe, it's . . . you just can't."

He smirked. "Shy? After what we did before? I'd say that was more intimate than a bath."

Nadua flushed and made a frustrated sound. "That was different." Well, it wasn't that different. "Our clothes were on, and you surprised me."

He shrugged.

The idea of being naked in front of this aggressive male was as frightening as it was titillating.

"Marik, this isn't funny. Are you prepared to strip in front of me?" she challenged.

Marik reached to remove his shirt and Nadua got a glimpse of tightly corded abs and a rock solid chest with light scars rippling over each muscle. Cheeks heating, she flipped around, yet was imaging licking every inch of that flesh.

She heard his soft chuckle. "You really are shy."

"I haven't been naked in front of a man since Evlon," she admitted. She never used to be shy about things like sex. She wasn't entirely sure why she was now.

"What about back in the prison tent? You weren't shy then."

"If my face had been uncovered you would have seen how nervous I was. Besides, you were restrained."

"Not as well as you thought. If I had wanted you, I could have had you."

Nadua wasn't sure how to respond. Did that mean he hadn't wanted her? And why was that the first thing she thought, rather than how dangerous a situation she had put herself in?

"Look, I don't want to push you," he continued. "Although now, I can think of nothing but your wet naked body before me." He let out the slightest groan, as if he couldn't help it.

She could imagine it too. And it excited her.

His voice lowered to a more serious tone. "I don't know this place, and I nearly lost you before. There are so many scents in here that I can't pick yours out. So there is no way I'm leaving you alone, even for a second. Either accept that or go without a bath."

Grumbling, Nadua snapped back around, keeping her eyes mostly on his face. "You are not to come in with me." She shivered at the idea. Was that what she wanted?

"I'll stay right here," he agreed.

She raised a brow. "And you can't watch."

His lips thinned. "Fine."

"You really won't look?"

Was that disappointment in her tone?

"I promise." He turned his back to her.

Nadua snorted. "Like your last promise?" The memory of him yelling that she would never see Ava again still stung. Was that why she was doing this? To punish him?

He gave her his profile. "I never promised you would see Ava again. I promised to try and make it happen. And I still will, Nadua, but I can't guarantee it. I can't see what will happen in the future." With that he turned his head away from her, giving her free reign to study his bare back, smooth and tan, and just as ripped with muscle as his front.

He couldn't see the future, but *she* could—every so often—and she was reminded of the first vision of him, red-eyed and tearing through a wall of men.

Her brows knit together. Before, he'd been angry with her for trying to run, but nothing like in that vision. His gentleness when he'd stroked her to orgasm, and the desperate way he had held her in the cavern after she'd nearly fallen, was all too confusing in comparison. Once again she cursed her lack of control with her ability.

"Are you getting in or not?"

"I'm getting in. Don't move."

There was no way she was giving this up, even if he had insisted on watching. The notion had actually thrilled her, but Marik gave in much easier than she would have guessed.

It was probably better this way. They had been too intimate already. She didn't really know Marik, and her cryptic visions were only adding to the mystery.

* * *

With every sound of Nadua peeling off her clothes and stepping into the water, Marik couldn't help visualizing what she might look like with the lantern's dancing light caressing her silky skin, her fiery red hair damp and clinging to the soft curve of her breasts.

When she groaned with contentment, his shaft jerked and he had to stifle one of his own.

Not being able to scent her down here made him incredibly uneasy. If she disappeared, he wouldn't know unless he stole a look. And that would surely piss her off, though it would no doubt make his day. He'd never wanted to break a promise so badly in his life.

"How's the water?" he asked, to get her talking.

"Perfect," she replied in a deeply sexy voice, which made him harder still.

Damn it. Why didn't she want him in there with her? He'd proven he would do nothing to hurt her, hadn't he? Although that was his fear, he knew she worried about it too. With her, he'd been gentle, had restrained his desire while badly wanting to settle her under him and shove inside her, until they both screamed with ecstasy.

The thing that was most surprising to Marik was that he hadn't blacked out while she'd given him the most powerful orgasm he'd ever experienced—with only her hand. It made him wonder if being with her for a night might be different than his past experiences.

Again he thought that maybe it had something to do with her gift, that he had remained himself during the height of pleasure. He had been eased by her presence from the beginning. Perhaps that was her talent.

Or maybe her gift was something else altogether.

At first, he thought they'd only gotten lucky with the sinkhole. But if Nadua hadn't called out like she had, he would have been well in the middle of it. Only now did he recall that she'd yelled his name before there had been any hint of a problem.

His teeth gnashed together at the memory. While watching Nadua dangle on the edge, Marik's heart had wrenched in a way he'd never felt before. Neither the arena nor any of his other masters had been able to inspire the crippling dread of that moment.

He told himself that it was for Anya's sake that he'd been so alarmed for her safety. But for whose sake was it when, later, he had to forcibly release her from his relieved embrace? It had resulted in a rush of anxiety that was only appeased when she allowed him to take her hand. An anxiety that was returning now with her out of sight.

Marik was grateful when she found the soap. The sounds of water calmed him, but it did nothing to hinder the images running though his mind, keeping him hard as steel.

"I can't believe this has been here the whole time," she practically moaned.

His cock jerked once more and he shifted in his pants. More water sounds resonated, as if she lifted it to drip over her body, and it was trickling through all the crevices where his tongue should be.

Mine.

Marik mentally shook himself.

The sudden thought reminded him of the comment Rex had made in their first meeting. Marik had been ready to tear his throat out for the way he'd been looking at Nadua. But in Demonish, Rex had said, "Easy friend, I would never encroach on your mate."

At first, Marik had been flabbergasted. After brief consideration, Marik had informed him that Nadua wasn't his mate. Rex's response had been, "Are you sure?"

How could he not be sure? Demons were supposed to be able to scent their mates instantly, from miles away. Rex should know that. Sure, Nadua was getting under his skin in a bad way, but that was only because he'd gone without a woman for so long. As he always did.

Breaking him from his thoughts, Marik noticed Nadua had gone quiet. Unthinking, he turned to make sure she was still there. She shrieked, shielding herself with her arms and ducking into the water.

"You looked!"

"I'm sorry, I didn't hear you . . . I thought—"

"What? That I left? Where would I go? You're standing by both exits."

"I didn't see anything," he lied. His painfully stiff shaft was punishing him for it. Had she just been about to . . . ? Surely her hand wasn't . . . "Make some noise or something, so I know you're still there."

"I-I was just . . . wondering about your scars."

Marik went tense. How could he have forgotten his own marred body? He contemplated putting his shirt back on, but because he hadn't perceived any kind of distaste in her tone, he decided to leave it off.

"Could you tell me about them?"

"No." He tried not to growl the word.

How would she react knowing what he'd been forced to do? She'd be disgusted.

When Nadua went silent again, he almost turned. He needed the expression of her eyes to give away her thoughts.

Instead, he changed the subject. "How about we talk about your abilities?"

Still, she said nothing.

"Nadua?"

He heard movement in the water again. It sounded as though she were getting out.

You can turn around now," she said.

But when he did, he regretted it. She was perched at the edge of the pool, dripping wet, with only a thin cloth wrapped around her to conceal her otherwise naked body. Did she realize how revealing it was? He swallowed hard.

Soaked crimson locks fell heavily over her shoulders. She tucked a thick strand behind her ear. "I left the soap over there for you."

He didn't look where she pointed; an explosion couldn't have ripped his eyes from her. Not when her nipples beaded through the cloth so perfectly. Droplets of water rolling over the soft skin of her thighs claimed his attention next.

Nadua remained still, allowing him to drink in the sight of her. When he was finally able to drag his eyes back to hers, he found they had gone violet. He clenched his fists, struggling to control his need.

Her heated expression relentlessly traveled his body. If he didn't put an end to this, they both might regret what happened next. Unfortunately, his actions were no longer his own. His lust had quickly overpowered his common sense.

As she watched his every move with heavy lids, he found himself undoing his pants to show her just what she was doing to him. She licked her lips.

With the last of his restraint, he offered a reprieve. "Do you want to turn around?"

Liquid lavender swirled in the depths of her irises, and she gave the slightest shake of her head. Marik let the fabric slide free of his grip. Her breath hitched, and her throat worked hard as swallowed. The softest shade of pink filled her cheeks.

Entering the warm pool, Marik crossed to her. To his delight, she didn't back away when he found a slender ankle dangling under the water. He traced his way up to her thigh. Her body shuttered. He kissed one knee and used his other hand to pull her leg to the side. She offered no resistance.

Lightly touching, he kissed his way up the skin of her inner thigh. Nadua's breath caught. The sweet scent of her desire claimed his mind, demanding he continue.

Pushing the cloth aside, he swiped out with his tongue and was instantly addicted. Nadua softly gasped as her head lolled at that simple caress. Needing more, Marik pulled her closer to the edge of the pool and took her with his mouth, delving through her soft folds.

Leaning back on her elbow, Nadua ran her fingers through his hair and boldly lifted one leg over his shoulder as if to keep him in place.

As if he would go anywhere.

Marik gripped the thigh resting on his shoulder, keeping *her* in place.

Her moans echoed off the walls, encouraging him as well as tormenting him. He needed to be inside her. But when he met the spot that made her cover a scream of pleasure, he did not relent. Unable to hold herself up, Nadua's back found the stony ground. Her hands lay at her sides, digging into the soil.

When she came, her back bowed and she sucked in one long hard breath, obviously trying to temper her passion. Marik didn't like that. He wanted her to scream until all of Undewla could hear how he pleasured her.

"Of all the things I've missed, that would be the greatest," she breathed, sitting up.

"I'm not done with you yet." Marik's voice sounded far too husky to be his.

She didn't argue when he found her waist and lifted her, cloth and all, back into the pool. Her intense gaze held him captive as his body came in contact with hers. Hesitantly, her slender hands came to his chest, and she rested them there for a moment before allowing them to roam his skin with palpable curiosity. In the water, the tan cloth danced free of her body, leaving her open to him. It was driving him wild.

The top was still tightly wound around her chest—a problem soon remedied.

* * *

"You make me crazed," he whispered as he pressed his hard erection against her.

Nadua must be a little mad herself, because she couldn't bring herself to stop this. Her body ached for him.

Watching him while she bathed had been a bad idea. She wasn't sure if he knew it, but his muscles would flex every-so-often and the movement had fascinated her. The combination of being naked while he stood sentinel, and her hands roaming her body with the sweet smelling soap, had aroused her beyond comprehension.

She'd just been about to release the tension when he'd broken his promise and turned on her. Embarrassment at what he'd almost caught her doing stamped out any anger she should have felt.

Getting out of the water was supposed to break the spell, but his eyes grew dark, filled with such promises of pleasure. She knew he could deliver, and her need had turned urgent.

Nadua couldn't explain it, but the moment her desire hit, he'd changed. He became a predator. And now he had her in his grips. One arm held her around the waist, caged against his body. The other was caressing the soft flesh of her thigh that he had pinned high against his hip. His skin was both hard and soft at the same time. The masculine scent that was distinctly his filled her head.

As if testing, his hand came up to grip the edge of the cloth wrapped around her upper body. Her breath was coming hard, her heart blasting within her. But she didn't protest when he gave a tug and the material came loose. His eyes dipped to her breasts, half buried under the water. She shuddered under his riveted scrutiny.

Her head lolled as he tenderly cupped her. She fit perfectly in his palm. And still, he held her tight. As if she would try to get away.

Never.

Just when she was ready to let out a moan, he swallowed it with a kiss. So warm and soft, his lips were gentle, yet powerful.

She remembered there was nothing between them now. Nothing to stop him from taking her at any moment. But he hesitated, continuing to kiss and pet her with such light touches.

She traced her fingers down his thick arms and back, trying to keep steady, while memorizing the feel of his warm flesh. The smell of a man's desire.

Intoxicating.

Why was he not inside her already?

She began undulating her hips, briefly wondering if tempting a demon like this was wise. After all the stories of their terrible brutality, she shouldn't be practically begging him to take her. But Marik wasn't like that. She was sure of it.

Mostly.

In any case, she was about to find out. Lust was rolling of him in waves, and her own desire was like a drug causing her brain to focus only on one thing.

Satisfaction.

As she moved her hips again, a deep rumbling emerged from within him. But instead of going wild like she expected, he stopped, and pushed her away. Nadua's back met the warm ledge of the pool. For a moment, he held her in place as he gathered his breath with his eyes closed.

"What are you doing?" She was still panting from his attention.

The pleasure had been a shock to her body, bringing it back to life.

At first, he said nothing. She waited, feeling he needed a moment. The stark look he gave her made her heart lurch.

"I don't want to hurt you." His grating voice told her he was on the verge of losing control.

"You won't hurt me, Marik." She reached for him, but he put more distance between them.

"I could. I have before." He seemed to shake a memory away.

Have what? Hurt her? Hurt another? But if he were anything like the demons in the stories, wouldn't he have hurt her from day one? And he wouldn't stop himself now, when he so obviously wanted to keep going.

"I don't believe that." The vision of him maddened and bloodthirsty circled her mind, but she pushed it away. She didn't believe he would ever harm her. There had to be something more that the vision wasn't showing her.

To Nadua's relief, he stayed where he was as she slowly moved toward him, though he was flexing those magnificent muscles again. As if she might scare him away, she lightly brushed her lips against his. To her delight, his softened and molded to hers.

She whispered, "Marik, I need you."

With a groan, he was on her, kissing her with renewed fervor. She found herself once again backed up to the edge of the pool. Her legs wrapped around his waist so tightly that he would have to peel her off him to get away. His strong hand gripped her backside, kneading the soft flesh.

She could feel the tip of him near her entrance and pulled him closer with her legs. A noise that sounded partly defeated and partly triumphant reverberated through him.

He slipped into her.

Gasping, Nadua gripped his shoulders, nails digging in hard. She wasn't used to being filled so thoroughly and he didn't give her a chance to grow accustom to his size before he started thrusting his hips.

Through gritted teeth, she said, "Marik, wait. Give me a second. It's been . . . a while."

He stilled, growing rigid. His head shook as if clearing it and he squeezed her ass hard, but she found she liked it. After a moment longer, she rolled her hips, and he began moving again.

Blissful fire crashed through her core, up through her spine, materializing as a deep moan. Arching her back, she rocked her hips again, straining to take more of him. Sensing what she wanted, he gave one hard thrust and she cried out from the pleasure.

The water around them broke into tiny waves that licked at her breasts and arms, as Marik continued to move in and out of her. It was surprisingly erotic.

He buried his head in the crook of her neck and teased the sensitive flesh there with his tongue and teeth. She shuddered. Then she felt the tiniest of bites, and an orgasm the size of Undewla itself exploded through her every cell. Her head fell back while the waves repeatedly assaulted her. All she could do was cling to Marik to keep from slipping under the water from the power of it.

Both his hands were gripping her hips, holding her in place as his body pounded furiously. His head flew back with a roar as his seed began to spill. The sound of their heavy breaths bounced off the cavern walls. When he eased up, his eyes were dazed.

They slowly cleared.

She felt something was wrong even before his expression grew confused.

He seemed to note her nudity with surprise, as well as their closeness. "Did we just . . . Shit. I didn't hurt you, did I?"

"What?"

Dread blanketed his features the moment he fixated on her neck. He lifted a hand to move her chin and hissed in a breath. Then he let go of her and backed away so swiftly that she dipped under the water before she was able to right herself.

She spat out a mouthful of water and muttered, "Well, that was romantic."

He was already out of the pool and, for some reason, thumping his head against the hard wall.

She watched for a moment, confused. "What is the matter with you?"

"I blacked out. I don't remember doing it. I'm . . . so sorry, Nadua."

His cryptic words spiked fear in her. What was he sorry for? It was only sex. Mind-bending sex that shattered every erotic dream she'd ever dared to have.

"You didn't do anything wrong."

He just gave her a pitying glance. "Get out of the water. Get dressed."

The clipped order and the abrupt way he'd left her—as if she'd suddenly become diseased—transformed her chagrin into something more like fury. "What do you mean you blacked out?"

"I mean I don't remember most of what we just did. I don't remember . . . biting you."

"You don't remember?" she said in a flat tone. "It happened two seconds ago."

It was the most amazing, overwhelming . . . And his bite? My gods, he could come back and bite her again right now, even with how pissed she was becoming.

She touched the mark on her neck and figured it should at least feel tender, but it didn't. Was that what this was about?

"It didn't hurt, Marik. I actually kind of liked it."

What an understatement.

"You shouldn't. I didn't give you a choice."

"A choice for what? Sex? If anything I pushed you—"

"No!" The word echoed loudly, causing her to jump. "I just claimed you as my mate!"

Chapter 18

Nadua wasn't sure what all this mate gibberish was about, but Marik seemed pretty broken up about it. He'd refused to say anything more on the subject, and it was hard not to feel hurt, or like she'd done something wrong. Initially, she hadn't intended for things to go that far. And obviously Marik was unhappy that they did.

Then why didn't you stop, acta.

She realized then that he had tried to stop but she hadn't let him.

After she had dried and dressed, she'd made her way back to the chamber where Rex waited with a welcoming fire and a nearly cooked carcass. When she approached, Rex regarded her neck briefly and shot her a surprised look before masking his features.

Marik had stayed behind, joining them later with a neatly shaved jaw. Nadua refused to notice how handsome he looked.

Beside the fire lay three thick and exquisite looking blankets.

Nadua raised her brows at Rex. "Stolen?"

He winked. "Do I look like I sew?"

She should have been more curious as to whom he was stealing from out here, but Nadua was too tired to care. She was just grateful that there were three, and not two. Snuggling up to Marik after what just happened didn't sound like something she could handle at the moment.

Maybe if he hadn't looked thoroughly disgusted with what they'd done.

A strange silence fell between them during their meal, which was a little tough and overcooked. She thanked Rex for catching it, and noticed that he kept sneaking glances at the both of them, somewhat confused.

Join the party.

Fighting a bout of melancholy, and a poking need to study the disquiet demon to her right, Nadua settled in to her blanket. She let the flames hypnotize her, and her mind began drift.

She wasn't expecting another vision so soon after the last, but then, she never did expect them. Their sudden frequency was both unsettling and a relief.

Clouds of white faded away. Nadua stood in the familiar coliseum. It was just as she'd left it, though the faces in the crowd were different. Their screams assaulted her senses. Covering her ears did nothing to drown them out.

Fresh welts covered Marik's back and arms as he fended off the whips. With a roar, he gripped one just as it lashed at him. He yanked hard, causing its owner to surge forward into the bars meant to keep him safe from the demon he was coaxing into a rage.

As the man's head split by the force of the blow, Marik caught him around the neck, squeezing till his eyes bulged, his body thrashing.

Shaken by the sight, Nadua took a step back. But she couldn't keep her eyes off Marik.

Baring his fangs, muscles bulging, eyes and horns molten in color, Marik matched perfectly the image of what she imagined a bloodthirsty demon would look like. He was magnificent . . . and fearsome.

The clamor of the crowd grew deafening while the second guard continued his beating. There was a harsh snapping sound and the body in Marik's possession went limp. Nadua barked out a cheer, never knowing she could rejoice so thoroughly in the death of another.

Marik dropped the shell of a man, tilting his head to focus his searing gaze on the other. The man hesitated for a second before resuming his assault.

Another entered the fray, taking up the fallen man's whip and together the two pushed Marik back to the center of the arena. His anguished roar ripped through the coliseum.

Just as before, at the height of Marik's arresting madness, a female was tossed at his feet. Bile rose in Nadua's throat. How many times had Marik endured this? She feared the answer.

His chest rose and fell as he gazed down at the woman huddled like frozen prey, awaiting her fate. The crowd began to boo and hiss as Marik stood there.

Confusion was etched in the creases of his wild eyes, mixed with another familiar expression. Desire. Eyes darting, his mind working, he reached for the girl. But when she whimpered in fright, he gave a harsh sound of frustration and backed away.

Suddenly, as if everything were made of some fragile material, the vision faltered. The familiar sound of wind rushed past her ears. In jagged bursts, the arena dropped away, replaced by a harrowing war zone.

Wind whipping through her hair, Nadua stood at the edge of a cliff, one that she recalled from a distant memory. By the vibrant green landscape, blue sky, and two distinct suns, she knew it to be Evlon, her home planet.

The air was choked with flying contraptions, reigning destruction on the land. Below was a frenzy of bodies, tearing viciously at each other.

There were others with her on the cliff. One person she recognized as Marik stood at her back, fending off ugly creatures aside several other towering males.

Most of what she was seeing was blurred as though she were seeing it through solidified fog. Some actions were moving out of sync with others. This was the kind of vision Nadua was used to. A vision of the future. Or rather, as her father would say, "A possibility among possibilities."

Nothing in the future was a certainty. Everything was changeable, pliable. Like soft dough. If Nadua decided not to continue on with Marik, this future would never exist for her, but it might still transpire for him.

The vision transformed again.

She saw Marik, clawing and snarling, pushing toward her. An army of Cyrellians holding him back. His face twisted into a chasm of malefic intent as he held her gaze. He looked even more enraged than in the arena

Overpowering the soldiers, he lunged.

The vision shattered on a gasp.

Both demons glanced over at her with concern. She reassured them with a wave. Marik looked away first.

Three separate visions at once were rare. And the last two were a conundrum. Was she being shown two possible futures? Either Marik fights with her, or against her, in lieu of some event that has yet to take place? Or, was it a warning of some sort, that she be wary of Marik? Or of doing something that would cause him to seek her life? What could she have done to anger him so?

Since deciphering the visions was nothing more than a guessing game at this point, she might have no choice but to find out.

* * *

From the corner of his eye, Marik watched Nadua's sleeping form. The gravity of the situation caused his insides to twist painfully. She was his.

His mate.

Now that his mark was on her, there was no denying it. But there was also no taking it back. Since he claimed her during one of his blackouts, he was sure she hadn't had a choice in the matter.

More twisting.

Of course she'd had no choice; she didn't even know what it meant.

Marik never fathomed that he could unknowingly do such a thing. How was it even possible? The fact that she was his mate shouldn't have come as such a shock.

Again he peeked at Nadua, unsure how he could conceivably make this right with her.

Just after she had fallen asleep, Rex put distance between them, out of respect for Marik's claim on her.

Good man.

His confusion as to why she wasn't bunking with Marik was evident, as was Marik's need to bring her to his bed and hold her within the protection of his body. To have her scent clinging to him all night.

But he resisted that urge.

Nadua was angry over the admission that he didn't remember making love to her. If she were more familiar with his culture, she would be even more livid. Claiming a female against her will was considered an extremely disgraceful and depraved act.

How much more dishonor can I bring upon myself?

Rex seemed to have known Nadua was his from the start, and

Marik wanted to know why that was. In Demonish, Marik asked, "How could I not have known she was mine?"

Until it was too late.

Rex raised his head slightly, responding in kind. "Sounds nice to hear my language spoken again." He paused, brandishing a sad smile before continuing. "It's different when a mate is not of our kind. Not as obvious, or easy to accept."

Marik recalled Sebastian's turmoil over Anya. "How is it you knew Nadua was mine, when I did not?"

Rex chuckled softly. "Your initial reaction to me, for one. You were on the Edge before you even realized you were awake. Then, afterward, your body language made it clear. You often herd her away from me if she gets too close."

Marik hadn't realized, but thinking back, he knew Rex was right.

"Also, I've been witness to a mating such as yours before."

Interest piqued, Marik motioned for him to continue.

"When the Kayadon attacked our home planet, I was captured and taken aboard a slave ship, along with several others. While docked at a station, a group of us escaped the slavers and hijacked a nearby ship. The crew was of mixed lineage and we had intended to remove them from the ship at our earliest convenience. But since we were unfamiliar with space at the time, our leader, Orson, struck a truce with their captain."

Rex picked at the last of his carcass and Marik waited for him to go on.

"It was uneasy at first, but over time, we grew to depend on each other. All this time my friend, Grayton, acted strangely toward one particular female named Elyra. A dragonshifter. Do you know of their kind?"

Marik nodded.

"Well, Grayton grew more and more obsessed with Elyra. He tried everything to keep his mind from her, but he could not. None of us thought it was possible to find a mate outside our race, and many believed Grayton was nearing madness. It wasn't until Elyra made her feeling for him known that Grayton became himself again." Rex shrugged. "A few weeks later, we were celebrating their matehood."

Marik digested this. It wasn't far off from Sebastian's story. But deep down Sebastian had known, hadn't he?

I should have known.

If Marik had had the slightest inkling about Nadua, he would've taken better care around her. He wouldn't have allowed himself to imagine her naked body writhing under his, her screams echoing in his ear. He wouldn't have been tempted to lose control with her.

He had told Nadua that he didn't remember what happened between them, and that wasn't entirely true. He remembered her barely stifled moans, her scent, like a drug, and, ah, gods, her taste. He recalled her soft flesh giving way under his. Being with her had been the most amazing experience of his life.

But then, she had asked him to be still, and he feared he'd hurt her. Flashes of the arena assaulted him . . . and the rest dimmed to black. When he came to, he was spent and her neck held his mark. Shame had never been so consuming.

Rex interrupted his thoughts. "So, what's your story? What happened to you after the war?"

Marik lowered his gaze. "I didn't escape."

* * *

Ava gave Wren a withered look as he took her hand and gave it a light kiss. Normally she would have done something silly like giggle or blush.

Not today.

"You look lovely," he said. He was dressed neatly in his best uniform. His decorative sword tucked by his side.

She didn't feel lovely. She felt like going back to bed for the next two years. But her aunts and Wren and even Terina, who had held her through the worst of it, were imploring her to make an appearance.

Sr. Baret, with his oh-so-important lineage, had requested the use of the throne room to throw a ball for his daughter's day of birth. It was a wonder his daughter, Jestina, hadn't acquired the same sense of entitlement as her father. She was a good friend, and Ava wished she could feel some happiness for her today.

But how could she possibly go down there and see all those people, dancing and being merry, while she had just barely stopped crying over Nadua.

Both of Ava's aunts stood by the door, impatiently waiting. Idesse, in her tight purple bodice and flowing skirts, and Odette, in her black ensemble with a matching hat woven into her shimmering white locks.

Ava had chosen a simple pale gown.

Odette stepped forward and placed a hand over Ava's shoulder, giving her an encouraging smile—which ended up looking rather painful. "Avaline, dear, if there is any hope of you keeping your crown, you must retain the support of the Nobles. And that means going to this little party and showing off that pretty face of yours."

Odette was usually, what Nadua called, a hardcore bitch. And Ava knew she was struggling to show some compassion at the moment.

"Unless you don't care that your father wished for you to be queen."

Ah, there she is.

With the news of Nadua's death spreading, the future of the

kingdom was quickly becoming uncertain. Peace was tenuous, and nobles were positioning themselves to take her place as proxy. They all expected Ava to announce her recommendation tonight. Then later, she, her nominee, and the highest nobles would meet, and discuss the future of the kingdom.

The last time a decision like this was made was when Nadua took the throne, and she had needed to utilize the army to keep it. Throughout her life, Ava had been in awe of Nadua's diligence and strength.

Ava had asked her one day how she'd managed it. Nadua's reply had been, "Whoever controls the army, rules the land."

It made sense because no one could stand against Nadua. She'd been fierce and confident, but at the same time benevolent. Could anyone rule as well as she had?

Reading her thoughts, Idesse asked, "Who will you choose?"

"I've not yet decided."

"You must decide quickly. This decision could affect all of us. This is not a game, child."

"I'm well aware, Aunt Idesse, how important this is. If I am to claim my title when I come of age, I must choose someone who will not try to overthrow my rule when it comes time for them to step down."

But I don't know who to trust.

Both her aunts had offered themselves, of course, along with half the kingdom. If only she were a few years older. All of this would be irrelevant.

"Come, Idesse." Odette motioned for her sister to leave with her. "Our Avaline will make the right decision."

When they were gone, Wren held out his arm. "Are you ready?"

"Give me a minute." Ava straightened her dress and took a

few deep breaths. Then her shoulders slumped. "What should I do, Wren?"

With the crook of his finger, he lifted her chin. "Whatever you do, don't let them see your fear. A leader must be a source of strength and courage."

"But I am neither of those things."

"Aren't you? You have a spunk that cannot be tempered. You're tenacious when you want to be. Self-possessed and poised when you need to be. And your heart is as true as your father's." Taking her arm, they made their way through the hall. "You will make a fine queen one day."

In the throne room, soft music played while couples danced. Ava sought out Jestina right away. Like always, Wren stayed close.

"It's good to see you," Ava greeted.

"You, as well," Jestina replied, then she placed her hand on Ava's shoulder. "I haven't had a chance to see you since . . . well, I'm so sorry—"

"This ball is lovely," Ava interrupted. The last thing she wanted was break down in fresh tears. "Your father did a wonderful job putting this together for you."

Jestina smiled. "You know very well my father had nothing to do with the décor, or the food. The servants are to be credited. And the people? They're all here for you, I'm sure."

"Unfortunately, I think you might be right." The room was packed.

"At least I can boast that my ball was attended by all the great families. Look"—she pointed—"even the Muray's are here."

"Ah, Irina will be so jealous."

"Not if she can procure a husband from tonight. I saw her dragging Destin onto the dance floor." At Ava's consoling look, Jestina shrugged. "She can have him."

Sr. Baret appeared beside his daughter. "How wonderful to see you again, Princess Avaline. We are honored."

"Thank you. I'm glad to be here."

"Have you decided who you'll be nominating? A few of us have a bet going and I would love to know if I should bow out now." He winked.

"Father!" Jestina chided.

Ava unclenched her teeth, and spoke as kind as she could. "I'm delighted, Sir Baret, that you can find some entertainment under the circumstances and I would hate to ruin your fun."

Sr. Baret paled. "Of course I meant no disrespect, my dear. I offer my condolences for your loss."

Wren spoke from behind. "Princess, would you care to dance?"

She turned, thankful for the excuse to step away. "Yes, please."

Wren led her onto the floor and they started moving to the elegant music.

"You okay?"

Throat tight, Ava gave a nod.

Be strong, she told herself.

Over Wren's shoulder, her eyes settled on her father's throne—elaborately decorated, and elevated by rows of delicately curved steps. It was where her father, and then later Nadua, once sat. She was reminded of their unwavering dedication to both her and the Cyrellian people. Her people.

In a low voice, Wren asked, "Do you know who it will be?"

Ava had been to nearly every gathering, learned every family name, and had studied the characters of each. Though some have shown more dignity than others, none could take the place of Nadua or her father. None could be what this kingdom needed. Yet all flaunted a desire for the crown.

Ava replied, "The obvious decision would be one of my aunts, but they are both so frivolous. I fear they would focus more on how a queen should look, rather than how she should act, or what she should be doing for the people."

"Do you think they could ruin the kingdom in a few years?"

"A few years is an eternity for those in need. We are at war, though not many like to see it that way. A competent leader is necessary."

Wren gave her an approving look and their eyes met. "What about you?" she whispered.

His smile faded. "If you could choose me, I would be honored. But you know it's not possible. I am not of noble blood."

Nor was most of the guard. But Wren would make a better leader than any of the choices allotted her. In truth, she cringed at the thought of any of them being in charge. A wild idea that had been tickling the back of her mind solidified.

"I've made a decision," she declared.

Wren pulled back to look at her. He must have seen something in her eyes because he released his hold, bowed at the waist, and backed away, leaving Ava alone while jubilant couples continued to dance around her.

It felt somewhat symbolic.

Resolved, she crossed toward the throne and reached the first step. When she took it, a few nearby conversations went silent. By the third step, half the room had stilled. The fifth step increased her determination. And on the last step, the musicians had ceased playing and she felt the entire room watching her.

Trying to slow the pounding of her heart, Ava turned to face them.

"Welcome," she started. "Many of you have come to celebrate Jestina's day of birth, as I have. But I suspect that many of you present are eager to hear who I will nominate as successor to Queen Nadua."

Ava could no longer see Wren among the large assembly. Her aunts, however, pushed through the crowd.

"I have read that, under my father's rule, we built this amazing city from nothing. Under Nadua's rule, I have watched us thrive. We have seen tragedy, as well as victory. Through tragedy, we have worked together to overcome. And with each victory, we have celebrated as one."

Applause rang out.

"My father loved his people. As do I."

Ava took a moment to breathe, preparing herself for what she was about to do.

"There are many of you who would make a wonderful king or queen." She paused before continuing. "And there are many of you would not. I'm sure you all have an opinion on the matter . . . but I won't be hearing them. I will be offering no nomination."

A few gasps and grumbles came from the crowd.

She swallowed hard and stood straighter. "Here and now, I, Avaline of the House of Dion, daughter of Fineas of the house of Dion, will be taking my rightful place as queen." With as much elegance as she could muster, Ava sat upon her father's throne.

A slow rumble of outrage rose.

She let it go a moment. Then her voice rose with a kind of authority that surprised even her. "If anyone objects, I invite you to come forth and speak your mind."

The room went still. She caught the eyes of her aunts who looked stunned into speechlessness.

Movement in the crowd claimed her attention. Ava's heart nearly stopped when it was Wren who stepped forward.

Pausing just before the first step, he pulled his sword. The sound of more metal being unsheathed echoed around the room, but she kept her eyes on Wren. If he wasn't with her, then she was lost.

Balancing his weapon on two palms, Wren knelt before her and placed it on the ground. More soldiers moved beside him and did the same.

A significant silence coated the room. Ava's chin lifted to the crowd expectantly, though her heart was still beating harshly. Some of the Nobles nearest to the throne gingerly knelt. Then, in a wave, the rest followed.

Wren peeked an eye up at her and grinned with pride. Ava finally swallowed the lump in her throat.

She was queen.

Chapter 19

Today was a bad day.

Normally, Sonya had three willing demons to spar with, to take out her frustrations on. Bastian, Cale, and Marik didn't realize it, but their sessions quite often kept her from spiraling toward the Edge. Fighting kept her sane while allowing her to bury other, more embarrassing, needs.

After a long morning in the control room, she'd handed over command of the ship to her chosen second, Aidan, and was now on the hunt for a sparring partner.

Sonya prided herself on being a fierce fighter, and had built up quite a reputation that she was normally very proud of.

Unfortunately, with the only three people who would engage her in battle gone, she was having a difficult time convincing someone to join her for a bout on the mat.

With every shake of the head, and hands flying up in immediate surrender, Sonya was beginning to lose ground on another kind of battle that had been raging inside her since last night. She pushed the memory away as she stomped down the hall.

Don't think of it.

She'd been telling herself the same thing all morning, but her mind always seemed to drift back to the way his lips had felt.

Damn pirate! This was his fault. Hours of training, meditating, and vigorous exercise, all designed to keep her from focusing on such things, shattered by a kiss.

She'd only enjoyed it because she'd been a little tipsy. Not because it was passionate, or demanding, or any ridiculousness like that.

Sonya thought back to the last time she'd been kissed. Surely it had been just as heated. She couldn't recall. What she did remember was that, soon after, the man had started to grow increasingly uncomfortable around her brothers. He hadn't stayed on the ship long.

Sonya didn't think that her brothers intentionally kept males from wanting to pursue her. They didn't openly threaten anyone. Rather, it was in their manner, and a look that said, "If you hurt her, I'll kill you slowly and with great pleasure."

Eventually, Sonya had given up on the whole prospect, and instead focused on exercise and fighting. It had worked for her thus far.

But she'd already gone through her normal routine, and this time it wasn't helping. She needed a good fight, and there was only one person aboard who might be ignorant—or arrogant—enough to comply. And because he was the cause, he owed her a solution.

Entering The Demon's Punchbowl, Sonya headed straight for the bar. Ethanule's dark blue eyes followed her with a little too much intensity. Other than that, he was unreadable.

Sonya's resolve faltered as she wondered what he thought of her outfit—a tight purple bodice with a black skirt that fell just above tall boots threaded with purple strings. Scolding herself, she quickly morphed her inappropriate reaction into fury.

His own dress was the usual Ethan garb. An overly adorned neatly tailored coat, deep red and lined with gold trim, hugged a fitted tan shirt. Dark brown trousers tucked into heavy black boots with thick gold buckles completed the outfit. Typical pirate. She would use it as a reminder of why she hated him.

"Captain," he greeted with his usual cavalier smile, as if nothing had happened between them. "What brings you to my fine establishment?"

"*My* fine establishment," she corrected.

"Don't worry," he assured. "For you, drinks are on the house."

"They better not be for anyone else."

"Oh, only the most important people."

A nearby table of crew members raised their glasses and cheered at Ethan's words. The sound quickly died at Sonya's piercing glare, and the men pretended to look elsewhere.

She faced Ethanule, ready to give him the usual threats to his life, but he had moved to the other end of the bar and was pouring a drink for Jade, one of the few people aboard the ship who didn't work as part of the crew. She paid a hefty sum to be ferried around, with no real destination.

Like most of the people who chose to enter space, Jade didn't like staying in one spot for too long. *Marada* provided a safe way for her to travel, with a little more excitement than a standard cruise ship.

Jade took hold of the drink Ethanule offered, allowing her hand to linger on his a little longer than necessary. The sight made Sonya's teeth gnash together.

When Ethanule finally came back to her end of the bar, Sonya ground out, "This ship has rules, you know. Didn't Sebastian tell you? There's no consorting with anyone on the ship."

"Was I consorting? I recall it being a little more involved than that. Anyway, I thought that rule only applied to crew? Jade just informed me that she is merely a passenger." He paused thoughtfully.

"I do believe she was flirting with me actually, which I know must be alarming to you. Me being the lowly creature that I am." He grinned. "I will go straight to her room after work and let her know how off her judgment of character is. I'm sure she'll be grateful for the warning. Would you like a drink?"

The harsh sound of her teeth grinding rumbled in her ears. With effort, Sonya loosened her jaw, only to allow a string of Demonish curses run past her lips.

"That sounds sweet," he interjected. "But I don't think you should be coming on to me like that. You know the rules."

"The only reason I'm not pulling your spleen out through your eyeball is because I promised Anya I wouldn't kill you."

He gingerly placed his hand on his chest. "I am truly blessed."

"But she didn't say anything about not hurting you."

"Mm, I do like it rough."

Barely holding on to the last of her control, Sonya continued, "Look, you ass, I'm going to give you the opportunity to prove you're more than just a waste of air."

She knew she piqued his interest, even though the only response she got was a raised eyebrow.

"I need someone to spar with, who can offer at least a bit of a challenge." She let a little skepticism show in her tone. "I'm willing to believe you're not totally without skill."

"You want to fight me?"

"Spar. But yes, I really, really do."

"What do I get if I agree?"

Sonya snorted. "A sliver of respect."

He shrugged. "Not really high on the list of things I want."

Sonya guarded her features, making them as uncaring as she could. She couldn't let him know how badly she needed this.

In an offhanded tone, she asked, "What do you want?"

A sense of foreboding crept up her spine as he studied her closely, a knowing glint in his eyes. She was afraid he conceived that he had the upper hand.

"I want to be free to run the pub how I want, without you or your minions checking on me."

"My pub has rules. You would still have to follow them."

"*How ever* I want," he repeated.

Sonya glanced around her beloved bar. How badly could he destroy it, really?

"One week," she offered.

Looking thoughtful, he added, "And I want you to be nicer to me. That means saying things like please, and thank you, and not threatening to kill me every other day."

Sonya opened her mouth to argue, and then closed it. The Edge wasn't going to be contained much longer.

"Fine, for one week also." In the deeper crevices of her mind, Sonya wondered if she would be able to keep that promise.

"We have a deal then. I'll meet you there after I close tonight."

"No. Now."

"Who will watch the—"

Sonya turned to the room and bellowed, "Everyone get out! We're closed!"

Fifteen minutes later, Sonya was stepping onto the mat. Her skin sizzled with a familiar itch. Something inside was screaming to break free.

The entire way to the sparring chamber, Ethanule had walked quietly at her side.

How could even his silence sound arrogant?

He'd been watching her, though. Peeking at her from the corner of his eye. She thought he looked pleased, and she assumed he was as eager for her blood as she was for his. But it wouldn't be her who shed it.

Taking his place on the mat across from her, he broke the silence. "So you finally have me alone, what *will* you do with me?"

She pointed to the array of weapons lining the walls. "Pick your poison." She was hoping for something sharp and pointy.

His gaze traveled the selection. "I don't care for poison. Gives me indigestion."

"Fine with me, I love a good brawl."

And to prove her point, she leaped to attack. Expecting a solid hit, she put her full force into her right hook, but at the last second he dodged, throwing her off balance. She realized her mistake too late.

He took the advantage, but instead of retaliating, as she would have, he placed himself at her back, grasped her forearms and pulled her against him to whisper in her ear. "I know what's going on here."

Her eyes went wide and she slammed her elbow into his stomach. His grip loosened as he huffed out a breath. Pushing away from him, Sonya continued with a high twisting kick.

Again he dodged, and began circling her with an infuriatingly sexy curve to his lips. Just as she expected the Edge to take over, something else began to happen within her.

"You don't know shit, pirate!"

Sonya lashed out again, left, right, left, right. She dropped to the floor, swinging her leg wide, then a backward flip had her back on her feet. He evaded her every attempt like a master.

Even with Cale she could land a hit! She lunged again, determined to find flesh with her fist.

He wasn't countering, she noticed. He wasn't attacking in any way.

"Fight me!"

Bouncing around her, he replied, "Just reading your style,

Sweetheart." The humor in his voice made her realize he was enjoying himself.

"Read this!" Now that she was used to his avoidance, she attacked using a wide kick as a diversion, which allowed her to wrap her tail around his wrist and pull him off center for a heavy punch.

Satisfaction filled her as his eyes bugged with the contact. She brought her leg up, but before her knee could find his ribs, he twisted his body away from her.

The split-second she had to regain control was not enough. Before she could react, he swiped her feet out from under her and had her on her back, resting his weight on top of her.

"Is this fighting really what you want? When we could be doing something much more fun?"

Shifting her weight, Sonya pushed him over, mirroring his position. She realized he went a little too easily, and she was now straddling him. Heat pooled at her center, causing her to hesitate. Ethanule's irises sparkled with delight, as though he knew the struggle raging inside her.

Determined to keep on track, she pulled out one of the small knives she always kept concealed in a small pocket at her side. Knowing how much it would anger him, she used it to pluck free one the gold pieces decorating his coat.

He grabbed her wrist, and she smirked.

"You're playing dirty."

"There's no other way."

The smile that spread across his face was wicked. "Agreed."

He reached behind him and produced a blade of his own. In one smooth motion, Ethanule sliced through the ties of her bodice.

Sonya gasped in surprise, as the garment slipped open and cool air met skin. She rushed to cover herself, leaving her vulnerable when Ethan pushed her back to the mat, positioning himself between her legs and pinning her arms beside her head. Her torn garment parted with every pounding breath.

Ethanule dipped his lips close to hers. "I don't think fighting is what you need."

Robbed of speech, Sonya violently shook her head.

"Wouldn't you rather I be touching you?" His lips moved to caress the soft cord of her neck. Her eyes rolled back involuntarily. "Tasting you?" With maddening slowness, he followed the line of her jaw with his mouth until his lips were pressing against hers.

Her mind flooded with something she couldn't describe, but it was fierce and commanding. Sonya summoned all her control, but this was a side of the Edge that had never possessed her before. And it demanded release. It didn't care that she could hardly stand the sight of the person willing to give it to her.

Ethanule pulled back to gaze into her eyes. His lids were heavy and the blue of his irises had deepened to that of a vast ocean.

He was waiting for something from her.

A decision? Could she do this? With him?

"Damn you," she breathed, lifting her lips to his once more.

After that, Ethanule didn't hesitate. He batted away the ruined material of her corset and palmed her breast. Sonya moaned at the contact. When he moved to swirl his tongue around one taut peak, she barely stifled a squeak of surprise.

With obvious intent, his hand skimmed down her belly, causing her to shiver with anticipation. He slid his hand under the hem of her skirt and lazily played there, teasing the soft flesh of her thighs at her apex. Her body shuddered as the need coursing through her fought with her brain. When he pushed aside the thin fabric of her panties, the battle instantly dissolved.

His finger glided over her sex. She suddenly grew aware of how wet she had become, and felt her cheeks burn—which grated because she never blushed. At anything. But then Ethanule found a spot that made her mind go blank. Her embarrassment was forgotten, replaced with a sharp thrum of electric current that racked through her.

He stroked her repeatedly, never letting her catch her breath, while he continued lavishing attention on her breasts. When her panting grew dire, Ethanule lifted his head to watch as she lost control. A moan ripped from her lungs as her body arched and an explosion of pleasure crashed over her.

As the vibrating waves began to dim, she looked up at Ethanule and recognized the hunger in his eyes.

Going to his knees, he tore off his coat and flung it aside. Next came his shirt, while Sonya sat up to eagerly undo the buckle of his pants, where his bulge was straining against the fabric. As she pulled them down, he reached for her panties, practically ripping them off her.

"Finally, I can get you out of my head," he grated.

She didn't know what that meant, but his tone was rough, which sent chills clamoring through her. The sight of his thick erection made her mouth water.

Once again between her legs, Ethanule grabbed a hold of her thighs and roughly pulled her toward him. Then in one smooth motion, he kissed her hard, just as he shoved into her body.

Sonya cried out from the pain.

Freezing completely, lips still at hers, Ethanule opened his eyes. They grew wide while hers burned with unshed tears.

He pulled back fast to study her, his shaft sliding free. Even before he looked down in horror, she knew there would be blood.

"Fuck!" His voice shook the room. He pulled up his pants and had them zipped and buckled in no time. He grabbed his shirt and coat, heading for the door. "How could you not have told me!"

His anger fueled her own, but her throat was too tight and she could only stare at him through narrow blurry eyes.

Just before he disappeared she heard him mutter, "I'm so fucking dead."

A wretched tear streamed down her cheek. There had only been one other time in her life when she had cried, and Ethanule would forever remind her of both of them.

Chapter 20

Nadua woke to an unusually chilly morning. The blanket worked well enough, but there was no wall of warm muscle pressed at her back, or a heavy arm draped over her. The lack was felt deep in the pit of her stomach.

Rex sat across from her, poking at the fire. He smiled when he saw she was awake. "Good morning."

Although she had slept through the night, Nadua still felt tired as she pushed herself up. Her body was sore in places she had forgotten could even get sore. Remembering the reason almost made her smile, until she recalled Marik's behavior afterward.

Glancing around, she noticed he was not with them. "Where is Marik?"

"He said he was going to hunt down an edisdon."

"What?"

"I told him they're not easy, but . . ."

"*Acta*, demon! He'd better not kill one. They are intelligent, compassionate creatures. Don't you demons care about anything but yourselves?"

Rex raised a brow. "We care about survival. Marik said you need their fur to stay warm. And besides, you and he have mated. He'd do anything to provide for you."

Nadua tilted her head.

He knows?

"Uh, did he tell you that?"

"No, but I can tell."

She stifled the urge to cover her neck. "Well, it was only the one time. It is never happening again."

From his seated position by the fire, Rex reached to pluck a fresh log from the pile. "Well, yeah, it can only happen once."

A dark sense of foreboding slowly crawled through her. "Um, Rex? How permanent is this mate thing?"

His body froze. The log hovered in his grip as his head turned back to her. The disbelief and astonishment in his face was alarming. She was sure now that she didn't want to know the answer.

"Didn't Marik explain?"

Oh, gods.

"Explain what?"

"He didn't explain?" Rex repeated louder.

She shook her head.

Standing, he scrubbed a hand down his face and began to pace. "You're his mate." He spread his hands out and shrugged, as if he wasn't sure what else to say. "It's forever."

"What do you mean forever?" She scoffed.

"What other kind of forever is there?"

"But, there's a way out of it. Right?"

Rex shook his head, his face growing pained. "Not for him there isn't."

"Stop being cryptic. What does that mean?"

Rex slouched against the wall and ran his hands through his hair. "He should have explained before he claimed you."

"Well, obviously he didn't!"

With a ragged breath, Rex began, "According to our legend,

there is only one mate for each of us, and it is fate that brings us together. However, the belief is highly controversial, even among our kind. Anyway, when they are near, a demon can usually identify his destined mate instantly. If it is another demon, that is. When it is not ...." He looked at her pointedly. "It seems there are complications."

"No kidding." Nadua waved him on.

"When our mate is recognized, we are driven by a desire to claim her, or him, in a female demon's case. When our fangs are inserted, a type of chemical is injected—"

Her hand flew to the bite on her neck. "I've been injected! With what!"

"Uh ...." Obviously uncomfortable, Rex continued. "It is so all others will know you are taken and who you belong to."

Nadua gasped. "I do not belong to Marik!"

Rex swallowed hard, growing more agitated.

"What else, Rex?"

"After the claiming, we only desire our mate's touch. There are very rare cases of any demon ever straying. But you? You don't have any such restrictions." Concerned, he added, "Did he not tell you any of this?"

Her stomach was crumbling and she was afraid the meal from last night was about to be her only response. "Not a word," she whispered.

"It was not right of him. He should have told you all this before he asked if he could claim you."

"He didn't ask," she replied in a flat tone, staring at the fire.

A snarl lifted her gaze back to Rex.

Blood red eyes swirling with outrage stared back at her. "I will kill him for you."

"What? No!"

"But it is against our law." His eyes dimmed back to normal.

Pinching the bridge of her nose, Nadua sighed. "I don't want him dead." Besides, it probably wouldn't be Marik who ended up dead, she added to herself. "I need to think. I'm going to go down to the pool for a little bit. Don't kill anyone while I'm gone, okay?"

Down in the warm chamber, Nadua plopped onto a jutting boulder and leaned her back against the wall. Her mind swirled at a nearly painful speed, like it was stuck in a twister. She tried to slow it by focusing on the natural heat and the mirrored surface of the water.

Demon mating was much more serious than she could have imagined. How could Marik have done that to her without her permission? He'd practically wed her against her will, while distracting her with the most delicious orgasm.

And then he'd regretted it directly after.

No matter what Rex said, Nadua didn't believe there was nothing that could be done. She wasn't going surrender her future and allow herself to be tied to a brash demon forever.

Soft echoing voices interrupted her thoughts.

Her back went straight as she listened hard. It didn't sound like Marik or Rex. Again, a muffled male voice sounded. A feminine timbre followed. Nadua slowly stood, looking around for the source.

Then she noticed a tiny hint of light from behind the boulder she'd been sitting on. Setting the lantern down, Nadua pulled the hefty rock back, revealing a small opening. Tentatively, she lowered to the ground to peek inside.

The voices came louder. Definitely a woman and a male. The male was talking. Nadua could make out a few words. They were Cyrellian. She leaned in farther.

"We can keep you safe, Lidian."

Lidian!

Surprised, Nadua jerked up and banged her head on the roof of the small tunnel. "Ow." She rubbed the sore spot just as the voices went quiet.

"What is it?" the female asked.

"I thought I heard something."

More silence.

"Let's go back," she pleaded. "Being this far away worries me. What if Jaxsin comes searching for me?"

"I would kill him before I let him near you again."

Nadua mused, what is it with guys wanting to kill each other today?

Swift footsteps dimmed into silence.

By the sound of it, the boy who had spoken was around the same age as Lidian. It seemed they had been alone, as well. Nadua might not have any weapons, but she was certain she could take down a couple of Cyrellian kids if she needed to.

Scooting along on her belly, Nadua wormed her way through the narrow space. It was so tight she had to push the lantern ahead of her a few feet, move forward, and then push the lantern again. Loose sand fell from above, coating her hair and arms. More of it pressed down on her back and legs. After a few minutes, she had to bite back a growing sense of claustrophobia and a building panic. She had no idea if the tunnel would ever end, and she didn't think she could wiggle her way backwards.

Then the tunnel grew even smaller. To her horror, the lantern flickered, sucking the light away and then bursting back to life. She'd almost lost it then, but when the light had dimmed, she spotted the end of the tunnel only a few more feet ahead. With renewed enthusiasm, she surged onward.

Nadua had to inch one shoulder forward and then the other. Back and forth. Sharp rocks scratched her as she went, but eventually she was out. It wasn't until she stood that Nadua realized how fast her heart had been beating.

Entering that hole to return was now a terrifying thought. Why had she thought that was a good idea? Soft footstep in the distance reminded her.

She glanced around her surroundings, and found she was alone in a dark passageway. To her right, ancient looking rocks fanned out toward her in varied positions, as though there had been a cave-in long ago. In the other direction, the cave split in two.

Above were little keyholes in the stony roof, allowing natural light in and making her lantern unnecessary. Afraid someone might happen upon it, she stashed it inside the little tunnel. She then piled a few rocks in front of it.

Nadua crept along the path she believed the couple had taken, being careful where she stepped. Any small sound could alert whoever she was following.

A voice echoed from the far end of the cave. She planted her body in a tight, dark corner. After several moments passed in silence, she continued forward, stopping often to listen for sign of others approaching.

The light only seemed to be getting brighter, yet the air remained moderately comfortable. If she was approaching an exit, it should be getting colder.

Gradually, the edges of the cave transitioned from its natural rocky formation into something more contrived. Intricate pillars carved from the rock stood on either side of a wide arched opening. Rex had said there was a tribe living within the caves. She was now sure that she'd found their lair.

Curiosity tickled the edge of her mind. She peeked through the doorway and found she was looking over a balcony carved of rock. Past it lay a huge expanse, like a great hall. Near the ceiling, surrounding a sleek dome, was a circumference of windows. From them, light gleamed against perfectly smooth stone walls that seemed to sparkle.

Making sure she didn't give herself away, Nadua leaned out for a better view. Along the inside balcony walls stood rows of elegant tall doors made of a dark wood, finely etched and polished. Below, stairs led to an open area for gathering, with a large table raised on a dais and surrounded by empty chairs that were neatly tucked in.

A painful breath caught in the back of her throat as her gaze fluttered over an array of elaborate tapestries that decorated various walls. The designs on them were all too familiar. If she didn't know any better, she could easily delude herself into thinking she'd been teleported back to the palace. Any second now, Ava could come running out of her room to greet her with a catching smile.

But it wasn't until she noticed the symbol etched directly in the middle of the stone floor that Nadua became sure that she must be hallucinating.

The Dion family emblem.

* * *

Edisdons were more difficult to hunt than Marik initially assumed. At first glance, they looked to be the dimmest sort of creatures, but they had a hidden intellect that easily thwarted his every attempt.

Even the smallest in the pack of five he'd been stalking had anticipated his every move. And, by the gods, were they fast. Their heavy frames were misleading. They should be slow and sluggish, but no doubt they were ten times swifter than he on foot.

Among his attempts, he'd waited in the tree tops, only to be bucked free when he landed on a big male's back. After that, he realized they were migrating in a straight line. He had run ahead of them and buried himself in the deep snow, planning to burst out and surprise them. Later, when he was positive they should have passed, their trail showed that the pack had given him a wide berth and then resumed their track.

Marik had traveled miles, sniffing out their pungent scent. Nadua needed their fur, and he was determined to get it for her. Unfortunately, he failed to snatch even a hair and was forced to return to the cave with nothing to offer his beautiful mate. Perhaps they could stay in the warm part of the cave until they were found. They weren't too far from—

A crack to his jaw sent him reeling to the ground. Pain erupted and the metallic taste of blood tingled on his taste buds.

Fists clenched, Rex peered down at him with a mix of repulsion and disgust.

Marik should have expected this. Nadua would have questions, and had obviously directed them at the only other person she could.

Raising his fist again, Rex brought it down hard on Marik's skull. Marik didn't even attempt to avoid it. His head ricocheted off the hard frozen ground.

Rex was only following the old law, and rightly so. Nadua deserved better than a miserably dishonored slave who had unintentionally claimed her. She deserved someone who loved her, who would die to protect her.

Another hit darkened his vision.

"Fucker! Fight me!" Rex yelled.

Marik spit blood and replied, "No."

A kick to his gut had him gasping, clenching in agony.

"Fight me if you think you deserve her!"

"What do you care?" Fire rose in him, thinking Rex wanted her for himself.

She's mine!

"She doesn't deserve what you've done!" Two more swift, heavy kicks to his face.

I know.

"She's the only kind person I've known in centuries!" Rex kicked him again. "Do you think because she's not of our kind you can just take her as yours!"

Burst of pain indicated that Marik's face was bloodied and swelling. "I didn't mean to. I never meant—"

Marik wasn't sure if it was a kick or a punch that cut him off, only that it was painful. Was Nadua watching this carnage? Had she sicced Rex on him? He couldn't find her scent.

"Where is she?"

"She went to be by herself in the spring."

Dread settled in him. Rex swung again, but Marik seized his fist.

"Are you sure?" Something felt off. He didn't like her being alone down there. When Rex went silent, Marik shot to his feet. "When did you see her last?"

"It has been a few hours—Where are you going?"

"We can continue this conversation after I'm sure she's safe." Marik flew down the narrow passage with Rex right behind him.

Nadua wasn't there.

The Edge bubbled up.

He slammed Rex against the wall. "Where is she?"

"She came down here, I—" His eyes widened at something past Marik's shoulder.

Marik tilted his head at a boulder that looked to have been moved. Behind it was a tiny passageway. Too small for either of them, but perfect for a Faieara sized female. Kneeling down, Marik caught Nadua's scent.

Why would she . . . ?

He peered inside. There was a small amount light trying to get through, but a lump of something on the far end was blocking it.

"Nadua!"

"Shh," Rex hushed. "You don't want to alert anyone else."

"Anyone else? What the fuck do you mean, anyone else?"

Instinctively, Rex took a step back. "I told you, there are people living in the caves. I thought there was no access between here and their territory."

Marik raked his hands through his hair. Nadua had to have moved the rock to gain access to the small opening. Was she running from him again?

He took another desperate peek. Still that dark lump hadn't moved. A horrific picture of Nadua passed out or stuck inside the tiny hole assaulted him. He began frantically digging, pulling away rock and soil.

"You could cause a cave in like that," Rex warned.

"I must get to her!"

"Come with me. There's a larger entrance around the mountain."

"If anything happens to her, I will kill you."

"I know."

Chapter 21

Nadua stood shocked to her core and looking up at a shadow of her past—long dead, yet standing before her with a familiar smile on his face. At first she had raced down the steps to embrace him on sight, but then reality slammed into her and she grew furious.

He was supposed to be dead.

Cyrus was obviously surprised to see her, and his expression morphed into exuberance as though presented with an old friend.

Abruptly, Nadua slapped him. The sound of it echoed off the slick curved walls. "What is this, Cyrus? Fineas told me you died." She sucked in a devastated breath and looked around the massive room. "For three hundred years I have mourned the day!" Her fists clenched. "Have you been here? The whole time?"

Cyrus rubbed his cheek, reminding Nadua of a chastised child. "Nadua, girl, calm yourself."

"Calm? Calm! You are alive and you let us think otherwise! You let *me* think otherwise!" She could feel herself becoming hysterical. "Why?" she screamed. Her eyes burned, her throat tightened, and she feared she was about to break down and weep.

The noise she was making drew others, and Nadua registered that five rather common-looking Cyrellians had arrows and swords aimed at her. She didn't care. She stared at Cyrus, waiting for an explanation.

Cyrus slumped his shoulders and opened his mouth to speak, but was interrupted by a familiar, echoing growl.

Oh, gods!

A scream issued behind her. Nadua turned as a couple Cyrellian females rushed passed.

Marik, fully demonized, emerged from a darkened passageway. His muscles strained as burning red eyes promised pain and were fixed on her supposed attackers. She couldn't help but think he looked . . . magnificent.

Rex followed behind him, equally aggressive in form.

The weapons that had been on her were now turned toward the demons.

"Wait!" she called, rushing for Marik, her hands up in a calming gesture. "Marik. Stop."

He did, looking at her with dim confusion.

What had happened to his face? It was slightly swollen, and his cheek and lip were cut. He scanned the room and let out a terrifying roar that, days ago, would have made her cower.

Now she just snapped her fingers for his attention. "Focus."

Both he and Rex gaped at her.

Nadua turned back to Cyrus and the armed men. "Cyrus, these are my demons. I mean . . . not my demons, my friends. I mean, they won't hurt anyone." She turned back to Marik and Rex. "Right?"

Both gave halfhearted shrugs.

She looked at Cyrus again. "But your people need to lower their weapons. Now."

"Do it," Cyrus ordered.

The Cyrellians glanced at each other and relaxed their stance.

"Things have changed," Cyrus observed. "Have we established a treaty with the demons?"

"We? What do you mean by *we*? The kingdom? Or are you

talking about the living?"

"Nadua—"

"No, I need to know." She gestured to the room. "What happened to you? Are you allied with the rebels now?"

"Of course not. How could you think that?"

"Why have you not contacted me? Or Wren?"

Cyrus ducked his gaze at that.

Nadua gasped. "No . . . Wren knows? For how long?"

"I wanted news of you, and little Avaline."

Nadua felt her lip quiver. "I took it all on when your brother died. The kingdom. Raising Ava. You could have been there, this whole time? I needed you!"

Sorrow etched in his features. "From what I hear, you've been doing a wonderful job."

Tears fuzzed her vision. She marched forward, teeth clenched, and slapped him again. His entourage raised their weapons. Before Cyrus could wave them back, Marik had her behind him with a growl.

"Marik, this is my business," she snapped.

"When it concerns your safety, it's mine."

She pushed past him, and thankfully he did not try to stop her. "Well?" she said to Cyrus.

Cyrus gave a heavy sigh and replied, "You look tired. And why are you such a mess?"

Nadua looked down at her clothes, which were torn and stained from her travels. "It's a long story."

He glanced at Rex and Marik. "Indeed. Well, so is mine. Allow me to provide you with lodgings and proper clothing. And I will have a warm meal prepared for you. Let us talk then."

Curious faces gazed down at them from the balcony. Most were dressed in the standard aristocratic garb, and held themselves with an elegance that reminded Nadua of the palace.

"Who else is with you?" Cyrus asked.

"It's just us."

His brows shot up in surprise. "It's just you three?"

"Like I said, long story."

He motioned for a nearby female to approach. "Show them each to a room, please."

Marik wrapped his arm around Nadua's waist and pulled her closer to him. "She stays with me."

Cyrus slanted a gaze at her.

In a tone meant to pierce metal, she said, "He'll forget he said that in a couple of minutes. Three rooms will be fine."

Marik gave her confident look that said, "There might be three, but we will be using two."

We'll see about that.

"Uh, very well then. Please follow Collet. She will show you the way."

Collet bowed, slipping nervous glances at the demons. "This way, please." She started up the steps and glanced back as they followed.

Marik was still rigid and giving off I-will-kill-everyone-here vibes. Rex moved cautiously, scanning the large room. He was obviously unnerved by their close proximity to these Cyrellians—some of which had probably fought against his people.

"Cyrus is an old friend." Nadua felt she should reassure them.

Collet kept a few feet ahead and walked as though she were prepared to be tackled at any moment.

"You trust him?" Marik sneered.

"Yes, I do."

I did.

She hoped he was still the person she once knew, but she

couldn't be sure. It had been such a long time since she'd seen his beautiful, crystal eyes.

Questions pounded inside her head. Why did he leave so long ago and let her believe he had died? What was his purpose here?

Please don't let him be involved with the rebels.

Seeing Cyrus had been more than a shock—it had jarred her to the core, rendering her breathless. She had rushed forward without thinking. Now she prayed she hadn't just walked them into danger.

Collet paused, gesturing to a door. "For the lady." She moved to turn the heavy knob but jumped back when Marik approached. He burst through the door as if expecting an ambush on the other side.

"Uh, thank you, Collet. You can just point to the other two if they are nearby."

Collet let out a relieved breath and indicated doors at the end of the hall. Nadua dismissed her.

She turned to the demons and sighed. "Try not to scare the locals, boys. Oh, and Marik, your room is over there."

He snorted, ignoring where she pointed and advanced into her room. Nadua gave Rex a look beseeching him for help, but he shook his head.

"There's nothing that can make him leave your side right now, short of killing him."

"I suppose we should talk. Will you be alright by yourself?"

Rex nodded. "These people have never hunted me like the others."

"Nice blanket!" Marik call from inside her room.

Nadua poked in her head. A familiar looking blanket lay neatly across a high bed. She raised a dubious brow at Rex. His guilty smile nearly made her laugh. "You thieving demon."

After watching Rex enter his own room, Nadua took a calming breath and shut the door behind her. Small windows against the wall let soft light in, making the space surprisingly bright. The room was magnificent.

Marik sprawled out on the bed, arms bent behind his head and a wicked grin on his face. His legs were crossed and his dirty boots hung off the edge of the mattress. He looked too sexy and, for a split second, she imagined straddling him there. Then her sanity returned.

She crossed her arms and narrowed her eyes. "What happened to your face?"

"Rex."

The way he was looking at her made her feel like she was in the den of a prowling beast, and she wished it didn't send a small thrill through her.

I am angry with him, she reminded herself.

"Rex told me what you did to me was against your people's law."

He frowned. "Aye."

"And irreversible?"

Losing all resemblance of humor, he repeated, "Aye."

After everything that had happened to her: being attacked, abducted, forced to travel the countryside on foot. Having the most erotic experience of her life, followed directly by the most devastating. Finding out that she'd been lied to by a dear old friend, as well as her oh-so-loyal captain of the guard. Nadua's emotions were held together by a frayed thread of sheer determination.

"How could you?"

Marik's lips thinned but he watched her with eyes full of regret.

"Say something."

"I have no excuse. It was a huge mistake that I cannot undo."

"A mistake! No, this is a disaster!"

He raked a hand down his face and mumbled, "Aye."

"Stop saying that!"

"I don't know what else to say. I never thought I would find my mate this way."

"I am *not* your mate." She pointed to her neck that was now fully healed. "Orgasmic bite does not equal binding commitment."

"Orgasmic?"

She pinned him with a hard glare.

"I wish I could dismiss it as easily as you. But I can't. Every fiber in me says you are my life now."

Nadua frowned. She opened her mouth to respond, but for a moment nothing would come out. Finally, she said, "I didn't agree to this. You don't own me, and I can be with anyone else if I want."

His features twisted with a mix of agony and anger. "You'd be risking the life of anyone that you show interest in. I won't be able to help it." His voice turned into a rumble. "To me, and to all other demons, you are mine."

Rendered speechless once more, Nadua began to pace. "There has to be a way to reverse this. The Serakians are old allies of my father, and their magic is great. I have no doubt that they can work a spell to fix this."

* * *

Marik shot to his feet, alarmed by her words. Fix this? Like they were broken?

"Is that really what you want?"

She stilled. "Isn't it what you want? You yourself said it was a mistake."

He did, but he meant the way it had happened. He'd bungled the claiming, but he couldn't be more satisfied with his mate. She was powerful and sexy as hell. He enjoyed talking with her, and her lovely eyes commanded the beating of his heart.

The Serakians are a secretive race, and little was known of them other than they were not borne. They were recruited from remarkable individuals found all over the universe. What Marik did know was that Nadua was right, they were renowned for their prowess with magic. If there was any way to affect the finality of demon mating, they would know if it.

"Right?" She prompted. "You don't actually . . . want me? Forever?"

Keeping his voice steady, he replied, "Of course not." Marik's heart sank the moment her shoulders relaxed. Up until he had claimed her, Marik had been looking forward to the time they would spend together, not just on Undewla, but on *Marada*. Even though he hadn't realized she was his mate, he'd been excited to have her to himself for as long as he could.

Had she been imaging the opposite? Being away from him? With other males? Ethanule?

Feeling himself slip toward the Edge, Marik lowered his eyes so she wouldn't see them change and worked to pull himself under control. He should have realized early on that he was falling for her. Perhaps things would have gone differently if he had. Now he would need to woo her.

But there were two problems. First, he'd never wooed anyone in his life. The second was his little problem of blacking out at the worst possible times. If he was going to make love to her again, he needed to be fully conscious.

A knock sounded at the door.

Nadua called, "Come in."

Collet eased the door open and peeked in. "Hello miss, I have clothing for you and your . . . male."

"He's not my male," she grumbled.

Marik stifled a protest.

"I can help you dress if you require assistance." She held out a formal gown. The fabric looked beautiful and elegant, just like everything else in this place.

At the woman's question, Marik thought he noticed Nadua cringe and recalled that female garments could be difficult to get into, requiring a lot of touching. She had probably been burned many times by those who helped her in the past.

"I'll assist her." He crossed to accept the clothes, forgetting that his eyes had reddened.

The frightened girl backed up so fast she knocked into the wall.

Nadua moved between them. "I'll take the clothes. Thank you for—"

Before Nadua had finished the sentence, the girl thrust the bundle at her and darted into the hallway.

"You're real good at making friends, aren't you?" She separated the gown from the rest and tossed Marik his clothing. Then she ducked into the bathing room. "And I won't be needing your help."

She slammed the door.

* * *

The gown was nice, but a bit old fashioned with its low cut and crisscross laces on the back of the bodice. She contorted her body for what felt like eternity, first trying to reach over her shoulder, then behind her back while bending forward. With a huff, Nadua admitted defeat.

She poked her head out the door while holding the dress up at her breasts.

Marik sat on the edge of the bed, already dressed in his new outfit. They'd guessed his size well. The dark top hung like a robe and flared at his midsection. Defining his waist was a strip of fabric that split in the front and was decorated by a pair of silver clasps. His dirty boots should have made the pristine black trousers look out of place, but on him it looked . . . sexy.

Damn it.

When he spotted her, he tried to hide his smile but it showed in his eyes.

She narrowed her gaze at him. "I need you to tie the back of this."

Instead of making a snarky comment as she expected, he rose from the bed and made his way toward her as if trying not to seem too eager.

Nadua gave him her back. A soft rumbling sound escaped him, followed by his finger running down her spine. She clenched her teeth to keep a shiver in check.

"Just tie, no touching."

The gods knew what happened last time he touched her. And this time her body sprang to life at that tiny hint of contact, making her remember in perfect detail how his body slipped easily into hers, his hands running over her heated skin. She mentally shook herself.

At the base of her back, he started pulling the strings taught, slowly moving his way up. Every now and again a finger would graze her flesh. She suspected on purpose, but it affected her nonetheless. When it happened again, just below her shoulder blades, she couldn't prevent a small shudder of pleasure. He briefly paused, then continued.

When he neared the top, Nadua lifted her hair out of the way. She felt a current of air brush her neck, as though his lips were close. She looked back and he gave her an innocent expression that screamed guilt. He was enjoying this way too much, and it was like sensual torture for her. And it wasn't over.

With the strings tight, he now had to do a second pass, and secure it with a knot at the bottom. Grinding her teeth, she remained still as he went even slower this time, having to slip his fingers under each crossing strand against her skin.

Nadua gripped the fabric of the dress, convincing herself that she was doing a wonderful job of steadying her breath.

Finally, the knot was tied. She turned and caught his eyes, glowing with barely contained passion. She gulped because she liked it. And so did her body. Way too much.

"Thanks," she choked out, and rushed back into the safety of the bathing room.

* * *

Marik shifted in his pants. Such a normal act had turned into something so damn erotic he couldn't think straight. Each stolen touch had his shaft lengthening, growing hard as steel. He had hardly kept himself from pulling her to the bed, lifting her skirts, and working himself inside her.

By her responses, he was sure she had felt it too. The scent of her arousal still mingled in the air. Just before she scurried away, her eyes had been heavy with lust and glossed with a sheen of iridescent sapphire.

She still wants me.

But she had practically dove to get away from him. It was going to take a long time for him to make things right between them, but he was up for the task. Time, he had. Patience, he could fake. Yet, becoming the man she deserved? To be worthy of her? He wondered if it were even possible.

His thoughts turned dark as old memories assailed him. His sister, Misha. How she had begged him to save her. Shadowed glimpses of the arena, and the screams that still echoed in his mind. Losing himself to the pain of his later tortures, and selfishly enjoying the mindlessness it eventually brought. There wasn't a moment in his life where he had proven his worth.

But he was stronger now. Trained. Hardened. No longer the helpless young boy. For Nadua, he would prove himself. Every day if he had to.

One thing was certain: she could never know of his past.

Chapter 22

Eventually, Nadua calmed enough to re-enter the room. Almost immediately, another knock at the door saved her from having to finish the conversation she'd started with Marik.

A different woman stood on the other side, holding a small box. She was much older and tougher looking. Collet must have refused to return.

Without invitation, the woman barged into the room, eyeing Marik as though she would put up a hell of a fight if he tried anything.

Holding out the small box, she said, "Cyrus offers a gift to the lady."

Inside, a gorgeous necklace sparkled at her. Twisted silver vines wrapped around golden flowers, each with a different colored jewel at its center.

Long ago, Nadua would describe the plants of her home to Cyrus and he would paint wonderful images based on her words. This looked straight out of one of his paintings.

"Beautiful." Her voice was breathless.

The woman continued. "Cyrus requests that you wear this at the evening's meal."

"When might that be?"

"Soon. I will return for you when it is time." Curling her lip, the woman added, "He says the demons are welcome as well."

Without taking her eyes from the gift, Nadua replied, "Thank you." But the woman had gone. Throat tight, Nadua ran her fingers over the smooth metal.

In a strange tone, Marik observed, "This makes you sad. Would you like me to destroy it?"

She clutched it to her chest. "No! Why would I want that?"

His only response was an irritated shrug.

Was this jealousy? Marik saw her as belonging to him, which probably meant he didn't like that another male had given her something so beautiful. Good thing he didn't know how instantly dear it was to her. She slipped it on. The cool metal slowly warmed against her skin.

Telling a demon to check his attitude was probably like telling a rock to speak up. Still, she asked, "Is this how you plan on acting from now on?"

"Do you plan on wearing that from now on?"

She raised her chin. "Look, we're going to find a way out of this eventually. Until then, why don't we just go back to the way we were before . . . the incident."

"You mean when I made you come with a stroke of my tongue?"

Warmth flooded her cheeks, then between her legs. "I mean before that."

"When you were frightened and running from me?"

Is that what she was doing now? Running from him again? No. What he did was a betrayal. A dark part of her mind wondered if they could still enjoy each other now and end it later.

Mimicking her thoughts, Marik edged, "Since we know we will be parting ways, why not just use each other for pleasure? As a mated male, I crave it like you wouldn't believe. And I can tell you're in need."

Her jaw dropped. A nervous laugh bubbled up. "What? I am not."

With a knowing curve to his lips, he continued. "Plus, I could use your help."

Nadua raised a suspicious bow.

"As you're aware, I sort of have a problem with . . . blacking out during sex."

"Quite aware."

"Well, once we break the mate bond, I'll be able to slake myself on other women again." He paused, watching her.

Waving him on, Nadua decided not to analyze why the thought of him with another woman pained her.

"And I don't want to make the same mistake I made with you. You could help me. Like sexual training."

Another woman writhing in ecstasy with his fangs in her flesh?

"How could I possibly help?"

"With you, I felt I could have stayed myself, if . . ." He trailed off.

"If what?"

He looked like he was about to say something, then changed his mind. "I think, if I had another shot—"

"Another shot? Like I'm some kind of game?"

"No."

"You're just trying to trick me into sleeping with you again."

"Why would I need to trick you? You're dying to sleep with me again."

"Is that so?"

"Yeah, I can smell it on you."

"You crude . . . I can't believe you!"

"Believe it, luv. You can deny me, but you can't lie to yourself."

He was right, and it pissed her off. But she couldn't stop from contemplating all the "training" they could get in, until what he called the "mate bond" was broken.

* * *

She's actually considering this.

Marik hadn't meant to be so abrasive at the end and was afraid he'd just ruined his chances. He held his breath as he waited for her next response. She fiddled with a lock of her hair. Their eyes met.

He wanted to throttle the person when, once again, there was a knock on the damn door.

That old snooty wench, who had looked at him like he was worth less than dirt, greeted Nadua. "Cyrus would like you to join him for drinks before your meal is ready."

"That would be lovely."

"Yes, lovely." Marik sneered.

They both slanted their heads at him.

Nadua must have registered the determined look on his face because she reluctantly said, "Of course, Marik will be accompanying me." Then she shot him a look that said he'd better behave.

As the old woman led the way, he followed behind Nadua, eyes riveted to her smooth open back, the slim arch of her neck, the soft sway of her hips. He needed to get it together, before he forced her back into the room and threw her on top of that convenient bed.

It became apparent to him that she didn't understand the power of her easy sensuality, or she wouldn't be moving her hips in such an enticing way.

Marik peered over the edge of the balcony and spotted Cyrus, already seated at the large table. He looked regal in his stance. His straight white hair was pulled back from his pale face. He was thin, like most of his kind, yet his arms were defined, peeking out from his tunic.

Marik smirked at the memory of Nadua slapping the man, as well as the light red mark that still lingered on his face. Did she burn herself as well?

Concern spiked. He should have asked her before. "Let me see your hand," he whispered.

"No."

He gripped her wrist and saw her palm was red before she snatched it away. "You're hurt."

"It's nothing. And it was worth it."

Good.

Cyrus stood at their approach, looking far too happy to see Nadua again. His gaze dipped to her neckline. "It looks beautiful on you."

"Thanks," she replied. And damn it, she blushed.

He spared Marik a glance and nodded respectfully. A round of drinks were already in place. Three, as though Cyrus had known Marik would be here.

"Does this have alcohol in it?" Nadua asked.

Cyrus nodded.

Nadua claimed her seat and before Marik could stop her, had already taken a generous gulp of her drink.

Cyrus noted the outraged look on his face.

Poisons could be easily slipped into drinks. In demon culture, alcohol was imbibed as a ritual when done in the company of strangers. It was considered a sign of trust to take the first sip as a group.

He didn't trust these people.

Still standing, Cyrus lifted his drink, not taking his eyes from Marik. Quirking a brow, Marik did the same. Then they both drank.

Interesting. Cyrus knew something of his culture.

Nadua shifted her eyes between them but didn't mention what she must have thought was a strange exchange between them. Instead, she took another large gulp.

Marik frowned and sat in the place to her left. Cyrus claimed the spot across from her.

* * *

The sweet liquid warmed her belly. Cyrus had remembered her favorite drink, though it was a little light on the alcohol. Right now she could use a good stiff drink.

Finishing the glass, she wiggled it in the air. "Can I get another, a little stronger?"

Of course, Marik had something to say. "I don't think that's a good idea."

She pierced him with an annoyed glare. "You want to know what I think isn't a good idea?"

"I can imagine."

A moment later, a servant brought her another drink and she put it to her lips. Perfect.

Then she focused on Cyrus. His eyes were just as clear as she remembered. Before she could ask the millions of questions floating around in her head, he cleared his throat and spoke.

"What are you doing out here with demons?"

"Well, the daughter of a noble family was taken by the rebels. Lidian. Do you know her? I thought I heard her name spoken."

"I believe so. We raided a rebel group just last week and rescued two females. Lidian and Jusibell."

"I will want to speak with them later.

"Of course."

"Well, anyway, I was hunting the rebels when Marik saved my life." From the corner of her eye, she could see Marik jutting his shoulders back.

"How? What happened?"

"Tamir and Nakul were planning to assassinate me."

Cyrus took on a dubious expression. "Are you sure? I know them both. And I fought alongside Tamir."

"I didn't want to believe it at first. I really didn't. But, the more I thought of it, and the more I got to know Marik, I must consider it to be plausible."

"You trust these demons then?"

"With this? I do."

With other things? Not so much.

Cyrus turned to Marik. "I thank you for saving her."

"I didn't do it for you."

Nadua shot him a look of warning.

"Of course not, but I'm no less grateful. She is very important to me."

"Am I?" She tried to keep the hurt from entering her tone. "Then why the lies, Cyrus?"

Looking a little sheepish, Cyrus started to speak but was interrupted by the appearance of Collet. He seemed grateful for it.

"The evening's meal is ready, my lord. Shall I serve it now?"

"Please do," Cyrus replied.

Nadua stood. "May I go alert Rex? I'm sure he's hungry too."

"Collet will retrieve him. Please sit."

Collet partially hid her surprise at being volunteered for the task. Without a word, she scurried up to the balcony. A few minutes later, Rex was seated on the other side of Marik. He was stiff, and looked to Marik and Nadua for reassurance. Nadua smiled at him. Marik nodded.

Steaming plates were placed in front of each of them. The smell was glorious.

Rex started on the food like a beast, using his hands and ignoring the utensils. Marik was a little more refined, but still gripped his fork with his entire fist. Cyrus eyed them with repressed irritation.

The dish was delicious and it was a relief from their repetitive meals over the last few days. Nadua had her fill and then set her utensils aside, unable to wait any longer.

"Tell me," she said. "No more delaying."

After draining the last of his drink, Cyrus let out a heavy sigh. "Do you remember what happened between us before I left?"

"Before you died," she corrected, and then flushed, knowing exactly what he meant. A week before his *death*, they had shared a brief moment of passion. While attending a party arranged by one of the nobles, they had ended up spending the entire night together, dancing and drinking in a lonely side room.

In their inebriated state, they had forgotten what would happen if they kissed. It had been a brief touch, but their lips had been swollen for two days. She smiled, remembering.

Then she realized Rex had frozen completely in mid scoop. Marik's fork was bent at an odd angle and the sudden heat rolling of him brought her back from the fond memory.

Cyrus noticed this too, and watched both demons warily.

Nadua broke the tense silence. "A week later, Fineas told me you died fighting the rebels." She couldn't stop the quiver in her lip. It still hurt to think of it. She'd locked herself away, mourned for months.

"I'm sorry it hurt you. It hurt me to leave."

"Then why did you?"

His shoulders slumped. "Well, it wasn't difficult to figure out what we'd done. Fineas summoned me the day after. He thought we were growing too close, and he was right. We could never . . ." He trailed off.

A low rumble came from Marik.

In an attempt to get his attention, Nadua placed her hand on his thigh. Marik quickly covered her hand with his. The action seemed desperate.

She looked to Cyrus. "Perhaps we should speak about this in private."

"Over my bloody dead body," Marik barked.

She ground her teeth. "Marik, please don't—"

"Actually," Cyrus interjected. "I would like to speak with Marik alone."

Nadua looked up in surprise. "Cyrus, I don't think—"

Marik stood, as if ready for battle. "Let's go."

Nadua was too shocked to say anything. Cyrus led Marik out of the room. She turned her wide eyes to Rex, who had resumed the assault on his meal.

Chapter 23

Following behind the blue tinted asshole who was far too familiar with his mate, Marik could barely contain his building rage. He had to continue telling himself that Nadua would hate him if he took the life of this bastard.

Maybe. Probably. Anyway, it wasn't worth the risk.

They didn't walk far. Cyrus led him through a hall that broke off from the main room, and into a rather nice chamber. Books lined one wall. On the opposite side stood a small fire place. A few paintings hung above it, and one in particular caught his attention.

The woman's beautiful red locks, flowing freely, were unmistakable. He recognized the slender curve of her shoulder, peaking out of a soft frill gown. There was excitement in her eyes, as though she'd just been laughing. Her breathtaking smile made Marik jealous of whomever it was gifted.

"I painted that a little after I left her." Cyrus spoke from behind Marik. "I couldn't stand not seeing her any longer."

"Are you trying to make me kill you?"

"I know a little bit about your kind. I know you have more honor than we give you credit for."

"You're sure about that?"

"I'm hoping." He paused. "I fought in the demon war long ago. I was there from the beginning. We tried for diplomacy at first, but as often it does, fear and ignorance claimed the masses. Before we knew it, we were at war."

Marik kept his back to Cyrus, listening while taking in the happy image of Nadua. She'd smiled at him before, but never like that.

"One day, I followed a demon into the Caves of Kayata. My brigade had been battling a group of them for days out in the open. We were caught off guard when the cave-in started and we halted our fight to save ourselves. When the dust settled we found we were both trapped inside, and on separate ledges of a deep impassable cavern."

To Marik's surprise, Cyrus chuckled. "After what must have been two days of screaming curses at each other, we got bored and started an actual conversation. He was rather funny. I wish I could remember his name. Well, anyway, I have to believe your kind are honorable because that day the demon and I made a promise to each other. If one side of the cavern was open, we would free the other and go our separate ways without conflict. His was opened first."

Marik waited for him to continue.

"I fully expected him to betray me. Especially since his men were telling him to leave me to die. But he ordered them to dig me out too. He told them simply that he'd made a vow and then they didn't hesitate."

Finally, Marik turned to face Cyrus. "Would you have done the same?"

Cyrus looked him straight in the eyes. "Without a doubt."

"Why are you telling me this?"

"Is Nadua yours?"

Marik hesitated. "She is."

Cyrus shook his head and lowered his gaze. "I love her."

Red flooded Marik's vision. His teeth began to grind, and his claws itched for action.

"I've never told her." He paused. "And I never will. She is an impossible dream. I know this."

"Again, why are you telling me? Why did you bring me here to see this?" Anger marked his tone as he gestured to the exquisite painting.

"Because I figured you would need proof of my feelings. And so that you would know I will do anything to keep her safe—to put you at ease around me." His expression was sincere. "Another thing. I find it hard to believe Tamir or Nakul would plot against her. But if they did, I'll need to find out why. Please, tell me everything you know."

Marik hesitated for a moment. Sensing the truth in his words, Marik decided he could trust Cyrus and revealed what he could.

Cyrus looked saddened by the time he finished. "I will send a message to the palace immediately. You're welcome to stay here as long as you need. I'm assuming you'll be taking Nadua away from Undewla?"

"That's the plan." Marik's hatred for Cyrus began to dull, re-placed in part by pity. He couldn't imagine never being able to touch Nadua without causing her pain. The mere idea sickened him.

Cyrus nodded solemnly. "Take care of her."

"I intend to."

* * *

Nadua was growing increasingly irritated. Rex had already fin-ished his dinner and was back in his room. Now she sat alone and sipped her drink, feeling the tingle of the alcohol. She debated retir-ing for the night.

Finally, Marik and Cyrus returned, both grave and somber.

"What happened?"

They claimed their seats and requested refills from a waiting servant.

Cyrus spoke. "I've sent a message to Wren, warning him about Tamir and Nakul."

Nadua sighed in relief. "Did you add that I'm here?"

"I did."

"Good." She was sure there was more to their chat than that, but she was determined to make Cyrus finish his story. "Can you please continue? Why did you feel you had to fabricate your own demise?"

Cyrus's lips thinned, but he obliged. "When you first came to this planet, very few were happy about it. Fineas was a strong ally of your Father, so he didn't hesitate to grant you his protection. But when the news spread, our people were torn. There was great fear that the Kayadon would come here and destroy us to find you. Many are still afraid."

The drinks arrived, and both Cyrus and Marik swallowed half their glasses. Nadua took another sip of hers.

"People fled Sori, looking to hide in case their fears were realized. Fineas truly loved his people, and hated that they were suffering beyond the walls of Sori. So this place was built."

He gestured around the room. "A refuge of sorts. But Fineas needed to send someone of the royal blood line to represent the crown, and keep the peace. When he realized how close you and I had become, he decided it would be better for everyone if I disappeared." He paused. "Fineas understood that if you knew I was alive, you'd come looking for me. And because there was fear in the people who lived here, that wouldn't have been a good idea. So he told you I died."

Tears were streaming down Nadua's cheeks. She wanted to protest that she wouldn't have come looking, but that would have been a lie. Cyrus had been her only real friend until Ava was born. He'd been the one to teach her to fight, and to use a bow. How to be strong in the face of the Cyrellians who looked down their noses at her. Living without him had been nearly unbearable.

"I'll be leaving soon," she blurted.

"I know. Marik told me."

The mention of his name reminded her that he was still sitting next to her, surprisingly quiet, though she was crying for another man. His face was almost void of emotion. Only a slight tick in his jaw indicated his mood.

"I should retire." She stood and so did the two men. Nadua said good night to Cyrus and, as expected, Marik followed her up to her room.

A fire had been started in the stone hearth, making the room a comfortable temperature. Inside, she turned to Marik, years of loneliness crashing down upon her. Nadua found herself kissing him, loving the warmth and softness of his lips. She wanted him to dull her mind with his expert touch. But she realized he wasn't kissing her back.

He put distance between them. "Good night. I'll see you in the morning," he said coolly.

"What? But I thought you would want to . . . you know."

His eyes were shadowed and she couldn't read them. "You have no idea how badly I want to." He glanced away. "But you wouldn't be thinking of me."

With that, he was gone. The door closed heavily behind him.

Left to do nothing but mull over everything that had happened, Nadua's emotions flared out of control. She was overcome with sorrow for her lost time with Cyrus. Fear over her unsure future with Marik. Worry for her people, both the Faieara and the Cyrellians, as well as for Ava. Bitterness for being left alone, not only by Cyrus, but by Fineas, and her own father and mother. Finally, guilt, for thinking badly of any of them, when they were only doing what they could to help her.

In the hallowed pit of her stomach, she felt she'd lost control over every aspect of her life. After years of holding it together, Nadua curled up on the bed and cried herself unconscious.

Sometime during that blissful oblivion, a vision came on the edge of sleep.

Once more, Marik crouched in the arena, the same brutality befalling him. This time, Nadua witnessed the aftermath. With the bleachers empty and the blood turning brown with age, Marik's eyes finally dimmed to their natural green, marred by horror at the sight of the dead woman left behind. Cradling her broken body in his arms, his bellow echoed off the cold walls.

How could I? How could I?

It took her a moment to realize she was hearing his thoughts.

How could I do this?

Marik thought he was responsible for the woman's fate? Did he believe that of all of them?

* * *

"Did you sleep well?" Cyrus called from below when he spotted Nadua on the balcony. He was enjoying a morning meal alone.

"I did," she lied, heading down the stairs to join him. "Does no one else eat with you?"

"They usually do."

Ah, until she had come. These Cyrellians really did fear she'd lead the Kayadon here. Or maybe it was the demon presence that kept them away.

"Have you seen Marik?"

She had checked his room, but he hadn't been in it.

"I believe he went out early this morning."

"Out? Why?"

"I'm not in the habit of stopping demons for a chat when they look like they're on a mission. How did you meet him, anyway?"

Nadua told him the story, leaving out the embarrassing intimate moments, and subsequent biting.

"I'm glad you survived all that. I'll get some new furs made up for you. I recall how important they are to your comfort.

"You keep edisdons?"

"There are some that roam free near here. They've come to trust us."

"That would be wonderful, thank you."

He called to someone behind her. "Oh, Lidian, come here please."

Lidian approached with a large smile on her face. At seeing Nadua, recognition flared and she bowed. "Your Highness. How are you this day?"

"I'm good. How are you?"

"Just fine."

"Are you Lidian, daughter of Rin?"

"I am, Your Highness."

Nadua felt a small amount of tension leave her shoulders. "Your parents are very worried about you."

"I can believe it. I was so frightened when the rebels took me and I remember my father had fought them. Is he well?"

"I believe so." She tilted her head. "Why haven't you contacted them?"

Her cheeks darkened. "I am afraid they would demand I come home. I . . ." She trailed off, too embarrassed to say.

Nadua grinned. "You have a crush."

Lidian put her hands behind her back and gave a shy shrug.

"Well, that's fine with me, but you should send a message to your parents. It's not nice to leave them to worry. How would you like it if they disappeared, and then didn't write to tell you they were okay?"

Lidian frowned and slowly nodded. "I will, Your Highness."

When the girl scurried away, Cyrus said, "You sounded very motherly."

"I've been raising Ava since she was two."

"I wish I could have been there for her birth. How is she?"

"She's brilliant. Sweet. Tougher than you could imagine." Nad-ua grinned. "She could use you there, you know, once I'm gone. Her only family are those vapid aunts of hers."

"You mean my sisters?"

"Sorry, your vapid sisters."

They both laughed.

From the corner of her eye, she spotted Marik watching them. He stood across the room. Snowflakes were still melting in his hair. Again, she couldn't read his expression.

Cyrus craned his head to see what she was looking at, and as he did, Marik started up the stairs toward his room.

In a low voice, Cyrus asked, "Do you want to tell me what's going on between the two of you?"

The last thing she wanted was to speak with Cyrus about her very strange, very complicated relationship with Marik. She shook her head.

"Well, just so you know, I like him."

"You do?" She replied with more skepticism in her voice than she had intended.

"Yes. From what you've told me, he's done everything he can to protect you. He inadvertently brought you back to me so I can say a proper goodbye this time. That alone earns him my gratitude, even if I am a bit jealous."

"Jealous? Of what?"

Cyrus went silent for a long moment. "You both get to go have a real adventure, while I'm stuck on this cold planet."

"You like the cold."

He met her eyes and his demeanor became serious. "Not always."

It was she who looked away first.

Chapter 24

Marik was busy pacing the room when a knock sounded. The enticing feminine scent told him it would be Nadua standing on the other side.

Reluctantly, he let her in.

"Are you okay?" she asked.

"Splendid."

"Where did you go?"

"Hunting edisdons."

"Oh. Well, no need. Cyrus said—"

"I know, I overheard. He will be providing for you."

That was the reason he was pacing the room like a caged animal. His mate was in need of something and it wasn't he who could supply it for her. Cyrus gave her a bed, beautiful clotting, expensive jewelry—which she was still wearing!

He tried not to eye it with anger. That, and the fact that she laughed with him, spoke to him with an ease and familiarity that was not affected by three hundred years apart.

Cyrus had said he loved her, and she obviously returned the sentiment.

"Something's bothering you."

"Aye," he growled.

"Well. Will you talk to me?"

"It involves a topic you're not fond of. So, no."

She was quiet for a little while. "Then I have something I need to speak with you about. It's regarding your past."

Marik went tense. "I've nothing to say about that."

"Well, I do. You asked me about my gift, but I didn't get a chance to tell you about it."

Marik stopped pacing and, for some reason, a thick choking tension bubbled in his stomach.

"I inherited part of my father's gift for seeing the future. But lately I think I've been getting glimpses of the past."

The tension turned into a heavy sick feeling that clawed at his insides.

"My past?" His tone was sharpened with an edge of hopelessness.

"I believe so, but I'd like to verify some things with you if you don't mind. So I can be sure."

"What did you see?"

"I witness you in . . . um . . . something that looked like a coliseum—"

"No!" Marik's world collapsed. Had she seen what he'd done? What he couldn't stop himself from doing? No wonder she was so repulsed by the idea of being stuck as his mate

Marik laughed at himself for thinking that, just maybe, she had come to him to declare an inkling of feeling for him.

How delusional I am.

Her voice was ringing in his ear. Marik realized he was on his knees, face buried in his hands. She was asking him to look at her. Never again would he soil her beauty with his gaze. She deserved so much better.

"Marik! Look at me, please."

He raised his gaze, but didn't meet her eyes.

"Please don't do this to yourself. It wasn't your fault."

Of course it was his fault. If he had trained harder when he was a youth, he could have controlled himself. He could have mastered the Edge, and restrained himself from hurting anyone. Perhaps he could have even saved his sister and kept them both from being slaves in the first place. If only he had been stronger.

"Those women's deaths weren't—"

"Enough," he bellowed. "Get out!"

"No. I need you to understand."

Marik pushed her toward the door.

"Marik, stop."

"I don't want to see you again until we leave this planet. We'll find your Serakians and break this bond." He shut the door on her astounded expression.

* * *

"My Queen." Wren bowed, just outside Ava's door. She greeted him with a smile and, together, they made their way down the hall.

After a short distance, Ava commented, "That sounds so different now."

"What does?"

"When you call me 'My Queen.'"

"But I have always called you that."

Ava shrugged. "Yet your tone has changed. And you are more serious around me now."

Wren went quiet.

Exiting the east wing, they strolled over a bridge that connected it to the west, headed to the first council meeting since Ava's arresting declaration.

The air was sweet, as it always was after a heavy storm. She stopped to lean against the low wall, not wanting to admit she was nervous.

"I suppose I am more serious, My Queen. I have taken the ancient oaths. My only duty now is to protect you."

Ava recalled the day. Each member of the guard and representatives from the noble houses had knelt before her, swearing allegiance to the House of Dion and chanted the old oaths. But there was something different in Wren that day, and had been ever since. His words had been so strong she'd almost felt them in the air.

"But I liked it when you would tease me."

"It is not appropriate for a guard to tease a queen."

She wanted to protest, but he was right. She was entering a new phase in her life. Her charge was the management and preservation of an entire kingdom. The whims of a child were no longer her luxury.

Her eyes traveled the edge of the land, where white hills met frosty skies. A sharp glint out of place caught her eye. "Wren? What is that?"

"Looks like a couple," he replied.

From her distance, she could see that the larger of the two had dark hair, and the smaller was covered in an equally dark cloak. Her heart spiked and all she could do was suck in an excited breath.

"My Queen," Wren warned, reading her thoughts.

"But who else would cover themselves in a cloak like that? And the male is not of our kind." She sprinted back the way they came.

Wren was directly behind her. As they made their way to the palace entrance, he yelled for every guard they passed to follow.

"What's going on?" Tamir was at their side.

"There are strangers on the hill outside the palace," Wren answered.

Ava rushed through the elaborate archway, her light blue gown flaring out as she stepped foot on the packed snowy ground of the courtyard.

"My Queen," Tamir beseeched. "Let the guard go ahead. This could be a trick."

Wren was suddenly in front of her, blocking her path.

"No! It must be her!"

"We will not risk you for a wish," Wren bellowed.

His tone gave her pause and she took a step back, calming her beating heart. No matter what she wanted to believe, she had to concede that this could be a rebel trap.

High on the bluff, the two made slow progress toward them.

"Then I will take a sword and a small group of soldiers. We will approach with caution."

"Please, my lady," Tamir replied. "Let me go and assess the situation. There is no need for you to put yourself in danger."

"I will not be some timid queen who hides behind her army. That's not how my father ruled, it is not how Nadua ruled, and it will not be how I rule." She turned to one of the soldiers at her back and demanded his sword.

He obliged without argument.

Marching forward, Wren called out names of soldiers who were to join them. With Wren on her right and Tamir on her left, Ava started up the hill.

The couple spotted them and halted, seeming to speak back and forth. Ava realized her men had their weapons drawn.

She stopped and ordered, "Sheath your blades. You're making them uneasy."

She was now sure that the cloaked one was not Nadua. Nadua would have come running to embrace her on sight. The twinge of hope sank into despair once more. She kept it hidden though, so the others would not view her as weak.

As Ava moved toward them, the male placed himself in front of the other and bared his fangs.

Tamir pulled his sword again. "They are demons! Kill them!"

Soldiers rushed forward at Tamir's command. The large demon snarled, but the one he protected moved forward. A blast of distorted air rushed at them, originating from the small cloaked creature. Her men were launched back. Wren covered her with his body as it hit them. Next thing Ava knew, she was digging herself out of the snow. Wren had already stood and was shielding her, weapon drawn.

The powerful creature removed her hood, displaying a fierce determination. But that wasn't what made Ava's pulse leap into her throat. Those eyes were Nadua's, in shape and color.

"Stop! Don't hurt them," she ordered.

Wren glanced back, incredulous. Ignoring him, Ava considered the strangers. The demon was once again using his body to block the girl, a mirror of Wren's stance. Though she wanted to hate this demon as she hated the one who murdered Nadua, she would wait to pass judgment.

"They have assaulted our queen," Tamir hollered. "They will die this day!"

The men looked torn between the conflicting demands.

"I said no!" Ava shouted, pulling herself to stand.

The expression Tamir gave her was shocking in its anger. No one had ever looked at her like that before.

"I am your queen, Tamir. Do as I command."

The rest of her soldiers had already backed away, joining Wren at her front.

"Your Highness," Tamir started. "They are here to conquer us. We mustn't show weakness now."

"If you will take a moment to observe, you will see that that woman looks just like our former queen. She is obviously of Nadua's race and we are their allies, are we not?"

"You dishonor our queen, Tamir," Wren warned.

Tamir stepped back. Ava realized she was being studied with a curious expression by the golden-haired Faieara.

The male looked uneasy but the female spoke to him in a soft voice. "All is well."

Ava recognized the tongue as an off world dialect. Her tutors had insisted she learn the many outer languages for when merchants would come in their crafts.

"I am Avaline, queen of this land," she proclaimed. "Declare yourselves and your intentions."

"I am Sebastian, and this is my mate, Anya. We mean you no harm. We seek a friend of ours who was captured by a group of your people, and a woman named Nadua who should be living somewhere on this planet."

Ava's stomach sank. "You say you mean no harm, but this friend you speak of has in fact murdered Nadua, and is currently evading justice."

"Impossible. Marik would never do such a thing. What proof do you have?"

"Two of my guards witnessed the act. If you were not standing here with a Faieara at your side, I would have assumed you were the culprit. Demons have not been here in centuries."

Sebastian tilted his head at that.

Anya spoke. "Excuse me, but you are misinformed. My sister is not dead."

"Sister?"

"Yes." She turned her head as if seeking something in the distance. "Traces of their essence have been coming and going. I think they are together but every time I get a read they disappear again." She turned her clear eyes on Ava and it felt as though she were seeing into her soul. "Then I felt you, and was reminded of Nadua. Your energies are similar in flow."

"Nadua was like family to me. I dare not hope that you are right. I have mourned her loss greatly and if I were to believe what you say and it turned out you are wrong, it would be like losing her all over again."

Anya shivered and Sebastian pulled her close. The cloak she wore was a heavy fabric but was probably inadequate for this weather.

"Please accompany me inside. I will grant you sanctuary and protection." Ava repeated herself in Cyrellian so the guards understood.

"I must request this man be kept away." Anya pointed toward Tamir, whose features twisted with worry. "His malice is a bitter taste on my tongue."

Ava hesitated at the odd phrasing, then ordered Tamir back to his post. "I apologize for him. He fought in the demon war and still holds on to old prejudices. Please come with us, we have much to discuss it seems."

* * *

Anya walked the elegant palace halls—Wren and Bastian in tow—chatting with the young queen, Avaline. She had provided her with a marvelous fabric that shielded her from the worst of the cold.

Avaline was like honor dipped in purity and coated with innocence. She desperately wanted to believe that Nadua was alive but strove to keep her hope buried. Anya loved that this girl felt so strongly for a member of her family, and envied that she had been able to spend so much time with Nadua.

At first, Bastian had been on edge, stating that he didn't trust these strange people. Anya had reassured him that their intentions were to find the truth, same as them. It had taken some time for Sebastian and Wren to stop sizing each other up. Anya still wasn't sure if they were through, and neither realized how extraordinarily similar they were to each other. Protectiveness fell from them in misty waves.

There were those around that Anya did not like. A dangerous turmoil haunted this place, filling the corners with dull energy.

"You seem to have a unique gift, Anya." Avaline's soft voice was amplified by the structure around them. "But I don't understand why you would not be able to feel your sister at all times."

"I cannot say myself," she replied. "Sometimes I feel them both and other times it's just Marik. The last time I sensed them, a massive storm kept us from entering the atmosphere."

"It could be the caves blocking you in some way," Wren suggested from behind them.

"Caves?" Bastian asked.

"The Caves of Kayata. A labyrinth of sorts inside the mountains to the south. If the demon took Nadua alive, I'd have to assume he'd taken her into the caves."

"Well, let's go to these caves then." Bastian sounded as though he were ready to head out right away.

"It would be no small task to search the caves. They are thousands of times longer than the whole of Sori, and there is no known map of their passageways. Plus, they are considered to be cursed by the ancients."

The young queen lowered her head. "Wren is correct. There would be no hope of finding them."

Heavy footsteps echoed just before a guard appeared.

* * *

"My Queen." The guard rushed toward them, bowed. Ava saw his urgency and nodded for him to speak. "Wren, Tamir has gone mad. He is attacking a young messenger in the courtyard."

Wren shot ahead of Ava and she rushed to follow. Their guests trailed behind them, confused by the sudden commotion.

Tamir stood in the courtyard, sword out straight. On the other end of it was a frightened messenger, yielding a blade of his own. A red line ran down his arm.

"Give it to me!" Tamir hollered.

"What is this?" Wren demanded, striding forward and drawing his weapon, unsure of who was in the wrong.

Tamir's eyes went wide and he looked between Wren and the group of newcomers. Without answering, Tamir's metal lashed out for the messenger's throat.

A high pitched clang resonated in the air. Wren stood, blocking the young man, his sword holding back Tamir.

"Tamir!" Ava glided down the small set of stairs that lead from the entryway. "What are you doing? Drop your weapon."

He didn't. He just glared at Wren, their blades still pushing together.

"Now!"

With a sneer, he obeyed and stepped back, yet the hilt stayed tightly in his palm. "I recognize this man, Your Highness. He's a rebel. Here to spread lies. I meant only to protect the kingdom."

The messenger stowed his weapon and stood straight. "I am no rebel. I am here on behalf of the royal House of Dion. I was ordered to give my message to Wren of the guard and Wren alone. No one else. This person"—he pointed to Tamir—"tried to take it from me by force."

Ava struggled to hide her confusion. "On behalf of the House of Dion, you bring a message to Wren?"

"Yes, my lady."

"Queen," Ava corrected. "Queen Avaline, of the House of Dion."

The man's jaw dropped. Recovering, he knelt in the snow and bowed his head. "Forgive me, My Queen, I did not recognize you."

A wave of surprise iced through her. She gaped at Wren then

and realized he was not meeting her eyes. "Which of my family would send a messenger who does not know his queen, to a person we all see on a daily basis?"

"Prince Cyrus, My Queen."

Ava's shock was replaced with indignation. "Prince Cyrus is dead," she snapped. She had never known her father's brother, but had read about him in her history books. Nadua had always spoken fondly of him.

Wren finally looked at her. A hidden knowledge blazed from within the stormy depths of his eyes.

Ava couldn't find her voice. She was so immersed in the disturbing idea that Wren was keeping something from her that she hadn't heard Anya murmur in her mate's ear, and she hadn't noticed Sebastian slip out of sight.

"Well," her voice cracked. "Give him the message."

Wren stowed his blade and reached for the small piece of parchment. He was silent as he read. Then his body went tense and his head snapped to Tamir.

Tamir's blade rose swiftly and he struck at Wren.

Ava screamed.

From seemingly out of nowhere, Sebastian appeared behind Tamir. His fist clamped around Tamir's wrist, halting his swing just in time. A loud crack sounded and Tamir cried out in pain as his blade fell from his grip. His free arm formed an angry fist aimed at Sebastian, but the demon easily subdued it and broke his other wrist.

Wren nodded in thanks and called for a garrison of soldiers to take Tamir to the dungeons, adding that Nakul should be found and arrested as well.

"What is going on?" Ava demanded.

Wren gave her a guilty expression. "We need to talk."

Chapter 25

Marik hadn't left his room in four days.

The first day, Nadua left him alone, hoping he only needed time to cool down. The second, she knocked, but it was as if he knew it was her at the door and didn't answer. The third, she demanded he let her in and kicked at the thick wood but he yelled for her to go away. The forth, she warned that she would have Rex knock down the door, but when it came time, Marik threatened to leave him here to rot and Rex caved.

Today was day five.

The only people he opened for were the servants, who were apparently ordered to keep his supply of alcohol coming. Scared out of their minds, they would leave pitchers by the entrance, knock, and then scurry away.

Often, Nadua would pace her room, worrying about him, wondering if she had approached him wrong, or it he would have reacted so badly no matter what.

At night she couldn't sleep, missing her demon's breath on her neck as he cozily slumbered, molded against her. One night she crept down the hall and rapped lightly on his door, asking if she could but sleep with him. He had given a gentle no. It was hard not to feel like a beggar.

Cyrus was true to his word, gifting her with an exquisite edisdon cloak and matching boots. The decorative chain at the neck matched her necklace. It was beautiful. Yet, all she could think was how upset Marik would be if he saw it.

Or maybe he no longer cared.

Before he'd locked himself in his room, he sounded totally on board with her Serakian plan. His voice had been so harsh when he said it she almost wanted to cry—suddenly horrified by the idea that she might lose him. But wasn't that what she wanted?

Then later she realized all she was doing was thinking about Marik. His absence made her feel strangely hollow.

When had she grown to care for him so much?

Rex was becoming more comfortable with his surroundings, and had even begun striking conversation with the people around him. They'd been fearful of him at first, but seemed to tolerate his presence more and more each day.

Desperate for advice, Nadua asked Rex what she should do about Marik.

He looked uncomfortable with her direct questions, but replied, "I've never been mated, but demons in any state respond most strongly to physical persuasion. Fighting or, uh, other physical contact."

Nadua was afraid Rex was going to ask her if she wanted him to beat Marik senseless, but he left it at that.

After watching yet another servant produce a pitcher, an idea sparked. Nadua followed a short ways behind the girl and waited for her to knock before rushing away. When the door creaked open, she caught it with her foot.

He tried to force the door shut, but she faked a sound of pain, hoping it would weaken his resolve. It worked. He backed away from the door and she barged in, slamming it closed behind her.

His room looked just like hers. A small hearth with a fire bathed everything in a soft orange glow.

Voice like gravel, he ground out, "Are you hurt?" His eyes were rimmed in red, and didn't make contact with hers.

"Yes."

"How? Where? Do you need a doctor?"

"No. My heart is hurt."

Marik snorted, and took a large gulp from the heavy pitcher. "Whose isn't?"

She supposed she deserved that a little. "I want you to talk to me about what happened to you."

"Not going to happen." He paused, swaying slightly. "Didn't I tell you I don't want to see you? Go be with your ice man while you can."

"I don't want to be with Cyrus."

Marik shook his head and drank deep again.

"It's true. I want to be with you."

"Well *I* don't want to be with *you*. So—go—away."

"You're lying."

"Am I?" He snapped. "Look at you. Tiny little thing with barely any meat on you. Nearly helpless without your army and that beast you ride. More trouble than you're worth." He put his finger in the air as if he remembered more. "You whine over some young chit. What's her name? Ava. How you miss her and wish only to see her again."

Nadua crossed her arms and held her tongue.

"At least you handle a bow like a seasoned warrior. Watching you wield it is . . . your hair and skin are too soft." He shook his head as if he'd forgotten his point. "You're not even my kind." He lifted the pitcher to his lips, but looked at her over the top of it, waiting for a response.

"I need you to stop drinking, and to stop pouting."

"Get out, Nadua. Leave me be." He gave her his back, gulping from the pitcher. "I don't pout."

"I'm not leaving this room until I get through to you one way or another."

"I can force you out." He continued to drink and made no move toward her.

"Look at me."

He didn't.

Sighing, Nadua pulled at the tie of her bodice and began removing her clothing. His shoulders went stiff but he still didn't turn when the fabric hit the ground, pooling around her feet. She stepped out of it and sauntered toward him, pressing her hands against his back.

No response.

She tried to move in front of him but he sidestepped her.

"Marik, please look at me. I want you to touch me, hold me, kiss me like you did before. Bite me, I don't care." He made no reply. "Are you afraid you'll blackout again? We can work on that too, like you suggested. I want to help you."

"You don't get it. I'm done. Just go."

Her throat tightened. "You're just giving up? Because I saw something you didn't want me to see?"

"It's more than that, but that is part of it, yes."

"What more?" Nadua held her breath, surprised at how badly his words were hurting her.

Marik was cold and dismissive, speaking to her as if she were no more important to him than any other person. She suddenly felt as though she had lost something magnificent. Something few experienced. Nadua couldn't describe it, but the loss of it was devastating.

He shook his head.

Something snapped in her. "Just tell me already!"

"It's because I can't make you happy!"

Nadua halted in surprise. She swallowed the lump in her throat. "Yes, you can."

With his back to her still, he turned his head a fraction. "When can I? Maybe when I'm fucking your brains out."

She was taken aback, but knew he was only being churlish to make her want to leave. He thought she should find him repulsive and unworthy. But there was a deep sense of integrity inside him that he didn't even see. He had proven it at every turn.

"Now look at you. Naked as a whore and looking for more."

"You bastard!" She kicked out the back of his leg with her heel. He went to one knee with a growl, but sprang back up. So she did it again. "Do you want me to hate you? Fine, I hate you. Are you happy? Does it make it better?"

"Yes, it does."

"You don't care about me at all then?"

His shoulder twitched.

Nadua decided she needed to change tactics. Standing naked arguing with him wasn't working. Not to mention she felt quite silly.

"Fine, you stubborn demon. Prove it."

She crossed to the bathroom and hesitated next to the tub. The servants filled it with fresh water every morning, not realizing the freezing temperature did not appeal to any of them.

"What are you doing?" Marik leaned against the door jam. The fact that he followed her was a good sign.

"First, you will apologize for that comment. Then, I want your arms around me."

He shrugged and swallowed more alcohol. To her delight, he was drinking her in too.

"I'm not going to beg."

"Good, it wouldn't do you any good."

"But I *will* get what I want."

"How's that?"

Nadua stepped into the tub, hissing at the icy temperature.

"That water is not warm."

She lowered herself farther. Every cell screamed in agony, but she forced herself in until she was submerged up to her neck.

"You daft woman. Get out of there."

Her body went stiff from the icy shock. She had to rip apart her jaws to speak. "First, apologize."

"You can't stay in there forever."

After a moment she began to shiver, teeth chattering and skin turning nearly as blue as a Cyrellian.

Marik sat down the pitcher. "Damn it, Nadua! Come out of there."

She pulled her knees to her chest as if that would help. The water was so much colder than she'd expected.

Looking bewildered, Marik's features turned to concern. "Fine, I'm sorry. Stop this now. Your lips are turning purple."

Nadua wanted to speak, but she could no longer form words. Pain laced up her arms and legs. The task of breathing was increasingly difficult.

Then Marik went to her, pulling her from the tub and carrying her to the bed. She couldn't feel his hands. He wrapped her in a blanket, and then crossed with her to the fire and sat with her at the hearth. His arms folded around her.

"T-t-told y-you."

"That was stupid," he growled, staring into the fire.

Probably the stupidest thing she'd ever done.

Nadua laid her head to rest on Marik's shoulder and curled into his heat, but the shivers continued.

"Blanket's n-not helping. I n-need you."

Marik didn't hesitate. He stripped and wrapped them both in the blanket, pressing his warm flesh against her. She smiled with triumph, even though her skin was prickling with tiny explosions of pain.

"Why did you do that?"

"You w-wouldn't listen."

"So you hurt yourself?" He was shaking with anger.

"D-Didn't think it w-would be so bad." She wiggled closer to him.

"Do not ever do that again."

"I have to speak with you about your past. I have to tell you what I saw."

He went stiff. "Nadua, don't."

"You didn't hurt those girls. It wasn't you."

"Stop it."

"It's true."

"For the love of the gods, Nadua! I was there, I know what I did!"

"No, you don't. You were driven to madness but you didn't touch them."

He shook his head.

Placing her hands on either side of this face, she forced him to look at her. "My first vision of you in the arena was days before I let you kiss me. Do you think I would have allowed that if I had seen you do something so terrible?"

She could see the hope in his eyes, his mind working to believe what she said.

"How can you be sure?"

"Visions of the future are foggy and unclear. This was so clear it was almost like I was there with you."

The pain on his face broke her heart. As if he were gripping a lifeline, he clutched her tight and buried his head in the crook of her neck. She didn't know how long they stayed like that but her eyes had grown heavy and she had stopped shivering by the time he moved again.

Gently, he lifted her to the bed and settled next to her. She nuzzled up to his chest, and he offered no protest.

Just as she was about to sink into slumber, he whispered in her ear, "I'm sorry you had to see it."

She replied, "I'm sorry you had to live it."

* * *

Almost as soon as his eyelids closed, Marik was asleep. His dreams were mild compared to the previous few nights, and the sweet scent of his mate eased him as his unconscious mind warred with the new idea of his past.

When light drifted in, rousing him, there was a split second of fear that she would be gone and that everything from the night before had only been a drunken delusion.

But her lovely body was draped over his in the most gratifying way. Her leg trapped one of his, her arm folded over his chest, and her head rested atop his shoulder, a mess of red hair fanned out behind her.

By the slow pattern of her breath, Marik could tell she was still asleep. He took the opportunity to marvel at her beauty. Her plump lips were slightly parted, allowing her breath to tingle across his chest. With her hair swept back, a wee pointed ear with such a delicate odd curve was revealed. He knew her body to be just as perfectly shaped under the heavy blanket.

His cock grew hard at the thought and he couldn't help but gently palm her backside. He cursed himself when she began to stir.

Then she smiled up at him as though she were pleased, making him harder still.

"Good morning," she drowsily mumbled and kissed his chest.

When he softly groaned, a wicked glint grew in her eyes and she did it again.

He could come from that look alone.

"Morning," he replied in a husky voice, shifting his hold to the crest between her legs. She let out a slight gasp, but then smiled wider.

A demanding grumble came from his stomach.

Nadua rose up concerned. "How long has it been since you've had something eat?"

His lips curled into an evil grin. "Far too long." He flipped her to her back. She let out a delighted squeak and he placed himself between her legs. Her cheeks flushed when she caught his joke.

He started with her breast, licking and teasing till she moaned, circling one peak with his tongue while gripping the other. With his free hand, he felt between her legs, gratified to find her growing damp for him.

Unable to resist any longer, he slipped down her body, kissing and nipping as he went. The first taste of her exploded on his tongue and he knew then, he was a slave for her. Anything she asked he would do, if he could just keep her as his.

He delved between her folds, making her writhe. The sounds she made urged him on. She began chanting in Cyrellian, demanding him not to stop. Her tone became more frantic. Back arching, she grabbed a handful of his hair and cried out. He continued to lick her sex until her body went limp.

Needing to be inside her, he crawled up her body, but she pushed him away with her palms on his chest.

His heart dropped to his stomach. "What's wrong?"

"Will you forget again?"

"I can't be sure."

Without another word, she crawled out from under him. He dropped his head and let her go. But before he could chastise himself for ruining the moment, she pushed him to his back so their positions were reversed.

"What are you doing?" He watched her intently as her hands trailed down his stomach.

"Do you remember that night in the cave? The one where Rex nearly caught us?"

He nodded.

Her fingers began playing along his shaft. "Why do you think that is? That you remember, I mean."

Her hand wrapped around his length and she began slow strokes to the tip and back.

She wanted him to think while she was doing that?

"I'm not sure," he grated.

"Well, what was different then?"

"Damn it, woman. I don't know." His unsatisfied lust was making him irritable.

Her hand stilled. "I'm only trying to help," she snapped. "Get surly one more time and I'll stop completely. So what was different?"

He growled and pumped his hip. She began her slow, maddening movements again. The teasing wench wasn't going to go further until he answered.

Racking his brain, he said, "I wasn't inside you and I knew I wouldn't hurt you. Also, I was watching you as you came so I could memorize every second."

"What about when you . . . uh . . . when it had been your turn?"

"Still I watched you, your eyes had me mesmerized." His voice was strained. Her movements distracting. "The color of the finest gem, as they are now. Woman, you're driving me crazy."

"You didn't hurt me in the pool." She tilted her head. "But you did look away."

"But I thought I hurt you. I remember you went stiff and told me to stop. Everything's a blur after that."

Her grip tightened in reward, but she frowned. "I see. Well, you didn't hurt me. You are quite large though, and I needed to get used to your size is all." She paused, thinking. "Are you usually in control when you . . . um . . . with other women."

A thrill burst through Marik when her jaw clenched in a show of jealousy.

"Usually." He paused. "Always, yes."

Holding his gaze, she lowered her lips to his shaft, hovering just inches away. His breath caught.

"Then you're only allowed to watch. Understand?"

He nodded tightly, his shaft stiffening to the point of pain. She darted out her tongue to touch the tip and then looked at him.

He balled his hands into fists. "You can't be teasing me, luv. I'm about to lose it."

Then she laid out her rules. "If you touch me, I'll stop. If you look away, I'll stop."

As if anything could keep his eyes off her.

He nodded again, growing impatient, and struggling to keep his control.

Her plump lips came over him and he groaned in relief. The fierce pleasure almost made his lids close but he forced them open, fearing she would be true to her word.

The amusement in her eyes said she approved of his obedience. Her full lips began sliding up and down. She pulled out slowly and then sucking him back in as her tongue did wicked things to the underside of his cock.

In a teasing tone, he said, "My mate is talented." He worried he said the wrong thing when she paused and looked at him.

"I'm not a . . . what did you call me last night?"

He felt the blood drain from his face. Had he really called his mate a whore?

"I didn't mean it. You must know that."

She lifted a shoulder in a coy half shrug, giving him her profile: a picture of virginal modesty as she lovingly stroked his shaft, keeping his mind muffled by lust while trying to make him think clearly.

Sitting up, he tried to read her. Had his words hurt more than he thought? "I was just angry, and wanted to make you angry too. It was the only way I could keep myself from taking you then and there."

As soon as he saw the mischievous sparkle in her eyes, he realized she was teasing him.

"But then again you are showing me what an expert you are at handling a man's—"

With a gaping laugh, she pushed him flat to the bed and fell on top of him. "You're a jerk." She smacked his chest. "Now I have to punish you."

Marik chuckled. "And how does a tiny thing like you expect to punish a big demon like me?"

"Well, now you really aren't allowed to touch me." She sat up, straddling him.

His gaze fell to her pert breasts and he could feel her slick against his cock. His hips involuntarily bucked, seeking her entrance.

"Eyes up," she commanded.

With a huff, he obeyed.

"Arms out."

Her delicate brow rose when he hesitated. He stretched his arms out beside him.

Then she began her slow torture. Her hands caressed his torso as her hips slowly rode him, coating him in her wetness. But she didn't allow him in, not fully. Every now and again, she eased down on him, keeping him mad with need while showing him a hint of the pleasure she was withholding. When he moved his hips, trying to get farther inside, she scolded him and then started the torture all over again.

A thread of willpower alone kept his arms from gripping her and forcing her down his length.

"Nadua," he warned, when she pulled away from him once again.

"Eyes on mine," she ordered.

Her lids were at half-mast and her breaths were growing erratic, as though she were barely holding onto her own control.

Finally, she filled herself with all of him. His gaze was locked with hers and they both moaned as she began rocking. He grasped the edges of the bed to keep them in place. The need to touch her was almost overwhelming.

She broke eye contact when she threw her head back, arching as she began pumping her hips with fervor. Her wild red mane fell behind her, fanning his legs. A sheen of sweat glistened on her skin.

Her breasts were presented for the taking, demanding his attention. Thinking himself clever, he rose up and took one in his mouth.

She pulled away and he gave a menacing growl. He was almost overcome by his instinct to have her under him while driving into her soft flesh.

Hips still grinding, she panted, "Look at me."

He did. They were face-to-face. The clear violet-blue of her eyes were beautiful and filled with lust. They more than captivated him.

"Good boy. Focus on me."

"I need to touch you."

"I know." As if to appease him in some small way, her forehead came against his and she placed her hands on his shoulders for support, grinding harder.

"Then kiss me."

Desperately, she did, as if she couldn't wait another second to have his lips on hers. He took her mouth how he wanted to take the rest of her: hard and unyielding. He thrust his hips just as she came down on him, making her cry out.

Against his lips, she ordered, "Do that again."

With pleasure.

Together they ground their hips and moved in unison, increasing each other's bliss. Just when he was about to spill his seed, Nadua pulled away from the kiss and held his gaze. "Touch me."

The dam of his control broke. Instantly, she was below him, his hips thrusting into her core, one hand gripping her ass. Now he was holding her gaze as she moaned for him.

His release came hard, on the heel of her orgasmic scream. A few last pumps of his hips and they were both spent. He pulled her on top of him as he fell, exhausted, to the bed. Little sounds of contentment fluttered out of her as she molded her body around his.

Then her head flew up to look at him, her eyes searching.

Knowing what she wanted, he smiled. "There's no way in hell I could forget that."

Her lips curled and she lowered again to rest on his chest.

Chapter 26

Marik lay blissfully with Nadua curled around him. "Why didn't you tell me sooner?"

"Hmm?" Nadua was lazily tracing her finger over his chest.

They'd been lying for hours, content in each other's arms. Marik had never felt so sated in his life.

"Why didn't you tell me about your gift?"

Nadua hesitated. "Well, at first I wasn't sure that what I was seeing was part of my gift. I had never seen anyone's past before, only useless bits of their futures. Actually, I feared I was losing my gift altogether until you came along. I hadn't had a vision in years."

"Why do you think that is?"

"I can only imagine that it has something to do with our physical closeness. Before you, Ava was the last person I had real contact with. She would cry for me to carry her around when she was very little. I always made sure I was covered, but one time she reached for my face, and her finger grazed my cheek. I didn't realize the connection then, but I had a vision of her that same night. It was one of the last."

His fingers trailed up and down her spine. "What did you see?"

"I saw her grown, sitting on her father's throne, her people bowing. She looked beautiful and determined. A few months later her father died, and left me in charge. I wanted to make sure Ava had that future. I never told her about it though. Just because I see it, doesn't mean it will happen. Everything is changeable."

Outside the door, a few loud steps hurried past, followed by muffled voices that quickly died away.

Marik hated to ask the next question, but his curiosity was too much. "What about Cyrus?"

"What about him?"

"Did you see his future after you . . . touched?"

"Oh. Yeah, I did." Her brow furrowed. "I remember it was too fuzzy to make out. I thought it must have been of something in his distant future, but when he *died* I forgot all about it."

More voices came from outside. Marik recognized a note of distress.

Nadua sat up to listen. "Something's happening."

Another rush of footsteps marched past the door.

They were out of bed and already half-dressed when someone pounded on the door. Through it came Rex's voice. "There's a battle outside! The other tribe is attacking!"

In a flurry, Nadua was out the door, her gown still loose.

"Nadua! Wait!" Marik called, frantically searching for his other boot.

Rex poked his head in. "Do we fight?"

* * *

Bursting into her room, Nadua rushed to switch her gown for the new furs. She stuffed her feet into the tall boots, pulling them up to her thigh and yanking the straps close. Then she threw on the snug cloak before bolting into the hall.

Cyrus was downstairs, dressed for war and directing his soldiers one way, and women and children the other.

Nadua approached him. "Cyrus, what's happening?"

"The rebels are here. They've never attacked like this before."

"Have they made it inside?"

"No, we've pushed them back on the hill. But they have a Kaiy-lemi with them."

Nadua cursed. "I need a sword, a bow, and a dagger."

Cyrus pointed to an already half-emptied shallow storage room. "Check in there."

Marik was behind her as she picked though the weapons. "What do you think you're doing? You're not going out there."

"Of course I am," she said, checking the balance of a sword that looked to be just her size.

"My job is to keep you safe, not let you run out into battle to get yourself killed."

"Despite what you think, I'm not helpless."

Marik sighed. "I know you're not helpless, but you don't need to fight. These aren't your people."

She strapped a quiver on her back and pulled out a decent look-ing bow. "After so long, the Cyrellians are more my people than the Faieara. Ava is family, and Cyrus is my dearest friend. Those rebels would hurt them both if they could." Rummaging through the rows of blades, she mumbled under her breath, "Dagger, dagger."

Marik held something out in front of her. She plucked the hol-ster from him and pulled the knife out to study it. Sharp. Good hold. The sheath included straps to wrap around her thigh.

"Perfect." She gazed up at him in apprehension.

"Stay near me and only use the bow if possible." Marik snatched two heavy broadswords.

"Fine, let's go."

The great hall was nearly empty now. Rex was waiting for them by the exit. "Cyrus went on ahead."

Marching down the hall, Marik handed him a sword and muttered, "Don't let anyone near her."

* * *

Marik's nerves were like sandpaper against stone. His instincts were screaming to drag Nadua in the opposite direction. But the people she considered important were in danger and he didn't want her leaving here with the kind of guilt that plagued him.

As they traveled toward the exit, guards allowed them to pass, shutting and re-barring heavy gates behind them. They traveled through three such barriers before reaching the mouth of the cave. He hadn't noticed the cave was so fortified before.

Beyond the exit was a roaring frenzy of bodies and steel.

Rex grunted. "They all look the same to me. How can we tell them apart?"

Marik squinted through the melee, searching for a familiar face, but he hadn't exactly spent a lot of time getting to know any of them.

"It's easy." Nadua elbowed her way past them. "Whoever comes after me is our enemy." Then she loaded her bow and let her arrow fly. One less rebel.

Magnificent.

* * *

Between the hundreds of azure bodies and endless white hills wove strips of red, increasing by the second. Battle cries mixed in the air alongside screams of agony.

Eye on her next target, Nadua sent another arrow into the fray. Then three more, all perfect shots.

Next to her, Marik cheered, "That's my girl."

A corner of her mouth turned up.

Five men were climbing the hill toward them. Two wielded axes, and the other three gripped the hilts of their swords. The scowls on their faces were aimed at her, but they continued to give threatening glances at the demons beside her. The intelligence in their eyes showed they realized they would need to get past the demons before they could touch her.

Marik unsheathed his sword and rushed to meet them, calling back at Rex, "Stay with her in case they get by me."

Rex had his steel ready.

Marik launched himself at the closest foe, slicing a red stripe across his chest. The next was on his heels, swinging his ax overhead. With unmitigated power, he knocked the weapon out of the way and the tip of his blade slipped through the thick flesh of the Cyrellian's throat.

Nadua would have loved to watch him rip the group of rebels apart, but a second group came at them from the side. Rex engaged the two in front, their blades clanging with heavy grunts.

Another slipped past, wildly swinging his sword. Nadua ducked and dodged, giving herself time to drop the bow and unsheathe her sword. Their metal clashed. The Cyrellian rebel had power in his swing, but she could tell he wasn't the greatest swordsman. She easily danced away from his every attempt.

Down the slope, sounds of battle grew thunderous. More rebels poured out from behind the trees. She was sure her group was outnumbered.

Finding her opening in the man's poor fighting style, Nadua dodged again and then sliced cleanly through his neck. His head flopped to the side and he fell to the snow.

Rex was down to one foe. The others lay motionless on the ground. As the Cyrellian whirled his blade forward, Rex's arm whipped out to stop it in midair, then drove his broadsword up through the man's stomach. Bloody metal punched through his back. A gurgling sound left the man before he dropped. Rex kicked the lifeless body away before returning to Nadua.

She turned toward Marik who was marching to rejoin them, five bodies piled at his back. Nadua gave him a relieved smile that faded as the ground began to rumble.

For a fraction of a second, all fighting stopped in silent wonder. With a terrible screeching sound, thick shafts of ice sprouted from beneath the field. Nadua stepped forward, scanning for the Kaiylemi.

Without warning, the ground at her feet shifted, throwing her off balance. Falling to her hands and knees, she tried to right herself, as a solid circle of land began to lift her in the air. Nadua snatched her bow before it fell off the newly created edge.

Soon she was looking over the entire battlefield, on an unsteady pillar. Marik's angry bellow grew dimmer the higher she went.

Nadua pulled to her feet. Using her arrow as her line of sight and rolling her gaze over the onslaught, she sneered under her breath, "Where are you, you bastard?"

A Kaiylemi had to be close enough to see everything—that was the only way he could work his magic—and they were always guarded. Following the edge of the forest, she noticed a small assembly of stationary soldiers, watching but not participating.

The pillar started to sway to one side. It was still growing. She stowed her bow and arrow and reached for her dagger. Leaning over the edge, a thick gulp stuck in her throat.

* * *

Marik and Rex struggled to keep the swarm of Cyrellians away from the shaft of ice that held Nadua.

The horde was relentless, and worked as if they were of one mind. They aimed to hack at its base and bring her down. The fall would kill her.

Marik felt the Edge overtake him, and invited the surge of strength it brought.

Their Cyrellian allies rushed to help, slaughtering rebels as they went. Marik spotted Cyrus fighting to hold the enemy back. His technique was masterful and, for the first time, Marik was glad Cyrus cared so much for his mate.

When the pillar tilted, Marik let out a pained cry as fear spiked through him. Then he saw Nadua edge to the sloping side, and his heart nearly stopped. She was going to try to slide down.

She stabbed her dagger into the ice, and proceeded to make a swift and purposeful descent. Her feet, one in front of the other, led the way as the small blade cut a line down the face.

Marik yelled to Rex and Cyrus, "Make room!"

Their jaws dropped when they spotted her. Then they came together to push back the crowd and open a space for her.

"Marik!" she called, landing with a soft thud. Her bow was at the ready and she dispatched two rebels in seconds. She turned to him and pointed in the distance. "The Kaiylemi is there, beyond the trees. We need him taken out if we are to win this."

Marik looked over the carnage. Spikes of ice were sprouting up, taking out Cyrus' people."

"All this is done by only one?"

She nodded. "I believe so."

"Rex, stay with Nadua."

"No, take Rex with you. You'll be crossing the entire battlefield." Her voice was high with panic.

"He stays with you."

"I'll be fine without him."

"I'll go with Marik," Cyrus offered.

Nadua glanced between the two of them. Swallowing hard, she nodded. But before letting them go, she threw her arms around Marik and brought him down for a fierce kiss. "Don't die, okay?"

Marik grunted. "You, either." He shot Rex a look that promised pain if he let anything happen to her. Then he and Cyrus started down the hill at a brisk pace, carving their way through the melee.

The fallen bodies were so many that Marik couldn't keep from stepping on them. As for the ones that were still moving, Marik was unable to differentiate between Cyrus' people and the rebels, so whoever was bold enough to make a move at him died. There seemed no steel left on his sword, only deep red liquid that dripped a trail beside him.

Cyrus was gathering a following. Some of his men must have deduced they were trying to cross and were helping to make a path. Ice shards sprang up around them, but there was a detectable grinding sound before they sprouted and Marik was able to dodge out of the way.

An ax wielder ran for him, swinging brazenly. Baring his fangs, Marik shoved his sword through the man's right eye. The other eye rolled to the sky. Marik took his blade back, and continued on his way.

The soldiers at the edge of the forest noticed their approach and braced for battle. In an instant, all ice manipulation ceased. Two hefty Cyrellians came forward to block them, while the others moved deeper into the forest.

Escaping.

With his men holding their backs, Cyrus lunged for the soldier on the right. Marik took the one on the left. Sparks flared as metal bit into metal. Marik ducked a wide swing and, going to his knee, countered with a thrust into the man's shin. His assailant screamed but didn't falter, and brought his blade down on Marik. A loud clang sounded as Marik blocked it just before the sharp edge became intimate with his skull.

* * *

Nadua cried out. Marik was on one knee, with a rebel trying to drive his sword into him. But she had her own problems to worry about. A large group of rebels were fighting their way toward them, and she was running low on arrows. Rex was amazing at keeping them from her, but he couldn't go on forever.

At least the Kaiylemi had stopped his assault, but the damage left behind was substantial.

At the crest of the hill, edisdon riders appeared from the north. A lead weight settled in the pit of her stomach. More rebels? They were doomed.

Nadua sucked in a harsh breath as a familiar figure stood out from the pack. "Ava?"

Atop her edisdon, she was dressed in a soldier's tunic and metal breastplate. She looked like a warrior. Pride flooded though Nadua at the sight.

Then, like some sort of mythical creature, a small gray craft rose up from behind them, hovering ominously.

The rebels took one look and began a furious retreat. Only a few stayed to fight, hollering curses at their departing brothers. They were soon silenced.

Nadua scoured the field for Marik. He and Cyrus were caught between the forest and the escaping rebels, still fighting. From her distance, she couldn't tell if the blood drenching their clothes belonged to them or not. Bolting down the hill, Nadua raced across the field toward them, dodging corpses as she went.

She didn't notice a bloodied hand reaching up from the ground till it was too late. It wrapped firmly around her ankle and the packed terrain rushed at her, knocking the air from her lungs with a painful grunt. She glanced back and saw angry eyes glaring at her from a deeply slashed face.

Rex placed a heavy foot on the aggressor's back. Both let out a sneering growl, and the hatred wafting from the Cyrellian made her stomach roll. Blade aimed straight down, Rex slid it easily through the rebel's neck.

Nadua kicked his gnarled hand away. "Thanks."

Rex pulled her to her feet and gave a masculine grunt in reply.

To Nadua's relief, Marik was already headed their way. The field was now full of cheers and victory cries as the last of the rebels either perished or fled. Nadua leapt at Marik, clutching him tight in a cage of arms and legs. He held her just as tightly.

Brushing his blood soaked hair away from his face, she asked, "Are you hurt?"

"Now that I have you in my arms, you could cut off my leg and I wouldn't notice."

"I would notice when we're falling over."

His smile was exuberant.

To their left, a throat cleared. "My Queen."

"Wren!" Nadua jumped down from Marik. "Ava!"

Ava came forward, throwing herself into Nadua. "I thought you were dead!" Her voice cracked and cool fingers duck into her back.

"No," she cooed. "I'm fine. I missed you, though."

"I missed you too." Ava sniffed. They clung to each other for a long while. Neither wanting to let go. "You'll never believe what I did."

Behind her, Wren had a wide grin.

Nadua's gaze drifted to the large army waiting on the hill. "What did you do?"

Ava backed away and bounced in place. "I claimed my title as queen! My aunts were in shock, one nearly fainted, but it is done."

"You did?" Nadua looked to Wren. "How is this possible?"

"She spoke like a queen and took what was hers. Plus, she has the weight of the army behind her. As you did."

"But wait!" Ava cried. "Now you can come back and be queen again. I won't mind." Ava's expression fell when she registered the look on Nadua's face.

Nadua swallowed hard. "I can't come back with you, Ava," she said softly, glancing toward Marik, who was now in an excited discussion with a strange new black-haired demon. Rex was standing a few yards away, quietly watching them. Nadua turned back to Ava. "It's time for me to go. Do you remember what I told you?"

"That one day you would go home." Her lip quivered. "But you don't *have* to."

Nadua's throat clenched. "I do. My people need me now, just as yours need you."

Ava gave the tiniest of nods, but her eyes were glossed and brimming.

"I'm so glad I got to see you before I left."

In response, she buried her face in Nadua's furs and mumbled something incoherent. She grasped so tightly that Nadua was afraid Wren would have to peel Ava off her.

"Now, now, queens don't sniffle."

"Yes, they do. I say what a queen does now, and a queen can sniffle if she wants to."

Nadua laughed. "Yes, My Queen." It was then that Nadua noticed Cyrus, flanking her just as Wren was flanking Ava. "But I have someone I need to introduce you to." Ava wiped her tears and straightened. Nadua smiled at her. "Ava, this is Cyrus." She gestured toward him.

Cyrus bowed. "Hello, young queen. I am your father's brother."

Ava shyly nodded. "Wren told me about you on the way here. Thank you for your service to our people."

Nadua gave Wren a sharp look, remembering that he had kept the information from her all this time. He smiled, a little sheepish. To Ava Nadua said, "You should stay here a few days and get to know each other. He's the one who taught me how to fight."

"Speaking of," Wren chimed in. "We weren't expecting to come upon a war. What happened here?"

"It was the rebels," Cyrus replied. "Since this is the first time they've attacked us, I can only assume they were going after Nadua. They seemed to know she would be here."

Nadua noted the undertone in his words. Cyrus had a traitor in his midst.

"And what of Tamir and Nakul?" she asked.

Wren answered, "Tamir has been arrested. Nakul has not been found, as of yet."

That worried Nadua, but she would have to leave Ava and Wren to deal with it.

* * *

After Sebastian was finished slapping him on the back in greeting, Marik was relieved to hear that Anya was well and waiting for them in the shuttle. She waved with both hands and brandished a giant grin when he glanced through the window at her.

Sebastian's arrival couldn't have happened at a better time. A bit of weight was lifted from Marik, only to be replaced by a dozen heavy boulders.

What will he think of what I've done?

Marik was almost too ashamed to tell him. But there was no

way around it.

But before he could form the words, Sebastian asked, "Who is that?"

Rex was standing a few yards away, eyeing them both. Marik motioned him over. "This is Rex. He has been a great help to Nadua and myself."

Sebastian held out his hand. "Much appreciated."

Rex eagerly took his hand and nodded silently. Marik could see the stress marring his features.

"Rex would like to join us, and I vouch for him. He would make a good addition."

Sebastian looked him up and down. "Everyone works on my ship unless you can pay."

"I'll work. I worked the engines on my last ship, but I can do any job you need."

"You'll take your orders from me."

"Yes, sir."

"Also, I have a rule on my ship about sleeping with crew members. I don't approve of it."

Marik coughed, pulling Sebastian aside. After explaining Rex's unique situation, Sebastian grumbled, "Hell, I should just throw the rule out the porthole, no one follows it anyway."

Nadua chose that moment to join them. Sebastian took one look at her and shot Marik a stunned expression. Marik tried to keep the guilty look off his face, but feared he did a poor job of it.

Without hesitation, Nadua strolled up to Sebastian. "Hello, I'm Nadua."

"Sebastian."

Moving to stand by Marik, Nadua replied, "Oh! The captain of *Marada*. How is my sister?"

Nadua followed their gazes to the shuttle. Anya was pressed

against the window, staring straight at her with wide eyes.

"She is eager to meet you."

"As am I. Will we be leaving right away?"

"As soon as possible, yes."

She looked a little sad and Marik wanted to embrace her. "I will go say goodbye then."

Marik avoided Sebastian's hard gaze by watching his mate as she walked away.

"You're mated." The statement in no way accusatory, but it still felt that way.

"I . . . It wasn't . . ." Marik trailed off, hating himself anew. Rex was stepping away, obviously curious to see if Sebastian would follow the old laws. "It was not a proper claiming."

At first, Sebastian looked confused. Then, understanding, he closed his eyes in dismay. "Fuck."

The disappointment he saw in Sebastian was worse than a lashing. "She recommended we contact the Serakians. To see if they could undo it."

Head snapping up, Sebastian balked, "Undo it? I've never heard of such a thing." His brows knit together. "I suppose it's possible the Serakians could . . . Is that what you want?"

"If it is still what she wants, I will not argue."

They all looked to Nadua, who was leading the small white-haired girl their way. "Marik, this is Ava."

He nodded in greeting. The chit looked to be on the verge of tears.

Ava gave a slight bow. "I am in your debt. Thank you for saving Nadua. Is there is anything we can do for you before you leave?"

"Thank you, but no."

Ava looked desperately around the group, then to Nadua. She sighed, "Very well, perhaps in the future. Know that you are all welcome at the palace, any time." She turned to Nadua. "Please do come back and visit."

"I will try." They came together for one last hug. "I'm so proud of you. Your father would be as well." Nadua's breath faltered. "I love you."

"I love you too. Ouch." Ava pulled away, rubbing behind her ear.

"Oops. Sorry."

Marik quirked a brow at Nadua, who nonchalantly winked back at him.

After a few more goodbyes, they headed for the shuttle. Nadua took one last look behind her, and then bravely stepped into a new world.

Chapter 27

The shuttle ride was mostly a blur. Not only did Nadua discover she had developed a fear of flying—by the fact that her nails were digging into the cushion of her seat as the craft bounced through the clouds—but leaving, what had essentially been her home, was causing her emotions to run rampant.

Her sister, Analia, seemed to sense her distress and was trying to distract her with stories of *Marada* and its people. She was enthusiastic about it, which did lighten Nadua's spirit a bit.

The resemblance between the sisters was only clear in their matching blue eyes. Their fathers' eyes.

Nadua was proud to see that Analia had grown into a lovely young woman. After Marik told her about Analia's past, Nadua feared she would be dejected, but the opposite was true. Kindness oozed out of her.

When they first spotted each other, there had been a strong burst of emotion that had come from Analia and had nearly knocked her back. They held each other for long a moment, until Sebastian put his hand on Analia's shoulder and she finally let go, tears dampening her cheeks.

The shuttle had six seats, two by two, with a small aisle between them. Marik and Sebastian took the helm, Analia sat next to Nadua in the middle, and Rex was behind them watching out the window.

From his seat next to Sebastian, Marik kept glancing back to see if she was alright. She tried to give him a reassuring smile a couple of times, then gave up. Once they got out of the rough atmosphere, Nadua's stomach was almost ready to settle itself.

Then Sebastian spoke. "Once we dock, we will head straight for Earth, but I will contact the Serakians and see if they can be persuaded to send someone to meet with us on the way."

Apparently, it had been the first thing Marik suggested upon reacquainting with Sebastian.

After that, no amount of Analia's cheerful stories could ease her churning gut. Hadn't she told Marik she wanted to be with him? His bonding with her had been a complete accident, but she always assumed, deep down, that he had wanted her. With the possibility of an out did he no longer wish to be with her?

Her insides twisted at the thought.

Nadua recalled their lovemaking. She thought she had seen something more than lust in Marik's eyes, but it must have only been what she wanted to see.

Out the window, Undewla sat like a large heavy snowball against an infinite black abyss, melting away. It made her heart ache worse.

* * *

Marik feared she wouldn't protest at the mention of the Serakians. And she didn't. He had hoped their time together had changed her mind, but her indifference was clear as she gazed through the porthole.

It was not right how he had claimed her. So it was only fitting that he be the one to suffer. And being without her would be suffering—an entirely new kind of torture to add to his list. It would be difficult, but he would let her go. He had to.

Would she be with other men after him? Of course she would.

Ethanule's face flashed in his mind and he had to tamp down a feeling of sorrow, so strong it threatened to invoke the Edge. Then Calic's blond hair and arrogant face came into view. Marik's eyes burned, and his teeth gnashed together.

No, Cale would know that I'd kill him.

Sebastian was watching him from the corner of his eyes. It reminded him of the way he looked at Cale sometimes—with a good dose of pity. Cale's mate had done the unthinkable and betrayed him, nearly getting him, Sonya, and Sebastian killed when the Kayadon came to take their planet. No one knew what happened to her after they escaped the onslaught, only that she was gone. Cale had never been the same.

Now those glances would be aimed at Marik too.

There was no doubt the Serakians would send someone to perform the spell, if only because such a thing had never been attempted before. They were an innately curious people. Marik hoped it wasn't possible, but he knew he didn't have that kind of luck.

Would it hurt? Would his love for Nadua disintegrate along with the bond? He could only imagine it would be like someone tearing his heart out.

* * *

Sonya was thoroughly relieved when the transmission came in that everyone was safe and headed for *Marada*. But it also caused a sinking feeling in the pit of her stomach. Once back, Sebastian would take over as captain and she would go back to working in her pub . . . with Ethanule.

She'd been successful in avoiding him since the ridiculous incident, and did not relish the thought of facing him again.

It wasn't that big of a deal, anyway. Silly, in fact, when she really thought about it, though her brothers wouldn't think so.

That alone made her grin. Ethan would be so worried about her informing her brothers of his less than honorable conduct, that he would most likely do anything she said. But even that thought didn't help much.

She lifted her chin, resolved. She wouldn't let him see how badly he'd hurt her. It wasn't a physical pain she felt— although it had been a little painful, it had been more shocking than anything—but emotionally she was a mess, and had no idea why.

Aidan's voice interrupted her thoughts. "The shuttle is docking, Captain."

"Good. Keep us in orbit until further instructions. I'll go and greet them."

She was excited to see Anya again. No one else would understand what she was going through at the moment.

"Huh." Aidan's tone was baffled.

"What is it, Aidan?"

"There are five life-forces on board."

"Five?" Had they picked up a stray? A dark though filtered into her mind. Could they have been hijacked? "Are there any other ships in the area?"

"No, Captain."

That meant little; pirates survived by the prowess of their stealth.

"Run a physical analysis. Are they calm?"

"No, I'm reading three elevated heart rates, and traces of blood."

"Shit. I'm heading to the docking bay. If you detect conflict, seal off the area and alert the crew." No need to start a panic. Yet.

She stopped to gather weapons from the weapons locker. Because projectile guns could be detrimental to a ship's hull, they were outlawed on most civilized ships.

Sonya had convinced Sebastian to stock a few of the safer energy based weapons, though. The one she was currently strapping to her waist—and had been dying to try out—was a small hand held called a pulsar blaster. It directed a pulse of energy that could knock someone on their ass and crush the breath out of them, while leaving the heavy metal casing of the ship intact. Sonya also grabbed a couple of light weight swords before she hurried to her next stop.

Though she didn't like the idea of asking for his help, Ethanule had proven himself to be skilled in the art of combat. And, despite the fact that she was currently in shambles, her family was more important than her pride.

Poking her head into The Demon's Punchbowl, Sonya spotted Ethan, chatting across the bar with a couple crewmen. "Ethan! Come with me, now."

He looked up, bewildered at her tone but withheld the usual snarky comeback. A little uneasy, he approached. "Uh, do you want me to close the—"

"No time," she whispered now that he was near. "Sebastian is docking, and I'm not sure, but there could be trouble."

His demeanor instantly changed, and she caught a glimpse of the soldier he once was. Taking hold of the sword she offered, he followed without another word. When they arrived at the docking bay, the shuttle had already settled. But they could only wait and watch through the thick clear window pain in the bulkhead, as the room was in the process of being pressurized.

The wait was agonizing. Sonya could see two bodies through the front window of the shuttle. Sebastian at the helm, and Marik, who was covered in blood. Her tail flicked nervously.

Pressurization complete, the hatch whooshed open. Sonya moved in first, her blade in one hand and her blaster in the other. The door at the back of the shuttle slid forward, forming a set of stairs. A bloodied stranger, sword sheathed around his waist, filled the opening.

Sonya raised her pulsar gun as the Edge made its way to the front of her mind. If he had done anything to her family, she would make his suffering last years.

The unfamiliar man took one step before he realized Sonya and Ethanule had weapons drawn. His eyes flashed red. Sonya spotted the small horns atop his head and halted for a second.

Didn't matter. She'd take him down and ask questions later.

The demon pulled his sword and jumped forward, landing on the metal floor with a hard thud. Rising to his full height, he pointed his weapon at them.

Sonya could feel her own horns blanching red as they warmed. She was ready to squeeze the trigger and watch this bastard fly. But before she could, Ethan pushed her behind him and hurled himself at the other man.

A frustrated growl escaped her as the sound of their blades meeting bounced off the walls.

Stepping forward, Sonya was about to reclaim her right to battle when a woman's scream sounded from the shuttle. What came next happened so fast, Sonya's head spun.

A fiery-haired woman had started shooting Ethan with arrows as he continued to fight off the demon. Enveloped by the Edge, Sonya's body moved in a flash. Before she knew it, the woman was on the ground under her. The woman's head bounced off the metal and Sonya's sword settled at her throat. Then the weight of a thousand meteors smashed into her, so hard that she slid across the floor, only stopping when a wall got in the way. The impact was jarring, and she knew the ship now displayed a Sonya-shaped dent.

When her mind cleared, she was shocked by who it was that was growling maliciously at her. "Marik?"

Eyes swirling with liquid fire, he looked as though he were ready to rip her to pieces.

Sebastian was out of the shuttle, throwing himself between Ethan and the strange demon. Anya was hunched over the red-headed bitch who looked dazed as she pulled herself to sit.

Sonya's nostrils flared.

Oh no.

No wonder Marik's claws were still digging painfully into her shoulders. Sonya had unknowingly attacked his mate. The very idea could send a demon spiraling over the Edge.

Ethanule stepped toward them, looking as if he wanted to turn his sword on Marik. Sonya stilled him with her palm. "Hey, Red." She kept her voice calm, so not to further agitate Marik. "Call off your boy."

The girl gave her an icy glare, then softened at the sight of Marik in his deep rage. "Marik, it's okay."

Marik didn't move.

"Marik, look at me."

His breathing calmed, and his hold on Sonya began to loosen. "Eyes on me."

Marik's gaze shifted to Red. Sonya watched his eyes fade back to normal and his horns fizzle out. The moment she was sure he was himself, Sonya snipped, "Get off me, you jackass."

He rose to his feet. "What the fuck do you think you're doing?"

She reached to massage away the pain in her shoulder. "It looked as though you had been hijacked. Why is everyone so bloody? And who the hell is that?" She motioned her head toward the new demon. They had only expected to receive Nadua, Anya's sister.

After checking on Nadua, Marik gave a short explanation while throwing dark looks at Sonya.

"Maybe you should have mentioned that in your transmission! What am I supposed to think when everyone is bathed in blood?" She pointed an accusing finger at Ethan. "And you! Don't ever get in my way again. I brought you here as back up, not protection."

"Perhaps you should take your own advice and inform me ahead of time. It would be nice to know what I'm getting myself into."

She flushed at that, noticing at the same time two arrows had penetrated his side. The need to take Red to the ground arose, but she ignored the urge, as well as the reasoning behind such a desire.

Bastian spoke up. "Let's just get everyone mended and cleaned up. Anya, you can take your sister to our room to wash up and lend her some clothes."

That gave Sonya pause. Why wouldn't Red be going to Marik's room?

"Marik, show Rex to one of our empty compartments. He looks about my size, so I'll provide something for him to wear."

"Thank you," Rex said. He had yet to relax though, and his eyes were taking in everything around him.

"But first, everyone give me your weapons. I won't have you walking my ship armed as you are. Sunny isn't the only one who would jump to the wrong conclusion."

Sonya grumbled, "Don't call me that!"

Sebastian stowed their weapons in a bin and they all left, following Bastian's orders.

Sonya headed back to her pub and set to work wiping down the bar. She was grateful to be relieved of acting captain, and ready to get back to her normal routine.

In a teasing voice, someone at the end of the bar shouted, "Hey Ethan, nice accessories."

Sonya turned. Ethan had followed her instead of going to sickbay. "What are you doing?"

"I was going to get back to work."

Sonya gaped at him. "Are you just going to leave those where they are?"

"Of course not." Though the arrows were buried nearly halfway in, he looked unconcerned. "I can heal instantly, but since you're the reason they're in there I figure you should be the one to pull them out."

"I'm not pulling them out! Go to the doctor."

"You get me injured and you won't even help me?"

"I didn't tell you to jump in front of me and get yourself shot, pirate."

Ethan's eyes went dark. "Maybe if you had proved you could fight—"

Vision red, Sonya's hand wrapped around the butt of an arrow. She wrenched it, feeling flesh tear as she did. Ethan howled and nearly doubled over.

Sonya's teeth clenched. She didn't usually mind doling out pain, but this bothered her for some reason. The few people in the bar went quiet and watched with curiosity.

She swallowed hard and found her throat had gone dry. "There. Now go have Doctor Oshwald do the other one."

"No, just get it over with." He stood, blood gushing from the wound.

"Why aren't you healing?"

"I can't heal till the other one is out."

"Damn you." Sonya gripped the other arrow tight and yanked just as hard as she did the first one.

She could tell it hurt him just as much as before, but he was expecting it this time and only growled through his teeth.

Their eyes met.

"Was that supposed to be some sort of gesture?"

With a barely noticeable movement, his shoulder twitched.

"Just heal yourself and get out of my pub." Sonya turned to take drink orders, but when she asked one of the patrons what he wanted, he continued to stare at Ethan and the pool of blood gathering at his feet.

Sonya snapped, "You're getting blood all over the place! Heal already!"

"Not until you agree that we're even."

Sonya could only gape at him. "Even? How does this make us even?"

"I hurt you, you hurt me. Hence we're even."

"Is that a pirate thing?"

He shrugged.

"Well, there's nothing to make even. I'm a big girl and I knew what I was doing."

He grabbed her arm and pulled her close. "Well, I didn't! If I had known I wouldn't have . . . I would have been—"

"Enough!" She pulled away from him, suddenly embarrassed by their audience. "I don't want to talk about this anymore. So fine then, we're even. Go away." She paused. "But clean up this mess first."

She turned, resolving to ignore him for the rest of the night. Maybe the rest of the month.

By the glimmer of light refracting off her bar, she knew he was finally rejuvenating. A strange kind of relief had her stomach unclenching. She decided not to analyze that too closely.

Stupid pirate.

Chapter 28

The ship reminded Nadua of a luxury boat her family used to own. The rooms were comfortable, decorated in warm colors. The people were friendly, and always greeted her as if she was already one of them. Marik had been correct when he said she would like it here.

Unfortunately, he wasn't the one showing her around. Analia was. In fact, she hadn't seen Marik since they'd been separated a day ago.

Nadua didn't know what to think about that. She had wanted to talk to him about the Serakian thing, but she had no idea what she would say. She should by happy about his compliance to break the bond. Should be.

The constant debate in her head had kept her up most of the night. It could have also been because she was in her room alone. And though the bed was comfortable, it felt like something was missing. A surly demon, perhaps.

Was he avoiding her?

Analia led her to their next stop on the tour: The Demon's Punchbowl. They had just come from the Sanctuary, a mesmerizing wild garden that encompassed an entire deck of the ship. Nadua had been brought to tears by the sight. Until then, she had truly forgotten what a leaf looked like, the smell of flourishing life, the soothing sound of trickling water.

Analia had understood what she was feeling without even asking and allowed her to stay as long as she wanted. They both sat on a tuft of grass and took it all in. Trees and vines reached the ceiling, where false light provided warmth like a sun. A small stream of water curved and crisscrossed with a walking path.

It had reminded her of home. Evlon was a lively planet. Green and lush. Almost no land was barren, but for a few isolated spots. Nadua didn't know how she survived so long without it.

As they sat there, Analia had asked her about her life, if she had been happy and well treated, obviously hoping it was so. Nadua recanted her favorite memories. Memories of Fineas, Wren, and Cyrus. Then how Ava came into her life and had quickly become the main focus of her world.

Nadua wondered if her happy stories caused sadness in Analia, but her sister had remained quiet and attentive the whole time, never showing the slightest bitterness in her expression.

Now they entered the pub. Nadua followed Analia to the bar, where that woman, Sonya, stood serving drinks. Their first meeting had been intense, and she still felt uneasy around her. Once Nadua had calmed down, she could understand the mistake. She probably would have done the same, if Ava had been in a similar situation. But she and Sonya wouldn't be hugging it out any time soon.

Whenever Sonya glanced her way, Nadua got the sense she was imaging slitting her throat. Naturally, Nadua returned the look in kind.

Sonya had been incredibly fast. So much faster than Marik. If it came down to a fight between them, Nadua would most definitely lose.

Sebastian occupied one of the many stools surrounding the bar. At Analia's approach, his face lit up.

A twinge of jealousy spiked in Nadua's veins. Had Marik ever looked at her like that? She mentally scolded herself and pushed the thought away. Analia deserved her happiness, more than anyone.

Ethanule emerged from a back room, causing Nadua's mood to greatly improve. She hadn't recognized him right away, in the docking bay. Now she could see hints of his former self in his features. He was somehow harder, rougher, especially around the eyes.

Analia had informed her that their father sent Ethan to find them, and to bring them all home. To do this, Ethan had to team up with a brutal pirate faction and fight his way to become their leader, in order to utilize their powerful influence. So, for over three hundred years, Ethan had been masquerading as a pirate. Something from that way of life must have stuck with him. How could it not?

Nadua still felt like a Cyrellian in ways. Being here with Analia, calling herself Faieara once more, felt strange, like a dream. And being without Marik felt oven odder.

Where was he? She thought about asking Analia, but decided against it. She should just enjoy the company of her sister for now.

Sonya looked up, smiling at Analia and sparing Nadua a brief glance. "Hi, Anya. Can I get you something?"

Analia put her finger to her chin in thought. "A virgin."

Both Ethan and Sonya straightened, gaping wide-eyed at Analia.

"What?" they said in unison.

Sonya's eyes swiftly darted to Sebastian, Ethan, then back to Analia.

Interesting.

Sebastian didn't seem to notice, his attention was still riveted to Analia, who replied, "That drink you made for me once. You said it was a virgin."

Sonya's shoulders dropped and she let out a laugh that sounded a bit nervous. "That's not the name of the drink. That just means there's no alcohol in it."

"Oh. Well, whatever it was, I'll take that."

"Sure." Sonya turned to Nadua. "And for you?"

Nadua couldn't help but flash a knowing smile.

Immature? Maybe. But she suspected something was going on between Sonya and Ethan and, for whatever reason, they were pretending otherwise. Sonya's eyes narrowed dangerously.

Oh yeah, they were going to be the best of friends.

"I'll take anything that isn't a virgin."

* * *

Marik had been on his way to show Rex the exercise room when they walked past the pub and noticed everyone gathered inside. Showing only the slightest hesitation, Marik entered. Nadua was going to be on this ship for a long while, and he couldn't avoid her forever.

Sebastian raised his hand in greeting.

"Care if we join you?" Marik asked.

Nadua took a long gulp of her drink.

Sonya huffed. "I don't need you all crowding my bar. Pick a table." After they settled, she brought them a round of drinks before plopping down next to Rex. "Rex, how are you finding the ship? I hope everyone is being nice to you."

That was an understatement, Marik thought. At least where the women were concerned. They practically drooled every time he walked by. Marik hadn't noticed before, but apparently Rex was good looking. Cale might have some competition when he returned—hopefully with the last sister intact.

Marik mused that the way things were going, Cale might return with a mate of his own. He frowned, remembering Cale's fallen mate. There were no second chances for demons. The dark thought had his mind spiraling back to his own dilemma. He had claimed Nadua as his, but he didn't get to keep her.

Nadua's eyes were avoiding him as she played with the ice in her glass. Marik couldn't keep from studying her from the corner of his eye. A cute white top that stretched over plump cleavage made him remember in painful detail the sounds she would make if he fondled them just right. Her skirt was a mix between blue and green, and showed off her luscious, soft legs, bringing back images of her wrapped around him. Her red hair was loosely pulled back, and curled down the delicate curve of her spine.

She was so breathtaking, his heart ached. One look at her had him craving her touch once more, but he would have to hide it. He didn't want her feeling guilty about her decision. That's why he had been avoiding her for as long as possible. Well, that, and he didn't want to stoop to begging for her love. He feared he was too close to that point already.

Marik realized he wasn't following the conversation and had missed Rex's response to Sonya's question. They were on a different topic now. Ethan was talking about what he'd learned from the book.

"—your father suggested that the Kayadon may be close to learning her location."

Sebastian added, "That's why Cale was sent ahead, to find your sister and act as her guard till we arrive."

Nadua asked, "What do you know of Earth?"

"Not much. Our database shows that it is inhabited by a primitive people."

Ethan continued. "In the book, your father gave us a location. A land called New York."

"And this Cale? Is he capable . . ." Her gaze flickered to Marik. "I mean, he must be a powerful warrior to have been sent alone."

Sonya snorted. "Actually, I was supposed to go with him, but the ass left without me."

Marik thought he understood why Cale went on his own. Seeing Sebastian and Anya so happy must have been heart wrenching, reminding him constantly of the love he had lost. At least it was for Marik.

"He is capable, though," Sebastian assured. "Your sister should be just fine."

Nadua smiled at him. "Thank you, everyone, for all that you're doing for us."

"Your gratitude is unnecessary. We are all eager to face the Kayadon in battle."

"Ah, yes, Marik told me what happened to your home." Nadua looked to Ethan, "Is Evlon still intact?"

"As far as I know. I haven't received news otherwise."

Nadua's frame relaxed a little. The need to comfort her was strong, but Marik resisted. Distance was what they needed now.

Suddenly, Marik felt exhausted. He finished his drink and stood to leave, telling Rex that he would continue showing him around in the morning.

* * *

Nadua watched Marik as he left, a growing sense of emptiness gouged a place in her chest. He had barely looked at her, and hadn't even spoken to her. Was this truly the end of their relationship? Nadua hadn't wanted to believe it, but could it be that he really did want the Serakians to work their magic?

So deep in thought, she didn't notice everyone's eyes were on her, silently watching her.

She absently asked Sebastian, "Have you contacted the Serakians?" Her tone sounded hollow in her ears.

"I have."

Her heart sank farther. Until now, she had been holding onto the hope that Marik would change his mind. She expected him to declare some measure of feelings for her, something that went beyond the mysterious mate bond. But she knew she was clinging to an empty fantasy. After all, he hadn't really meant to bond with her in the first place.

Sonya pushed away from the table with a noise that sounded much like disgust, and storming her way back to the bar.

Rex followed her with his eyes, blatantly ignoring Ethan's killing look. If she wasn't feeling so terrible at the moment, Nadua would have found the scene humorous.

Sebastian leaned over to give Analia a tender kiss on her forehead. "I need to get back to the control room." Then he whispered something in Analia's ear that made her blush furiously.

"Jade!" Ethan called to a woman walking past the pub.

The woman entered with a sly smile. "Good evening, Ethan." Her eyes traveled the table's occupants, finally coming to rest on Rex. Jade's smile grew wider as she noted his horns. "Please introduce me to your new friends."

"This is Princess Nadua, and Rex," he offered.

Rex nodded in greeting, thoroughly distracted by the short, tight clothing that Jade draped herself in. The kind of clothing that begged for a male's attention.

"Rex hasn't seen the whole ship. Why don't you show him around a little?"

"I would love to." Jade grabbed Rex's hand and pulled him from the room.

He went without protest. Nadua had a feeling the only part of the ship Jade was going to show Rex was the inside of her room.

Ethan leaned back in his chair with cocky grin in place. His lips fell when he noticed Nadua's scrutiny. She raised an eyebrow in response.

After another drink, and a little more catching up, Analia offered to take her back to her room. They said goodnight to Ethan and left the pub. Analia fully sober, Nadua only a bit tipsy.

That is, until a bright vision knocked Nadua to the floor.

Snow softly fell from above, settling on the edges of her hair and tickling her eyelashes. The air was so crisp in her lungs, Nadua could have sworn she was back on Undewla. Her legs were knee deep in a blanket of white, and an unmistakable trail of red led up a gently sloping hill.

Trudging to the top, Nadua squinted past silent flakes. Sori stood not too far in the distance. But closer, stretched out over a white plateau, was a scene of gore and blood. Cyrellians once again fighting Cyrellians, brutally driving metal through flesh. On the edge of the melee she recognized Wren, hunched over a body, pain etched on his face. Nadua didn't have to look at the girl to know who it was: Ava.

Dead.

Behind Wren, Tamir raised a blade. Wren didn't even try to move, though he must have known someone was at his back.

Nadua found herself on the floor of the ship. Analia was leaning over her with concern, frantically calling her name.

"Oh, gods. I have to go back!"

"What?"

The vision was so clear . . . too clear. It would definitely happen if Nadua didn't find a way to warn them.

Though there was a transmission receiver jumbled with some other technology in a palace room, it was only turned on when they wanted to barter with space merchants—which wasn't often.

"Are you okay? Do I need to get the doctor?"

"No, no. Analia, I need a really big favor from you."

* * *

Marik paced his room, stomping a path into the carpet. He couldn't keep his mind from drifting to his mate. His beautiful, soft Nadua, who should be here, in his bed, rather than in a completely different part of the ship.

Sebastian had already received word from the Serakians. They agreed to send someone and were scheduled to rendezvous within a week. One week and he would be mateless.

Could he even last a week? Seeing her in the halls, catching her scent everywhere he went. Could he serve her food in the galley while watching her enjoy the company of other passengers? Other males.

No!

His mind screamed, the thought driving him to the Edge—a place that was threatening to become his permanent residence.

Or maybe he had screamed out loud. He could no longer tell the difference. His mind was slipping. His head pounded, anguish finding a corner of his brain to make a home.

The Serakians couldn't possibly remove this pain, short of killing him. How could even the strongest magic take away someone's love?

Marik stopped mid-step.

His love.

The thought solidified, taking hold and digging in. He was in love with Nadua. The truth of it was like a physical punch to his gut, only it didn't hurt. It was freeing. The only thing left to do was find her and tell her she had better get used to him, because he wasn't letting her go.

Marik nearly smashed into Sebastian as he flung himself out the door. He would have pushed him out of the way if it wasn't for the fearful look in his eyes.

"What is it?"

"A shuttle has been launched."

* * *

It had taken a lot of convincing, begging, and pleading to get Analia to agree. Analia had suggested they speak with Sebastian about going back, but Nadua couldn't risk him rejecting the request.

"Please, Analia! I cannot let Ava die." Nadua had gone to her knees, tears brimming.

Analia had gazed down at her in a way that made Nadua believe she understood. Her lips thinned and, at length, Analia nodded. After stopping to gather Nadua's furs, they'd headed straight for the shuttle, ripping past the pub to get there.

Unfortunately, Sonya must have seen them because she appeared just as they were ready to start up the contraption.

"What in the name of the gods do you think you're doing?"

Nadua and Analia exchanged worried glances. Nadua tried to explain the urgency of the matter with a quick revelation of her gift and a recap of the vision she needed to prevent. Sonya listened, calm and rigid. But she was also calculating, and Nadua feared the demon was going to stop them.

After she shot a questioning look at Analia, Sonya gave a curt nod and moved to gather the weapons Sebastian had taken from them earlier. To Nadua's surprise, she said, "Well, we'd better hurry then."

Maybe she wasn't so bad, after all.

With them settled inside, the craft rumbled to life and they jetted into the black abyss.

Hours passed by, yet Undewla was nowhere in sight. Just never ending darkness dusted with twinkles of light. Nadua's gut wrenched. What if they didn't get there in time? She'd never forgive herself for leaving.

Analia was piloting the shuttle, concentrating on the many confusing buttons and screens. From the passenger seat, Nadua had already stopped trying to make sense of it all.

Sonya sat behind them. She'd folded up the remaining chairs to lay out the weapons and inspect them.

Nadua's bow leaned against the hull. Next to that was her quill, which held only two arrows. Still, that was better than none. A couple of daggers rested on the floor beside a set of swords. Hopefully they wouldn't have to use any of them.

Silence filled the space as Nadua watched the stars, keeping her eyes out for a speck of white that stood out among the rest.

Sonya spoke from behind her, her tone venomous. "So, Red, what's the deal with you and Marik?"

Nadua glanced back at her. Sonya was studying the edge of a blade. Her violet eyes tilted up at Nadua, not even trying to hide her contempt.

"You first. What's up with you and Ethan?"

Sonya's lip curled.

Before she could respond, Analia added, "Yes, there is something strange with you two. Your energies fluctuate wildly. I can't figure it out."

Sonya frowned and her deep blush was a satisfying sight. The silence stretched on again and Nadua was sure she wouldn't respond.

Finally, she did. "We fought."

Analia groaned, a bit of disappointment seeped into the sound. "I thought you were going to make an effort to be nicer to each other."

"We were sparring," Sonya corrected.

Analia still didn't look mollified.

"He was, uh, really good at it, and we fought for a while." Sonya shifted uncomfortably. "And then we were . . . doing more than just sparring, which was different for me. And really nice, at first." A faint smile fluttered over her lips, then she frowned again. "But then . . . it hurt, and . . . he freaked out and—he just left. Left! What the hell is that about? No wait, first he yelled at me, then he left."

"He hurt you?" Analia asked. "Did he stab you with a sword?"

"Uh, you could say that."

Ignoring Analia's sweet naivety, Nadua interjected, "Well, it only hurts the first time, it gets better after that."

"No, swords hurt every time." Analia looked at her like she was daft, and then spoke a little slower. "They're metal."

Sonya snorted, at the same time Nadua snickered. Realizing they were laughing together, both stopped immediately and took on a more a serious demeanor.

Sonya continued, "I know, and I was expecting it to hurt. That's not the problem. The problem is I hate his guts. More than hate his guts. I mean, he took advantage of me when I was in need of . . . sparring." She paused, as if wondering why Analia wasn't following along. "But then he goes and does this weird gesture that was . . . really stupid."

Sonya's expression said that, on some level, she appreciated whatever it was that Ethan did.

Analia shook her head. "I don't think you guys should be sparring at all. You can barely work together without killing each other."

Nadua and Sonya shared a comedic look before breaking into laughter.

Analia looked at them. "What?"

Chapter 29

"Your turn," Sonya said.

Nadua cringed.

"How is it you're mated to Marik, but he looks as miserable as the day we bought him out of slavery?"

Did he look that bad?

Nadua had only gotten a glimpse of him tonight, but he was no worse than when he locked himself in his room on Undewla, drinking, and refusing to come out for anything.

Nadua swallowed hard. Had he taken himself back to that place? And if he really was miserable, then why? Surely not because of her.

Nadua wanted to be with him. It was Marik who pulled away.

Well, whatever the reason, Sonya was blaming her for it. She was waiting expectantly, and her eyes said she was ready with a slew of accusations in response to anything that came out of Nadua's mouth.

"I'm not sure why Marik would be unhappy," she finally offered.

A soft growl came from behind. "How dare you! You're his mate, and yet you feel nothing for him?"

"I never said I feel nothing!" Nadua countered, anger pounding each syllable.

"Then what in the name of the gods is keeping you two apart?"

"Didn't they tell you?"

Sonya lifted her chin. "Tell me what?"

Hesitantly, Nadua explained the manner in which Marik had claimed her, steamy details extracted. That she had initially suggested the Serakians could fix it. And that she hadn't felt then what she felt now and was surprised to find Marik still wanted their bond broken. The last part had her eyes burning. She wished she had never suggested the Serakians.

Through it all, Sonya had sat, seemingly relaxed in her chair, but it was obvious by her expressions, and the random cursing under her breath, that she was hearing everything for the first time.

After a long moment, she pointed her intense gaze back at Nadua. "Well, do you love him?"

Taken aback, Nadua contemplated the question. Marik was abrasive and crude. Overbearing and overprotective. Possessive and irksome.

Despite all that, he was smart and funny, and made her go wild with a simple touch. A hint of lust in his eyes made her heart flip. And any time she thought about him, she wanted him.

But did she love him?

Nadua was overcome by the answer. She opened her mouth to speak, but a loud beep cut her off.

A computerized female voice bounced through the cabin: "Incoming transition."

"Anya! Nadua! You get your asses back here right now!" Sebastian's tone actually made Nadua shudder.

Analia, however, showed no reaction. "Sorry, hun," she chirped. "If you could feel how important this is to my sister, you would understand. We're going back to Undewla, just for a little bit."

Analia's phrasing was strange at first, then Nadua remembered what Marik had told her about her sister's gift. Analia could sense energy, as well as emotions.

"Absolutely not! No. Not going to happen."

"Hi, Bastian," Sonya said in a singsong voice.

"Sonya? *You're* with them? I am going throttle you for this! I am not kidding."

"You could try. I am in the mood for a good fight."

"Marik is going nuts by the way. If anyone cares."

Nadua got the feeling that last comment was intended for her.

Analia pressed a few buttons, mumbling to herself, "*Marada* is getting closer." More buttons. "Sebastian . . ." Her tone turning warning, "I'm not going to let you catch us." Then she flipped open a small side compartment, pulling out a thin wire.

"Oh, Anya." Sonya grumbled, strapping herself in.

The look of worry on her face was more alarming to Nadua than Sebastian's threat. Not really sure what was going on, Nadua followed her lead.

"Oh Anya what?" Sebastian sounded panicked.

"Bastian?" Anya asked sweetly.

"Yeah?"

"I love you," she said in that way couples do when they are about to get into trouble with the other.

Sebastian's resulting sigh was long. Then he let out a defeated, "I love you too."

What happened next had Nadua's mind reeling. Analia pierced her skin with the wire, and the ship went supersonic.

Nadua's back pressed into the soft chair. The stars in the distance began flying toward the cabin window.

The jaunt was short, thankfully, and Undewla appeared in their view. Analia seemed to know exactly where she was going. At least, she wasn't asking Nadua for her input.

The ship dived into a deep valley, surrounded by the familiar muted bare trees of the ancient forests. They were soon following the line of mountains that housed the Caves of Kayata where Nadua had made so many memories with Marik. When the Cliffs of Ashtel came and went, and the city of Sori grew closer, Nadua sucked in a horror-filled breath.

Were they too late?

It was like déjà vu of the previous battle, only now, Nadua was watching it from a different angle.

She spotted Wren, engaged with three hostile opponents.

"Take us down!" She leaned forward, asking no one in particular, "Where is Ava?"

While Analia lowered the craft, Nadua jumped out of her chair and began arming herself. Bow. Dagger. Sword.

Analia looked drained, and she agreed to stay in the shuttle. "*Marada* will be close behind," she reassured. "Bastian will be pushing the engines hard now." She smiled then. "And I've been secretly adding juice."

Sonya looked eager, her hand gripped the hilt of a sword. "Who are we going after?" She scanned through the window.

"Just follow me. I need to find Ava." The door flipped open. Nadua didn't wait for the stairs to fully settle before jumping out and landing on her haunches in the soft snow. Just as in her vision, flakes were falling, far too serenely against the backdrop of tangled bodies.

Sonya landed directly beside her, the corners of her lips turned up to reveal a small set of fangs as the violet in her eyes darkened, mixing into a deep maroon.

Nadua fired off the last two arrows in her quill and then discarded the weapon before the projectiles met their marks. Scanning the field, she searched for a familiar face. Unfortunately, the face that popped out was not the one she expected.

"Lidian?" She gasped under her breath.

The girl stood on the outskirts, surrounded by soldiers and looked to be in deep concentration.

Nadua's head snapped to a rising shaft of ice, interrupting a three way fight. The Kaiylemi? The traitor living with Cyrus? It was her! Disguised as an innocent!

Sonya asked in an incredulous tone, "Does ice always sprout up like that on this planet?"

Teeth gnashing together painfully, Nadua replied, "No." She pointed her sword at Lidian. "It's her. And we need her taken out. Do you think you can—?"

Sprinting forward, Sonya yelled back, "On it! Don't get yourself killed, Red!"

Nadua ran her eyes over the battle again. It looked as though every Cyrellian on both sides had come out to play. Even Cyrus was here, fending off a group of rebels with the grace of a dancer. He must have decided to escort Ava back to the palace.

The number of rebels seemed to have tripled, and she was horrified to see some of her own guards were turning on their fellow soldiers. Once again, patches of red mixed with white, smearing at the feet of those still standing. Nadua's heart broke for the unnecessary loss of life.

She spotted Wren in the crowd and moved through the chaos to reach him. He was never too far from Ava, and the fact that Nadua didn't see her was terrifying.

Nadua fought to get through, deflecting and dodging weapons, pushing against the rage and noise with every ounce of her strength. A rebel launched at her and nearly knocked her to the ground, but she caught her footing just in time and countered with a swift slash across his chest.

Nadua twisted through a string of spikes that seemed to be following her progress. As soon as she twirled around one, another would burst in her path. She hoped Sonya would make it to the Kaiylemi soon. Chest heaving for breath, Nadua hissed with rage at the shifting ice but managed to keep up her pace.

She yelled for Wren when she was close enough for him to hear. His wide eyes found hers. She'd never seen him look so maddened.

Confusion splashed across his face. The rebel at his front tried to take advantage of the brief distraction and leapt forward, but Wren was too good and his blade swiftly cut him down.

All the breath in Nadua's lungs escaped her when she saw a small body lying on the ground behind Wren. An arrow was protruding from it.

He was defending Ava. Was she still alive?

Heavy footsteps at her back alerted Nadua to a problem of her own. Someone was chasing her. Wren's eyes sparkled as he waved her forward with the slightest tilt of his head. Picking up speed, she went to her knees, using her momentum and the packed snow to slide smoothly under Wrens sword—in mid-swing. Whoever had been behind her cried out and landed with a hard thud, coupled with a pissed off gurgling sound.

Without looking back—she knew Wren was taking care of it—Nadua slid all the way to Ava. Her expression was shocked but her eyes were open and she was still breathing. *Thank the gods!* But the arrow was so close to her heart.

Nadua leaned over her. "Ava?"

Ava looked at her and, of all the things to do, she smiled. "You're here." She sounded weak.

"Yeah, I'm here." Nadua's tone quivered. "I'm sorry I'm late."

Ava shook her head. A bead of blood rested at the corner of her mouth. "You're not late. My last wish was to see you again." A line of tears drifted down her cheek.

"Don't say that." Nadua cursed, blinking back tears of her own. "You're not done."

"They were waiting for us." Her voice softer now.

"I know. Shh." Nadua felt helpless. Ava couldn't die.

Please gods, don't let her die.

The battlefield went quiet as the ground began trembling. Nadua lifted her head to see *Marada's* massive body, hovering in the sky.

The ice shafts had gone still as well. Nadua shifted her gaze to see Sonya standing over a bloody pile of bodies, her eyes wild, monstrous. In one hand she gripped the white strands of a severed head, and a sword dangled in the other.

Nadua was impressed.

Heart rate spiking painfully in her chest, Nadua recalled the end of her vision, only now it was her leaning over Ava, not Wren.

It was too late though. Tamir's arm wrapped around her neck, the cold edge of his sword pressed to the crook of her throat. Wren flipped around, sword high, but she knew there was nothing to be done.

Damn it! Not only did she not save Ava, but she'd gotten herself killed as well. Marik's beautiful face flashed in her mind. Her last wish? To have told him that she loved him.

As if her thoughts had summoned him, Marik was racing toward them, his eyes ablaze, his fangs lengthening. Marada had landed, and many of its inhabitants had joined the fray. A wall of rebels and some of her own traitorous soldiers put themselves between the enraged demon and their little group, but he was slashing his way through them.

Tamir whispered loathingly in her ear, "Time to clean away the muck."

"You will never survive this, Tamir," she said to buy time. "You see that demon right there? If you hurt me, he is going to make your death very painful."

"He'll never make it this far." He forced her to look toward Marik. "Look at all the wounds he's taking. The barbarian isn't even blocking them."

Tamir was right. Marik was no longer paying attention to those around him. He was focused on one thing—getting to her—while those around him repeatedly stabbed at him.

"Fight them!" she screamed. A sob bubbled in her throat.

Tamir hollered in pain. Nadua flinched in surprise, and managed to turn her head. Ava had inched toward them and planted a dagger in his foot. Tamir kicked out, knocking her in the jaw.

The move threw him off balance.

Wren launched his sword like a spear, piercing Tamir's neck straight through. Before he fell, Nadua reached up to take the hilt, ripping it out with a satisfying tug, then tossed it back to Wren.

Marik was still fighting. Blood stained every inch of his clothing.

Wren took command of Ava, placing pressure on her seeping wound. Nadua raced for Marik, all the way screaming for him to defend himself. His gaze was only for her. She saw the pain and panic behind the fiery depths.

Before she could reach him, a small group of rebels moved to block her. Marik's threatening roar made them jump and avert their gaze to the enraged demon. Nadua watched, horrified as he ignored his attackers, pushing forward with all her might as they hacked at him.

Her heart was ready to burst through her chest, but her body took over where her mind delved into hysteria. She thrashed her sword at the closest menace. Unsheathing her dagger, she launched it at the second rebel. It landed in his forehead just as the first slid to the ground, releasing her blade from his chest. The third had run off before his companions had hit the snow.

With the arrival of the large ship and their Kaiylemi down, the smartest of the rebels had started to scatter.

Marik finally broke through the thinning line of men, and Nadua caught him just when his knees gave out. His wounds were bad, deeper than she had imagined.

At some point, her hood had fallen away, but Nadua could hardly bring herself to care about the wind whipping her cheeks. Not when his eyes were hollow, lost.

"Baby, look at me." She splayed her hands on his jaw, directing his line of sight. "Love! Look at me."

He did then, his vision coming into focus. Marik threaded his fingers through her hair and crushed her against his chest. His heart was pounding fast and strong. At last, she lost control. Tears started flowing and she dug her nails into his back. He was going to be okay.

"Marik, we have to help Ava. She's hurt."

Reluctantly, he let her go and helped her to her feet.

Most who remained on the field were their allies, crowding around to get a hopeful peek at their fallen queen, sorrow etched in every movement.

Wren was comforting Ava, wiping her cheeks clean of blood and tears. His eyes were rimmed in red and she was coughing blood. Nadua knelt beside them and took her hand, unsure what to do.

In the distance, Sonya cursed in another language. Then she let out a grating, "I'll be fine. Leave me alone!"

Nadua turned to see Sonya approaching, Ethan by her side, trying to get a look at a deep slash across her torso.

"Ethan!" Nadua yelled. She'd nearly forgotten about his powers. "Ethan, come here, I need your help!"

Ethan rushed forward. "Are you hurt, Princess?"

"No, Ava is. Please help her."

Ethan joined them on the ground. "I'll need someone to pull out the arrow."

Sonya moved. "Got it." Without warning, she reached down and gave it a hard yank.

Ava screamed, clutching her chest.

Nadua tackled Wren to keep him from launching his big frame at Sonya.

"What are you doing?" he screamed at them.

Ethan placed his hands over the wound.

Light sparked under his palms, growing brighter with every breath. Around them, the drifting flakes of snow paused in midair, slowly melting and forming into droplets of water. As Nadua lifted herself off Wren, the droplets collided against her, clinging to her hair and face. Time around them seemed to slow down. Wren's eyes were wide, and she was sure he had no idea what was happening, but he remained where he was.

After helping Nadua to her feet, Marik placed himself at her back and wrapped his arms around her. Together, they watched Ethan work, shielding their eyes as the light became painfully bright. The air grew heavy.

When it was over, the light dimmed and Ethan leaned back.

Ava sat up, confused and holding the spot on her chest that was now healed. She looked up at Ethan. "Thank you."

Ethan nodded.

"That was amazing," Marik breathed.

Nadua turned in his arms. "Do you need him to heal you?"

Shaking his head, Marik gave her a meaningful look that stole her breath. "That's what I have you for." Then he bent to place his lips against hers. The passion of it exploded through her.

She leaned in to deepen the kiss before pulling back. "I've been meaning to talk to you about that."

His expression turned wary.

But before he could say anything, she blurted, "I love you. And there is no way I'm letting some magic-obsessed Serakian try and take you away. You belong to me."

Marik blinked twice, his face frozen in shock. Nadua's heart skipped a beat, waiting for his response. Then he gifted her with the most brilliantly wide grin, filled with a kind of boyish exuberance she'd never seen in him before.

In a flash, she was back in his arms, feet off the ground, with his lips claiming hers in fevered kiss that branded her to the bone.

Chapter 30

Nadua sat in the Sanctuary, *Marada* once again en route to the planet Earth.

After the battle, Ethan had healed as many as he could. For some reason, and maybe it was because of his gift, he could touch the Cyrellian's skin without any problem.

It was assumed that one of the disloyal guards had freed Tamir. Most of them had been killed or ran off with the rebels, but Nadua feared there might be more traitors still living within the palace walls.

Tamir was confirmed dead but, unfortunately, Nakul was still missing, perhaps plotting another attack.

Ava understood what it really meant to be a queen now, to risk everything for her people, even if there were those who didn't appreciate it.

And this time, when Nadua said goodbye, they knew it was for good. Nadua needed to look toward her own future, and think of the Faieara.

Marik returned to working in the galley, and Nadua was given the task of looking after the Sanctuary. Pruning, trimming, planting. It wasn't a difficult job, but she loved it.

She'd experienced one more vision of Ava, but it didn't reveal much. Only that at some point, Ava would venture into the Caves of Lost Souls.

Shortly after they left, Sebastian had sent a transmission to the Serakians, noting that their services were no longer required. They've yet to receive a response and there was no way of knowing if the message had gotten through. They would know for sure in a few days, when a Serakian was scheduled to show and work her spell. Nadua kept a dagger with her at all times, just in case the witch tried.

Nadua had moved into Marik's room and their physical relationship put the heat of a thousand supernovas to shame. It was like Marik was attuned to her every need and her darkest desires.

One thing continued to bother her, however. Nadua had told Marik she loved him, but as of yet, he had not verbally returned the sentiment. It shouldn't matter. His actions, and the look in his eyes told her it was so. But still . . .

Done with her tasks for the day, Nadua made her way to the pub.

Sonya had eventually allowed Ethan to heal her, slapping away his hand directly after.

A vision of Sonya's past gave Nadua insight into the animosity between them. Ethan reminded her of the men who had brutally murdered her father. Sonya had been but a child, hiding by her father's orders and made to vow not to come out for anything, as if her father had known what was coming. Sonya had spied everything through a small hole. But it hadn't been her vow that had kept her in place; it had been her fear.

Now Sonya sat alone at one of the tables farthest from Ethan while he tended the bar.

To see into someone's past was an interesting addition to her ability, but it felt incredibly intrusive. Analia had been able to learn to control her ability, but was admittedly still discovering new aspects of it. Nadua kept up hope that eventually she too would take command of her gift.

Nadua joined Sonya and was greeted with a smile—an expression she never though she would inspire.

"Where is Analia?" Nadua inquired.

"I think Bastian is still trying to figure out a way of keeping her from breaking into the docking bay."

Soon after their return, Sebastian had added new locks to the area, but Analia continued to prove them useless.

"He'll have to use a good old fashioned wooden barricade." Sonya laughed.

"Good evening, Princess." Ethan approached with a glass of her favorite wine. "How is the Sanctuary?"

"It's good to be around fresh air and greenery all day."

"I can imagine."

"Ethan?" Nadua started. "Why do you suppose my father never came to me? Analia told me he projected himself to her when she needed him most."

Ethan shook his head. "I cannot say, my lady. I have been out of touch with the palace too long. Perhaps he thought you didn't need him."

According to the book, the Kayadon kept their father alive to retain the compliancy of their people, but he was nothing more than a prisoner within the palace.

"Why have they not destroyed us like they had the demons? Just taken slaves and moved on?"

Ethan closed his eyes and his head lowered, yet he didn't respond. Had he feared this question?

Marik entered before Ethan could answer and sat himself next to Nadua. He placed a soft kiss on her lips, unaware of the sudden tension. Marik's mirth over the last few days had been like a living thing in her heart. Sonya kept giving Marik strange looks whenever he would smile, as though it were odd to see.

Ethan asked, "So, what can I get for you?"

"Anything that burns," Marik answered.

Sonya lifted her glass, indicating its contents by giving a small shake.

When Ethan turned to leave, Nadua barked his name.

Giving her his profile, he mumbled, "We'll talk of it later."

Whatever it was he didn't want to say, Nadua wouldn't let him withhold it for long. Something inside her hinted that she didn't really want to know.

They stayed for one more drink and then Marik led her back to his room—their room. It was larger than her previous lodgings, but it was blank. Apparently, the space was only used for sleeping and washing up.

To help it feel less like a dull compartment on a ship, Nadua had brought in a few low light plants from the nursery. Marik hadn't really said anything on the matter. He'd just watched her rearrange the pots with the same heat in his eyes that he was showing her now.

Nadua teased him with swish of her hips, easing her way to the bed. Marik followed as if it were impossible for him not to.

He caught her at the waist, stopping her in her tracks. Her body molded into his with the first hint of a kiss.

Against his lips she moaned, "I love you."

Next thing she knew, her back was to the bed and Marik's shirt was off. He was pressing his hard frame against her. Mind going fuzzy, she arched against him, encouraging him. His hands knew exactly where to go, and when to get there.

Through kisses, she pulled off her shirt while he worked on her pants. His fingers found her core, making her gasp at the contact. At the same time, his lips trailed down her jaw, her neck, then seeking one taut nipple.

She let her head fall back as he did wicked things to her body, driving her to a mindless need for more. Moving down, caressing as he went, his tongue took the place of his fingers and he groaned as though the mere taste of her gave him tremendous pleasure.

Her head thrashed wildly and she gripped the sheets at her side as her orgasm burst through her. He rode her though it, not stopping until she could take no more. He rose over her and she felt his thick shaft seeking her entrance.

Catching her breath, Nadua pulled back from the bliss and placed a palm on his chest. Marik halted, eyes at half-mast and burning with dark promises.

The sight made her shudder, but she had to ask before she lost her nerve. "Marik? Do you...love me?"

His brows drew together. For a moment he just gazed at her.

What if he says no?

Her teeth clenched.

"How could you not know that I love you?" He paused, seeing the doubt in her mind.

Nadua lifted one shoulder, hiding a satisfied smile. A knot in her stomach eased and she sighed in relief.

"I've loved you since the first time you called me an edisdon dicksucker."

She snorted out a laugh. "You jerk, I'm serious."

"So am I." His voice roughened. "You're the most amazing creature I've ever beheld. You're fierce, and wild. Brave, and sexy as hell." He gripped her thigh. "Your legs drive me out of my head. I think you knew that from the start, you naughty wench, because after seeing them, I was hooked."

She laughed at that.

"But it wasn't until that first night together, when I had you in my arms and your scent branded me, that my heart became yours.

And though I fought it hard, I fell in love with you in a dingy cave, under the cloak of darkness. And every time you look at me, smile for me, you cause my addiction to grow."

At some point during his speech, her jaw had dropped. She closed it and a smile spread over her lips.

"Satisfied, my love?"

Nodding, she could only reply, "Mm-hmm."

He kissed her hard, and held her hips as he slipped into her, their bodies joined, their eyes locked. "Not yet you're not."

Coming Soon...
DEMON RETRIBUTION
(Shadow Quest - Book 3)
By
Kiersten Fay

To learn more about Kiersten Fay, or to get info about
upcoming release dates, go to
www.kierstenfay.com

Or follow her on Twitter @kierstenFay, or on Facebook.

CPSIA information can be obtained at www.ICGtesting.com
Printed in the USA
LVOW031347161111

255238LV00004B/2/P